"ARE YOU ALL RIGHT?"

Her rescuer's voice, low and oddly compelling, reminded her that she wasn't alone.

Tessa looked up slowly, a shiver skating down her spine. Like the vampire, this man was dressed all in black. Was he here to help, she wondered morbidly, or was he another vampire, come to finish what the dead one had started?

"Are you all right?" he asked again.

When she didn't answer, he took a step toward her, stopped when she cringed against the wall.

"I mean you no harm." His voice moved over her like dark velvet, warm and comforting. "You're safe now."

Safe? She felt a hysterical bubble of laughter rise in her throat. Safe, with a dead vampire at her feet and a stranger blocking the stairway?

He lifted one brow. "Can you speak?"

She blinked at him, and then she did laugh. Laughed until tears ran down her cheeks.

The stranger muttered something in a language Tessa didn't understand and then, between one breath and the next, he drew her into his arms.

Other titles available by Amanda Ashley

A WHISPER OF ETERNITY
AFTER SUNDOWN
DEAD PERFECT
DEAD SEXY
DESIRE AFTER DARK
NIGHT'S KISS
NIGHT'S MASTER
NIGHT'S PLEASURE
NIGHT'S TOUCH
NIGHT'S MISTRESS
NIGHT'S PROMISE
NIGHT'S SURRENDER
IMMORTAL SINS
EVERLASTING KISS
EVERLASTING DESIRE
BOUND BY NIGHT
BOUND BY BLOOD
HIS DARK EMBRACE
DESIRE THE NIGHT
BENEATH A MIDNIGHT MOON
AS TWILIGHT FALLS
TWILIGHT DREAMS
BEAUTY'S BEAST

Published by Kensington Publishing Corporation

A FIRE IN THE BLOOD

AMANDA ASHLEY

ZEBRA BOOKS
KENSINGTON PUBLISHING CORP.
http://www.kensingtonbooks.com

ZEBRA BOOKS are published by

Kensington Publishing Corp.
119 West 40th Street
New York, NY 10018

Copyright © 2017 by Madeline Baker

All Kensington titles, imprints and distributed lines are available at special quantity discounts for bulk purchases for sales promotion, premiums, fund-raising, educational or institutional use.

Special book excerpts or customized printings can also be created to fit specific needs. For details, write or phone the office of the Kensington Sales Manager. Attn.: Sales Department. Kensington Publishing Corp., 119 West 40th Street, New York, NY 10018. Phone: 1-800-221-2647.

Zebra and the Z logo Reg. U.S. Pat. & TM Off.

First Printing: May 2017
ISBN-13: 978-1-4201-4250-1
ISBN-10: 1-4201-4250-X

eISBN-13: 978-1-4201-4251-8
eISBN-10: 1-4201-4251-8

10 9 8 7 6 5 4 3 2 1

Printed in the United States of America

To Bram Stoker's original Dracula,
who has been the inspiration for
countless novels since 1897.
My thanks!

Prologue

Tessa shook her head. "Lisa, I am so *not* going in there. You know I don't believe in all that nonsense."

"It's just for fun," Lisa said, tugging on her hand. "Come on!"

Tessa stared at the black-and-gold-striped tent. It sat a ways off from the rides and food booths. A tripod beside the entrance held a large, hand-lettered sign that read:

Madame Murga
Palms Read
Fortunes Told

Every time the carnival came to town, her cousin Lisa nagged Tessa to get her fortune told. Even though she was only thirteen, Lisa was really big on the paranormal. She read all the Young Adult books about vampires and werewolves, witches and zombies, watched all the movies, but she was too chicken to get her own fortune told, so every time the carnival came to town, she begged Tessa to do it.

Tessa blew out a sigh, knowing Lisa would keep

nagging her until she gave in. Might as well just get it over with.

"All right," Tessa said, "but just remember—you owe me big-time for this."

Grinning, Lisa pulled her toward the tent.

A small silver bell chimed when they stepped inside. The interior of the tent was appropriately dim. A small round table covered with a fringed, garish yellow cloth stood in the center of the floor. A pair of nondescript wooden chairs flanked the table.

Tessa stared at the crystal ball in the center of the table. Why had she let Lisa talk her into this?

A dark-skinned woman stepped out from behind a curtain. A bright red, purple, and blue scarf covered her long, black hair. She wore a white peasant blouse over a colorful skirt. Tiny bells affixed to the hem jingled softly when she moved.

"How may I help you?" Her voice was deep, husky.

Lisa gave Tessa a little push. "My cousin's curious about where she'll find true love."

"You seem very young to be concerned about such a thing," the gypsy woman remarked dryly. "How old are you?"

"Fifteen. But if I'm too young . . ."

"Be seated."

Tessa sat on the edge of one of the wobbly wooden chairs, her hands tightly folded in her lap. Suddenly, this didn't seem like such a good idea.

"Your hand."

Tessa placed her left hand in that of the gypsy, flinched when the woman's fingers curled around her own.

The woman bowed her head and closed her eyes.

A minute passed.

Two.

Tessa glanced over her shoulder at Lisa.

Lisa shrugged.

"I cannot see much of your future," the gypsy said, her voice sounding distant. "But I see a man. He is old. Very old. He will come into your life in a moment of danger. He will watch over you and protect you." The gypsy's hand gripped Tessa's tighter. "He will bring you death," she whispered, her voice like the rustle of dry leaves. "And life."

An icy chill ran down Tessa's spine. Jumping to her feet, she grabbed Lisa by the hand and ran out of the tent.

She didn't stop running until she was safely home with the door locked and bolted behind her.

Chapter One

Vampires. Tessa Blackburn shook her head as she scanned the front page of the *Cutter's Corner Gazette*.

It was hard to remember how it all started. The first hint of trouble had been a brief story on one of the major news networks. At the time, it hadn't made much of an impression on the citizens of Cutter's Corner, since none of the victims had been residents of the town. Gradually, as stories of people disappearing closer to home, of bodies drained of blood, appeared in the headlines more and more often, the people of Cutter's Corner began to pay attention. It soon became the main topic of conversation at the bank where Tessa worked. Speculation appeared in local blogs, on Facebook and Twitter. Such postings were frequently accompanied by lurid photos of the deceased and inappropriate comments.

At first, no one in town wanted to say the word out loud, but then, one reporter on a popular cable channel boldly stated that Cutter's Corner had a vampire problem.

Once the word was out in the open, people really began to sit up and take notice.

Had it only been six months ago that the word had first appeared on the front page of the *Gazette* in bold-faced type? At the time, Tessa's immediate reaction had been *Are they kidding?* There were no such things as vampires. Everybody knew that. Vampires were nothing but a myth, scary stories told to frighten children and gullible adults. A staple of old TV shows and spooky tours in New Orleans. Vampires were the villains—and sometimes the heroes—of numerous movies and books. They sold cereal, and taught kids how to count on *Sesame Street.* But real? No way!

Since then, every newspaper and magazine across the country—both print and digital—carried warnings for the public to stay inside after dark, and to never, ever invite a stranger into your home. And at least once a week, the news sources were plastered with a list of the various ways to identify a vampire, as well as the quickest and most efficient ways to destroy them.

Thus far, Tessa counted herself fortunate that, if the creatures did indeed exist, she hadn't run across one. At least, she was pretty sure she hadn't. After all, she was still alive.

No one knew how many vampires were in Cutter's Corner, what had drawn them to the city, or where they slept during the day.

The city council had issued a bounty of one thousand dollars in gold for every vampire destroyed, so it wasn't surprising that the population of Cutter's Corner had doubled in the last few months as self-proclaimed vampire hunters and greedy tourists armed with wooden stakes and bottles of holy water flocked into town, determined to rid Cutter's Corner of its infestation while collecting a tidy reward.

"Infestation," Tessa muttered. As if the creatures were no more dangerous than a colony of ants.

She turned to the last page of the *Gazette* and, sure enough, there were the familiar lists.

> *How to spot a vampire: hairy palms, pale skin, fangs, an aversion to sunlight, crosses, and holy water*
>
> *How to destroy a vampire: a wooden stake through the heart, beheading, incineration*
>
> *How to repel a vampire: holy water, any blessed artifact, pure silver, wooden crosses*

"What if the vampire's Jewish?" Tessa mused aloud. "Or Hindu? Or an atheist?"

With a shake of her head, she folded the paper and tossed it on the table, then lifted a hand to her neck, her fingers sliding over the thick silver chain she had taken to wearing whenever she left the house. It was a recent acquisition. Even though she doubted anything would repel a genuine vampire, if such creatures really existed, she had decided to err on the side of caution. The chain was pretty and if it wasn't effective, well, she still liked it. She'd considered getting a wooden stake, thinking it might come in handy if she could bring herself to use it. Had she been Catholic, she would have considered carrying a vial of holy water, as well.

Glancing at her watch, she quickly downed the last of her coffee, grabbed her handbag and keys, and headed out the door.

Vampires or no, she was a working girl who couldn't afford to be late. Mr. Ambrose was pretty easygoing, as bosses went, but he insisted on punctuality from his employees.

* * *

Tessa smiled as Jileen Hix plopped down in the chair across from hers in the cafeteria. They had started work at Milo and Max Savings and Loan on the same day and had quickly become friends. Tessa worked in the loan department; Jileen was a teller. They made an odd pair—Tessa standing five foot five and slender with long, blond hair and dark brown eyes; Jileen shorter and plumper, with spiked, black hair and bright blue eyes.

In spite of their physical differences, they shared a love for Starbucks's Cinnamon Dolce Lattes, strawberry shortcake, root beer floats made with chocolate ice cream, Lady Antebellum, Steven Wright, and anything starring Chris Hemsworth. Between them, they had seen *Thor* at least fifteen times. They met for lunch almost every day, sometimes eating in the company cafeteria, sometimes going out.

"Have you seen the latest headlines?" Jileen asked, as she sprinkled lemon juice on her salad.

"No, and I'm not sure I want to."

"Mrs. Kowalski is the latest victim."

Tessa's heart sank. Mrs. Kowalski had been the first person Tessa had met when she moved to town three years ago. "Why would anyone want to kill her? I mean, she had to be eighty if she was a day."

"I know," Jileen said. "She was always so sweet to everyone. Even Eddie Sykes, and you know what a bully he is."

Tessa nodded. "Are they sure it was a vampire that killed her?"

"Yes. According to the article in the paper, she had bite marks on her neck and—"

"I don't want to hear any more," Tessa said, adding a pack of sugar substitute to her iced tea.

"I guess it's not a very good topic for lunch, is it?"

"No." Tessa pushed her turkey sandwich away, her appetite gone. "This is a small town. There can't be that many vampires running around or they'd be bumping into each other. And what about all those hunters? There must be ten or twenty of them. As far as I can tell, most of them spend their time at Hanson's Tavern, guzzling beer and swapping stories that can't possibly be true."

"I met one of them here at the bank yesterday," Jileen said. "He was really cute."

Tessa shook her head. She loved Jileen like a sister, but the girl fell in love with a new guy every week. Last week, it had been the FedEx deliveryman. The week before, it had been the mechanic who worked on her Mustang.

Glancing at her watch, Tessa said, "Listen, I have to go. I have a client due in about five minutes. I'll see you later."

One thing Tessa loved about living in a small town was that, aside from knowing almost everyone, she could walk to work. But lately, she'd had the eerie sensation of being watched. And tonight, walking home alone in the dark, she wished she had taken her car.

She assured herself there was nothing to worry about. How could there be, with all the hunters stalking the streets? But the constant talk of vampires left her feeling vulnerable. She was sure there was a vampire lurking behind every tree or watching her from the shadows. She told herself she was just being foolish, that she needed to stop reading the newspapers and blogs, but she couldn't shake the feeling that she was being followed.

She glanced over her shoulder time and again, certain someone was creeping up behind her, but when she looked, there was no one there. No suspicious footsteps.

Just that creepy feeling.

Again.

Of course, it was October and every house she passed was decorated with ghouls and goblins, witches and tombstones. But that didn't account for all the other times she had been sure someone was following her.

Nearing home, Tessa quickened her pace. Then, feeling foolish, she ran the last two blocks. Heart pounding, she raced up the stairs to her apartment, thrust the key into the lock, and hurried inside. Slamming the door shut behind her, she shot the bolt home, then stood there, gasping for breath and feeling utterly ridiculous for letting her imagination get the best of her.

The vampire paused in the shadows outside the woman's house. The word was out, spread by a fledgling who had heard it from a gypsy fortune-teller: There was a woman in Cutter's Corner whose blood made new vampires stronger—something every fledgling would kill for.

His nostrils filled with the tantalizing scent of her blood.

Her fear.

He had missed his chance at her tonight.

He would not miss tomorrow.

Chapter Two

Tessa glanced at the neatly cut grass. At the tall pines in the distance. At the wreaths of flowers surrounding the graveside. At the fluffy white clouds sailing like ships across the sky-blue ocean. Everywhere but at the pale blue casket covered with a spray of red roses. She hated funerals. Granted, she hadn't been to many, and the ones she had attended had been for people who had been sick with no hope of recovery and for whom death had probably been a blessing. But Mrs. Kowalski hadn't been ill or infirm. She had been the town librarian, and one of Tessa's favorite people. When Tessa first moved to Cutter's Corner, Mrs. Kowalski had made her feel welcome. In spite of her years, Mrs. Kowalski had been filled with a zest for life. She hadn't deserved to die in such a horrible way.

Of course, neither had Mr. Holbrook, the town recluse, who had been Cutter's Corner's first victim. Or Miss Garcia, who had taught third grade. Or the two transients—one who had been found in a ditch alongside the freeway, the other in a Dumpster. Five mysterious deaths in as many months. And yet, if what the papers said was true, maybe not so mysterious.

When Jileen nudged her, Tessa looked up, startled from her morbid thoughts. "Let's go," Jileen said quietly. "It's over."

Tessa glanced at Mrs. Kowalski's family—her husband, Joe; their three daughters and seven grandchildren. "In a minute." Sighing, she made her way toward them.

It wasn't fair, she thought. Mr. Holbrook had been a widower who rarely left his house. Miss Garcia had been an old maid. Sure, Mr. Holbrook and Miss Garcia had had friends who would miss them, but Mrs. Kowalski had a husband and grown children who loved her, grandchildren who needed their grandmother.

After offering her condolences to Mrs. Kowalski's husband and children, Tessa headed for home. It was Saturday, the day she set aside to clean her apartment, do her laundry, wash her car. She usually had her chores done by early afternoon, but the funeral had thrown her off schedule.

It didn't take long to dust and vacuum her small apartment. After a late lunch, she pulled the sheets from her bed, then gathered up the rest of her laundry and drove to the Laundromat. As soon as she got enough money saved, she was moving to a larger place, one that provided washers and dryers on the premises. Or, better yet, inside every unit.

She sorted the lights from the darks, poured in soap and fabric softener, and settled down on one of the hard plastic chairs. E-reader in hand, Tessa soon lost herself in one of the mystery novels she had downloaded earlier in the week.

By the time her clothes were washed, dried, and

folded, and she had stopped at the gas station to fill up her gas tank, night had fallen.

Tessa paused as she lifted the laundry basket out of the trunk. Mouth dry, she glanced around the building's dimly lit parking lot. She felt it again, that same shivery sense that she was being watched. She told herself it was only her overactive imagination, but the creepy feeling remained.

Someone was watching her.

She slammed the trunk lid down, took a firm hold on the basket, and ran for the outside stairs that led to the second floor. If it was her imagination, she would laugh about it when she was safely inside, sipping a cup of hot tea. If it wasn't . . .

She had just reached the stairway when a hand closed over her shoulder.

Tessa shrieked, the basket falling from her hands, clothes scattering around her feet, when her attacker slammed her against the side of the building.

She tried to scream, but fear clogged her throat when she looked into his eyes—eyes that burned as bright and red as the fires of hell.

Fight! Her mind screamed at her. *You've got to fight!*

But she couldn't move, couldn't look away from those mesmerizing devil-red eyes.

Her attacker smiled, revealing a pair of very sharp, very white, finely pointed fangs.

Vampire! The word rang like thunder in her mind. *I'm dead.*

She was trying to accept the fact that her life was over when, suddenly, the vampire was no longer holding her, but sprawled facedown at her feet, a thick wooden stake protruding from its back.

Tessa slumped against the wall, one hand at her throat, unable to take her gaze from the dead vampire.

"Are you all right?"

Her rescuer's voice, low and oddly compelling, reminded her that she wasn't alone.

Tessa looked up slowly, a shiver skating down her spine. Like the vampire, this man was dressed all in black. Was he here to help, she wondered morbidly, or was he another vampire, come to finish what the dead one had started?

"Are you all right?" he asked again.

When she didn't answer, he took a step toward her, stopped when she cringed against the wall.

"I mean you no harm." His voice moved over her like dark velvet, warm and comforting. "You're safe now."

Safe? She felt a hysterical bubble of laughter rise in her throat. Safe, with a dead vampire at her feet and a stranger blocking the stairway?

He lifted one brow. "Can you speak?"

She blinked at him, and then she did laugh. Laughed until tears ran down her cheeks.

The stranger muttered something in a language Tessa didn't understand and then, between one breath and the next, he drew her into his arms. She struggled at first but then, realizing he truly didn't intend to hurt her, she sagged against him, her whole body trembling in the aftermath of the attack.

Gradually, she grew aware of him, of the strength of his arms around her, of the odd scent that clung to him. She spent a moment trying to determine what it was, but other sensations flooded her senses. The cloth of his jacket was soft beneath her cheek, probably expensive. He was tall, his chest solid as granite, yet his hand was gentle—almost a caress—as he stroked her back.

He held her until her trembling ceased. When her tears subsided, he offered her his handkerchief—fine linen embroidered with the initials *A. D.* It seemed a shame to use it, she thought as she dried her eyes and blew her nose.

"Who are you?" she asked.

"Just a concerned citizen," he replied, taking a step away from her. "Good evening."

A dozen questions popped into Tessa's mind, but he was already walking away. She stooped to gather her laundry and when she looked up again, he was out of sight.

Andrei Dinescu hovered outside the woman's living room window, shamelessly eavesdropping. She had notified the police earlier. Two officers had responded twenty minutes later. Now Andrei listened intently as she explained, slowly and calmly, what had happened.

The taller of the two cops—his name tag identified him as Officer Braxton—took notes while the other—Officer Gaines—asked questions, most of which were cut and dried where the dead vampire was concerned. They were, however, far too interested in learning about the man who had saved her.

The woman—Tessa—shook her head. "I didn't get his name," she said, glancing from one officer to the other. "I never saw him before."

"And he just showed up, staked the vampire, and left?" the shorter cop asked, his tone blatantly skeptical.

She nodded.

"You're sure you've never seen him before?"

"Of course I'm sure," she snapped. "What difference does it make?"

The cops exchanged glances.

"What aren't you telling me?" she asked.

The tall policeman shut his notebook. "Thank you for your help, Miss Blackburn."

She rose when the officers moved toward the door. "He was just a hunter, wasn't he? Wasn't he?"

"Good night, ma'am," Officer Gaines said. "In the future, you might want to make sure you're inside behind locked doors before dark."

She stared after them a moment, then double-locked the door.

Andrei drifted down to the sidewalk. Hands shoved into his pants' pockets, he strolled down the street. What was there about this woman that attracted vampires from all over the country into his city? But for his timely intervention on several occasions, she would have been dead weeks ago.

Or worse.

Perhaps in a day or two he would arrange to meet her, up close and personal, and see if he could discover her allure.

"A vampire attacked you?" Jileen stared at Tessa in disbelief. "Saturday night? At your place? Are you serious?"

"Of course I'm serious. Why on earth would I make up such a story?"

"Why didn't you call me?"

Tessa shook her head. She had spent most of Sunday trying not to think about what had happened. Or about the man who had saved her from almost certain death. "I know I should have called, but I just didn't want to talk about it, you know? It was still too fresh in my mind."

"Did he hurt you?"

"No, just scared me half to death."

Jileen put her sandwich aside and laid her hand on Tessa's arm. "You are so lucky to be alive. How did you get away?"

"I didn't. Some man I've never seen before showed up out of nowhere and drove a stake through its heart." Tessa shuddered at the memory. "It was . . ." She shook her head, unable to find the words to describe the shock. The horror.

"Girlfriend, I am so glad you're okay. I . . . what's wrong? You look like you've seen a ghost."

"It's him," Tessa whispered as her rescuer entered the café. "He's here."

"Who's here?"

"The man who saved me."

"Really?" Jileen glanced over her shoulder. "Where?"

"That tall, dark-haired man. Over there, by the door."

"*He* saved you? Geez, I hope you got his name and phone number. He's gorgeous."

"I hadn't noticed," Tessa murmured. But she was noticing now. As Jileen had said, he was drop-dead gorgeous. Tall, and again clad all in black—silk shirt, slacks, and boots—he had long, ebony hair, dark eyes, a blade of a nose, sensuous lips, a strong jaw.

He inclined his head in her direction and then started toward her.

"He's coming over!" Tessa exclaimed. "What do you think he wants?"

"I don't know," Jileen said. "Just be sure to introduce me."

The stranger smiled at Tessa. "You're well?" he asked. "No ill effects from your ordeal?"

"I'm fine, thanks to you," Tessa replied with a tentative smile. "This is my friend Jileen. Jileen, this is . . . I'm sorry, I'm afraid I don't know your name."

"Andrei," he said with a bow. "Andrei Dinescu."

"It's very nice to meet you," Jileen said. "Won't you join us?"

"Thank you." In a single fluid movement, he pulled out a chair and lowered himself onto it. "So, what are you lovely ladies up to this afternoon?"

"Taking a long lunch," Jileen answered, smiling expansively.

"Working girls?" he asked.

"Not *that* kind," Jileen said, grinning.

Tessa glared at her friend.

"What is it you do, Mr. Dinescu?" Jileen leaned forward, allowing him a glimpse of her generous cleavage.

"Andrei, please. I collect and sell antiques."

"Really? I *love* antiques," Jileen said.

"You must come by my shop sometime," he said, but he was looking at Tessa.

"Yes, well," Jileen muttered, sitting back in her chair. "I think I'll just go on back to work. See you later, Tess. Mr. Dinescu."

He nodded, his gaze still on Tessa. "Did you tell your friend what happened Saturday night?"

"Of course. I tell her everything."

His gaze moved over her. "Are you sure he didn't hurt you?"

"No harm done, but I'm not sure I'll ever be all right again. I hate to think what would have happened if you hadn't come along when you did."

He made a vague gesture with his hand. "I'm glad I was there."

Tessa nodded, her gaze trapped by his dark one, by the mellifluous tone of his voice. By the sheer beauty of the man.

Suddenly flustered, she reached for her drink. To her chagrin, she knocked the glass over, spilling iced tea across the table and into his lap. "Oh! I'm so sorry!"

"It's all right," he said, flashing a heart-stopping smile. "Unlike the Wicked Witch of the West, I won't melt."

Tessa handed him several napkins, her cheeks flushing with embarrassment at acting like such a klutz in front of the man who had saved her life. "I'll be glad to pay to have your trousers cleaned."

"No need. But there is something you can do for me."

"Of course. Anything."

"Go out with me Friday night."

She blinked at him. The man had saved her life and she was grateful, but he was a stranger. Granted, an extraordinarily handsome stranger, but still . . . "I'm sorry, but . . ."

He held up one hand, putting a stop to her protest. "I understand. We've only just met. Maybe we could double-date with your friend? Or I could meet you somewhere, say, at the movies?"

"I don't know . . . I don't think I want to be out after dark again anytime soon."

He nodded. "I understand. Perhaps a matinee on Saturday? I'll even spring for popcorn."

"You're very persistent."

He smiled, his eyes crinkling at the corners. "You have no idea."

"All right. I'll meet you at the Orpheum at two o'clock." The movie should be over no later than four thirty, giving her plenty of time to get home before dark.

Pushing away from the table, he took her hand in his and kissed it. "Until then, *dragostea mea.*" With a slight bow, he turned and headed for the door.

Her skin felt hot, tingly, where his lips had touched her.

Watching him walk away, Tessa couldn't help noticing that he looked just as hot from the back as he did from the front.

Hands shoved into his pockets, his thoughts turned inward, Andrei strolled slowly down the street, the distinctive scent of Tessa's blood lingering in his nostrils. Never in his seven hundred years had he encountered anything like it. Had he been newly turned and out of control, he would likely have dragged her into the nearest alley and drained her dry. Hell, as old as he was, it was still a temptation.

The question was, why did her blood smell differently from that of other humans? Each blood type had its own unique taste and smell, altered only by the individual's dining habits and addictions. But Tessa . . . her scent was like . . . like . . . Andrei shook his head. He had nothing to compare it with.

But one thing he did know: He had to taste her, at least once.

The thought of blood fired his hunger. Making an abrupt change in direction, he headed for his favorite goth hangout on the southern edge of the city.

The Crypt, built of gray stone inside and out, pandered to those who were fascinated by the undead or by death itself. Movie posters depicting Dracula in all his incarnations lined the walls. An antique, glass-sided hearse—complete with a stuffed horse and a manne-quin attired in black burial garb—stood in one corner. A life-size statue of the infamous count occupied an-other. It was a favorite spot for tourists to pose for pictures.

Music assaulted his ears when he stepped into the club. That alone told any vampire who entered the place that the Crypt was owned by mortals. Andrei tuned out the noise as best he could as he made his way to the bar, where he ordered a glass of red wine.

He stood there, glass in hand, and let his vampire glamor seep into the room. In less than a minute, three women made their way to his side. He smiled inwardly as he looked them over. The redhead was tipsy. The brunette was high on some exotic drug. The blonde reminded him of Tessa. Gazing deep into her eyes, he took her by the hand and drew her behind the hearse.

He whispered in her ear, soft words to soothe her as he lowered his head and sank his fangs into her throat.

Chapter Three

Tessa stared at the clock on her office wall. Usually, her days flew by, but not this week. For the first time that she could remember, her workload was exceptionally light, giving her way too much time to think about Andrei Dinescu. He'd said he sold antiques. So how was it that an antiques dealer just happened to be passing by her condo on Saturday night at the very moment she was being attacked? And how was it that he just happened to have a sharp wooden stake handy?

She grinned inwardly. Maybe he *was* some kind of superhero—mild-mannered shop owner by day, audacious crime fighter by night.

Or maybe, as she had first suspected, he was a vampire slayer, although he didn't look like any of the hunters she had seen in town.

She glanced at the clock again. Finally, time to call it a day. She planned to have dinner at Jileen's after work, but that wasn't the thought that had her smiling as she slipped on her coat, grabbed her handbag out of the bottom drawer of her desk, and headed for the elevator.

It was the thought of spending time with Andrei tomorrow afternoon.

Jileen was all smiles when she opened the door later that evening.

"What are you looking so happy about?" Tessa asked. "Did you win the lottery or something?"

"Better."

Tessa groaned. That dreamy look in Jileen's eyes could only mean one thing. "Who is he?"

"Shh. His name's Luke Moran. He's a vampire hunter. And he's in the kitchen mixing martinis."

"What? Jil, this was supposed to be girls' night. We were going to binge on pizza and brownies and watch the new *Iron Man* DVD. No men allowed."

"I know, I know," Jileen whispered. "But I met him at the pizza place earlier tonight and we started talking and I told him about your near-death experience and he said he'd really like to meet you . . . and . . ." She shrugged. "So sue me, I'm weak when it comes to hunky guys with big biceps and blond hair."

"How could you tell some stranger what happened to me?" Tessa asked, trying to hang on to her temper. "I'm trying to forget it."

"I know. I'm sorry. But wait until you see him!"

Tessa glanced at her faded jeans and *Avengers* sweatshirt. "If I'd known you were having company, I would have worn something a little more appropriate."

"You look fine. Come on."

Heaving a sigh, Tessa let Jileen drag her into the kitchen.

"Luke Moran, this is Tessa Blackburn. Tess, this is Luke."

It was easy to see why Jileen was smitten, Tessa

thought as she exchanged pleasantries with Luke. He was tall and quite handsome, with a shock of ash-blond hair and dark brown eyes.

Tessa and Jileen sat at the kitchen table while he poured drinks for each of them.

The table was already set with plates and napkins. Jileen opened the large pizza box in the center of the table with a flourish. "Dive in," she invited.

They made small talk over dinner. Tessa was content to let Jileen and Luke carry the bulk of the conversation until it turned to vampires. Luke, it seemed, had arrived in town only a few days ago, drawn by a story on the national news about the recent deaths in Cutter's Corner.

"How long have you been a hunter?" Tessa asked. "It seems like very dangerous work."

He nodded. "It is that, but it's exciting, too."

"From what I've seen, I'd hardly call it exciting," Tessa said. "Tell me, does someone pay you to hunt vampires?"

"You bet! There's a hefty government bounty on their heads. Of course, you can only get proof of death on the young ones," Luke explained. "Fledgling vampires don't wake up when you stake them and they don't disintegrate unless you drag them into the sun, so it's easy to get proof of death. Ancient vampires immediately turn to dust and ash when you destroy them. Unfortunately, the government won't accept a pile of ashes as proof."

Shuddering at the grotesque images his words had conjured, Tessa pushed her plate aside.

Noticing Tessa's discomfort, Jileen said, "This really isn't the kind of conversation to have over dinner. Has either one of you seen the new art exhibit at the museum?"

* * *

"I think I'm in love," Jileen confided later, after Luke had gone home.

Tessa shook her head as she placed another glass in the dishwasher. "Jilly, you're always in love."

"I know what you're thinking. I just met him. It's too soon to tell. Yadda, yadda, yadda. But he's . . ."

"Different." Tessa grinned. She had been down this road with Jileen a dozen times before.

"All right, I can't blame you for what you're thinking. But I really think it's different this time."

"Well, for your sake, I hope you're right."

"Enough about me. Have you heard from Mr. Gorgeous? You're still going out with him tomorrow, right?"

"I guess so." Tessa bit down on her lower lip.

"You mean he hasn't called to confirm?"

"I never gave him my number," Tessa admitted sheepishly.

"What? Girl, you really are out of practice, aren't you? Rule number one: Always make sure he has your number, even if you have to write it on his—"

"Stop! I get the picture."

"Well, make a note of this, too. I expect a full report of your date first thing Sunday morning."

"Yes, Mother dear."

Grinning, Jileen walked Tessa to the door. "Maybe Andrei Dinescu is *your* Mr. Right. Did you ever think of that?"

By Saturday afternoon, Tessa was as giddy as a teenager getting ready for her first date. She changed clothes three times before deciding on a pair of black skinny jeans and a pale pink sweater. She put her hair in a ponytail, then in a French braid, and then brushed it out and let it fall around her shoulders. She put on a pair of black heels. She put on flats, then put her heels on again.

Stomach aflutter with excitement, she drove to the theater, wondering if he would be there. After all, they'd had no contact in a week. For all she knew, he had forgotten all about her and their date.

After parking her car, she forced herself to walk sedately to the ticket window, but she couldn't help smiling with pleasure—and relief—when she saw Andrei was already there, waiting for her. "You're early," she said.

"Guilty as charged. I confess, I couldn't wait to see you again."

"Just let me buy my ticket."

"Already done," he said with a wink.

"But . . ."

"Is there a problem?" He ushered her through the door, handed their tickets to the young woman waiting to take them.

"I hadn't really thought of this as a date."

"No? What did you think it was?"

"Well, we were just meeting. . . ." She felt her cheeks grow warm when she realized how foolish that sounded.

She trailed behind him as he went to the concession stand and bought a large popcorn. Glancing over his shoulder, he asked what she wanted to drink.

"Root beer, please."

When they reached their seats, he handed her the popcorn bucket and the soda.

"Thank you." She ate a few bites, then whispered, "Don't you want any?"

"Not right now."

"I can't eat all this by myself."

"Perhaps later."

He settled back in his seat and, after a moment, so did Tessa.

The lights dimmed and after numerous trailers, the movie started. It was one Tessa had been anxious to see, yet she found herself more interested in the man beside her. Time and again, she found herself surreptitiously watching him instead of the screen. His profile was sharp and clean and strong, his lips firm, his hair thick and black.

She had never been so attracted to a complete stranger before. Of course, he *was* amazingly handsome but it was more than that. There was an air of mystery about him—even a veiled hint of danger—that intrigued her. Of course, if he was a vampire hunter, danger was likely a way of life.

With an effort, she forced herself to pay attention to the movie, although, at this point, she had no idea what was going on.

She nibbled on the popcorn, her thoughts turned inward. Maybe what she felt for Andrei was simply gratitude. After all, he had saved her life.

She glanced at him again, and found him staring back at her. At that moment, everything else fell away and there was just the two of them. His dark eyes seemed overly bright, almost hypnotic. Without conscious thought, she found herself leaning toward him. She moistened her lips with her tongue, closed her eyes as he lowered his head to hers.

His kiss was gentle, gradually growing deeper and more intense. His tongue swept over her lower lip, then dipped inside, sending heat sizzling straight to the core of her being. Feeling suddenly light-headed, she reached for him, the bucket of popcorn tumbling to the floor as her hands fisted in his shirtfront.

She was breathing as if she had just run a marathon when he drew back. For a brief moment, in the flickering light of the screen, his eyes seemed to take on a faint red glow.

"Did you enjoy the movie?" he asked as they left the theater.

"What? Oh, yes." *But not as much as I enjoyed your kiss.*

"Would you care to go out for a drink?"

Tessa glanced at her watch. It was a quarter to five. It would be dark soon. But the thought of spending more time with Andrei was far too tempting to refuse. "All right," she said, "but just a quick one."

"There's a little hole-in-the-wall club on the next block."

Nodding, Tessa fell into step beside him. She knew the place he meant. She and Jilly had gone there once. "Have you lived here long?"

"For about fifteen years. It's a nice town."

She hadn't lived here that long, but it seemed odd that she had never seen him before. It was, after all, a small town. "I used to think so, but lately I've been thinking of moving."

"Oh, why?"

She looked at him as if he was one brick short of a load. "Because of all the vampire attacks, of course. I'm thinking of going back home."

"Where's that?" He opened the door for her, then followed her into the club.

"Ashland, Nebraska. I moved here after I graduated from college. Look. There's a booth over there."

He slid in beside her, his thigh brushing intimately against hers. "Why did you leave?"

"Have you ever *been* to Ashland?" Her parents still lived there. She called them every week; went to visit them during summer vacations and at Christmas.

"Not lately." Nebraska hadn't been a state the last time he'd been there. "But I'm pretty sure there are vampires wherever you go."

"I suppose that's true, although it seems we have more than our share."

And she was the reason, Andrei thought. But there was no need to tell her that. At least not now. He crossed his forearms on the table. "Ashland's a small town, yet you moved to Cutter's Corner, which isn't much bigger. I can't help but wonder why."

"It wasn't the size of the town, so much, as the fact that everyone in Ashland knew who I was. They all expected me to get married right out of high school, settle down and have a family. No one really saw *me*. I wasn't Tessa. I was Alice and Henry's daughter. Here, I'm my own person. Does that make sense?"

"Indeed it does."

When the waitress came, Tessa ordered a vodka martini, Andrei ordered a glass of pinot noir.

"It's still hard to believe vampires exist," Tessa remarked. "I mean, it seems like one day they were just myths and the next, they were terrorizing the town." Now that she thought about it, it seemed as if the vampires had arrived shortly after she did.

"Terrorizing," Andrei mused. "Yes, so it would seem."

"Are you a hunter?"

"A hunter?" He laughed softly, genuinely amused. "Yes. And no."

"Which is it? Yes or no?"

"Depends on the prey," he replied with an easy smile.

When the waitress brought their order, Tessa lifted her glass. "What shall we drink to?"

"New friends?" he suggested.

"New friends," she repeated, touching her glass to his.

Tessa glanced around the room. The music was soft and low, the lighting discreet. It was a place for lovers, or for men and women who were cheating on their spouses, which was why she and Jilly had never come here again. *A place for lovers* . . . Her heart skipped a beat at the thought of being Andrei's lover. She quickly shook the idea from her mind. She'd just met the man, for heaven's sake!

Andrei sipped his drink, then put his glass aside. "Would you care to dance?"

Tessa hesitated. Being in Andrei's arms seemed dangerous somehow. Dangerous and exciting. *Like vampire hunting,* she mused.

When he offered her his hand, she quickly finished her drink, then let him pull her to her feet and escort her onto the dance floor. A tingle of awareness swept through her when he drew her into his arms.

The music was low, sensual. He held her close, his hand warm and firm at her waist.

"I knew we would dance well together," he murmured.

"Did you?"

He nodded, his gaze drifting to her lips. Her yearning for him filled the air, hot and musky.

Tessa loosed a deep, shuddering sigh as he slowly lowered his head and claimed her lips with his. As had happened before, the rest of the world seemed to fall away when he was this close. Desire spiked through her, stealing the breath from her lungs, the strength from her legs.

His arm tightened around her waist, drawing her body intimately against his as they danced. She had the oddest sensation that they were gliding above the floor, that they were encased in a silken cocoon that hid them from the rest of the world. For this moment, there was only Andrei, his voice whispering in her ear, his eyes darkly mysterious and compelling. . . .

He kissed her again and in the space of a heartbeat, reality returned.

She looked up at him, her brow furrowed in confusion. "What just happened?"

"I kissed you. Do you mind?"

"That's not what I meant . . . I . . . you . . ." She glanced around the room. No one in the club seemed aware of anything out of the ordinary. Several couples swayed nearby, their attention riveted on each other. The room was filled with the low hum of conversation, sprinkles of laughter, the clink of glassware. She shook her head. "Nothing. I think I must have . . . I don't know . . ."

"How do you feel now?"

"Fine." She smiled. "I guess I shouldn't have finished my drink so quickly. It seems to have gone right to my head."

"That's probably it," he agreed, leading her back to their table.

"I should go before it gets any later." She glanced at her watch. "Oh, no! How did it get so late? It's dark out."

"There's nothing to worry about. I'll walk you to your car and follow you home."

"Thank you. I know you probably think I'm a terrible coward . . ."

"Not at all. Would you like another drink before we go?"

"I guess so," she said, smiling, "since I have a bodyguard to see me safely home."

One drink turned into two, followed by another dance. She was feeling a little tipsy when Andrei suggested it was time to leave.

"It's a lovely night," she remarked as they walked back to the theater parking lot.

"Yes." He took her hand in his as they crossed the street. "Do you like the night?"

"I used to love to go walking after dark, or sitting on my balcony to look at the stars. Or at least I did until the vampires showed up. Thank you for tonight. It was fun."

They were at her car now. She unlocked the door, wondering if he would kiss her good night.

"Perhaps we can do it again?"

"Yes, I'd like that." She pulled her business card from her purse and handed it to him. "I wrote my cell number on the back. Call me."

"I will."

"Well, good night."

He caught her arm when she turned away. Pulling her close, he kissed her until her toes curled.

"Good night, Tessa. And don't worry, I'll be right behind you."

"Thanks."

Andrei followed her home, noting, when he glanced in the rearview mirror, that two other cars had fallen in behind his. Keeping a discreet distance, they followed him to Tessa's apartment complex.

Andrei drove past, nodding when the other two cars pulled up across the street.

He chuckled softly as he parked on the next block, thinking, as he dissolved into mist, that there would soon be two fewer vampires for Tessa to worry about.

Chapter Four

After parking her car, Tessa got out, house key in hand, and hurried up the stairs. She had expected Andrei to walk her to her door to make sure she got safely inside.

She wasn't sure what it was that warned her. A faint creak on the stairs or the way the hairs along her arms suddenly stood at attention, but she had no sooner slid her key into the lock than someone pushed her to the ground.

A large hand covered her mouth, stifling her scream.

It took her a minute to realize that there were two men on the landing, each tugging on one of her arms as if she were a wishbone.

And then a third man appeared, his hands slashing through the air like knives, and she was free.

"Get inside!" Andrei barked. "Lock the door."

She obeyed without question. After practically hurtling into her apartment, she slammed the door shut behind her and shot the dead bolt home.

Gasping for breath, Tessa went to the window and peered out.

Three men, all dressed in black, struggled on the

landing. She had no trouble identifying Andrei. He was taller than the other two and moved with the kind of speed and grace she had only seen in martial arts movies.

It was a silent battle, vicious, and quickly over.

Tessa covered her mouth with her hand when Andrei broke the neck of one vampire and drove a stake into the heart of the other.

She gagged when he pulled the stake—dripping with dark red blood—from the second body and drove it into the heart of the first vampire.

She had seen things a lot more gruesome and violent on TV shows. But this wasn't TV. It was real life.

Sick to her stomach, she bolted for the bathroom.

Andrei frowned at the sounds of retching coming from inside Tessa's apartment. He supposed he couldn't blame her for being sick. Still, she had seen him kill before. Then again, it wasn't something most mortals ever got used to.

He had intended to walk her from her car to her door, only there had been a third vampire lurking in the shadows by the sidewalk. By the time he questioned that one, then dispatched him, the other fledglings had already reached the landing.

Hoisting the dead vampires—one over each shoulder—he whisked them out of the city to the local dump. After tossing their bodies on top of a heap of trash where the early morning sun would quickly turn them to ash, he returned for the third vampire and added him to the pile.

A thought took him back to Tessa's apartment. He stood at the door a moment, pondering what he'd learned as he questioned the first vampire. In fear for

his life, the fledgling had gasped, "Madame Murga . . .
she tells of a woman named Tessa whose blood can
enhance a newly made vampire's strength tenfold."

Andrei hadn't waited to hear any more. At the
sound of Tessa's name, he had ripped the heart from
the vampire's chest and tossed the body aside.

He was still considering the fledgling's words when
Tessa's pale face appeared at the window. Her eyes
widened a moment and then, recognizing him, she
breathed a sigh of relief.

A moment later, the door swung open.

With a tentative smile, she invited him in.

Not a smart move on her part, Andrei mused as he
stepped across the threshold. But then, she had no
idea what manner of man she had just welcomed into
her home.

He glanced around her apartment. Several inex-
pensive paintings of flowers adorned the pale yellow
walls. A narrow cabinet held a collection of Disney
princess figurines. A striped sofa and matching love
seat faced each other in front of a small fireplace. A
half wall divided the living room from the combination
kitchen–dining room. There were two closed doors to
the left of the dining room.

"I knew you were a hunter," she said, gesturing for
him to take a seat.

"I'm sorry you had to see that."

"Me too. But it wasn't the first time." Tessa sank
down on the sofa. "I don't know why it bothered me so
much tonight." She shook her head, as if to clear the
memory. "Let's not talk about it."

"Whatever you wish."

"Have you killed many vampires?"

"I thought you didn't want to talk about it."

She made a vague gesture with her hand. "I guess I'm just morbidly curious."

"I haven't kept count."

"Oh. You told me you sold antiques. So, what are you, some kind of merchant by day and superhero vampire slayer by night?"

"Not exactly. Hunting is more of an avocation than a job." Better she should think him a hunter than what he truly was, he thought, amused.

"Well, you're certainly good at it. How did you know those two were following me?"

"I saw them pull over in front of your building while I was looking for a place to park. It made me suspicious."

"That's twice you've saved my life."

He nodded, pretty sure it wouldn't be the last time. He had mesmerized her on the dance floor earlier tonight, just long enough to take a little taste of her blood. In seven centuries, he had never tasted anything like it. Her life's blood was thick and rich, but, more than that, it had gone through him like fire, enhancing his vampire senses, his preternatural powers. Had he been a young vampire, unable to control his hunger, she would likely be dead now. But he was ancient and well able to control his hunger and his desire. But that added kick in her blood . . . It had given him a mild high, the kind humans experienced after one too many drinks.

So who was Tessa Blackburn? And who the hell was Madame Murga? And why had some gypsy woman told a fledgling that Tessa's blood would make him stronger? Had she actually foreseen such a thing? Or had she thrown out a name at random in a desperate attempt to save her own life? What if the rumor was true? And how the hell was he going to find out?

"Can I get you something?" Tessa asked. "A soda? A cup of coffee, perhaps?"

He glanced at the hollow of her throat, at the pulse throbbing there. The beating of her heart was strong and steady, the sound of the blood coursing through her veins a siren song that took all of his considerable willpower to resist now that he had tasted her. "No, thank you."

"Something stronger? I think I have a bottle of Scotch someone left here a few months ago." She frowned. "No, you're a wine drinker, aren't you? I have a bottle of merlot a coworker gave me for my birthday."

"Sounds good."

She went into the kitchen and rummaged through a cupboard until she found the bottle she was looking for. She pulled the cork, then poured a glass of wine for him, a soda for herself.

"I don't know why people keep giving me wine when I don't drink it," she remarked, handing him the glass. "Anyway, my friend assured me that 2009 was a very good year."

Andrei swirled the wine in the goblet, inhaling the bouquet. A good year indeed. Although it had been centuries since he had eaten solid food, he detected the rich aromas of chocolate and espresso. A sip carried the taste of dark cherries and plums.

"So, how is it?" Tessa asked, resuming her place on the love seat.

"Excellent."

"I must be the unluckiest woman in the city," Tessa remarked, curling one leg beneath her. "Or maybe the luckiest."

"How so?"

"Well, I've been attacked by vampires twice in a matter of days. I'd call that unlucky. On the other hand, you were there to rescue me both times. I'd call that lucky. For me, anyway," she said with a faint smile. "Maybe not so much for the ones who attacked me."

"I'm glad I was here for you."

The look in his eyes, the unmistakable hint of desire in his voice, sent a little thrill of pleasure down Tessa's spine. But who could blame her for being flattered? He was drop-dead gorgeous, after all, and sexy as sin on a Saturday night.

Andrei smiled inwardly. He didn't have to read her thoughts to know she found him desirable. It would be so easy to mesmerize her, to make love to her until dawn, and then wipe the memory from her mind. He had done so to countless women in the past, and while those encounters had been pleasurable, he much preferred his lovemaking to be spontaneous and his partners warm and willing.

"Do you really sell antiques?" Tessa asked.

"Indeed."

She frowned. "There aren't any antique stores in town."

"I sell them from my home to a select clientele."

"Oh." She was curious to know where he lived, but couldn't summon the nerve to ask.

Swallowing the last of his wine, Andrei stood. "I should be going."

"So soon? It's still early."

"It's for the best." He placed the goblet on the end table. "If I stay any longer, I'm going to take you in my arms and make love to you until the sun comes up."

Tessa blinked at him. Men had desired her before, but none had ever expressed it quite so candidly. Or tempted her quite so much.

Brushing a kiss across her brow, he murmured, "Good night, *dragostea mea.*"

Before she could decide if she should ask him to stay, he was gone.

Andrei. His face rose in Tessa's mind as soon as she woke in the morning. In the shower, she heard his voice softly threatening to make love to her until the sun came up.

While she dressed for church, she couldn't help wishing she had asked him to stay the night—a wish that no doubt required some sort of repentance on her part. After all, didn't the Bible say lusting after a woman—or a man, in this case—was the same thing as doing the deed? And if a thought was as bad as the action . . . well, she was already damned.

But how could she help but want him? Andrei was beyond gorgeous, beyond sexy, beyond description. She had never met a man like him. Doubted if there *was* another man like him anywhere in the world. A woman would have to be three years dead *not* to be attracted to him. And this morning, she felt very much alive.

She ate a quick breakfast, stepped into her favorite heels, grabbed her handbag, and ran out the door.

She managed to stay within the speed limit—mostly—and made it to church with a minute to spare.

"I didn't think you were coming," Jileen whispered, scooting over to make room for Tessa.

"Why would you think that?"

"I texted you yesterday and you never answered. I figured you were . . ." At a reproving look from the minister, Jileen fell silent. Until the choir began to sing, and then she whispered, "You were supposed to call me this morning with all the details."

"I'm sorry. I turned my phone off when we went to the movies and I guess I forgot to turn it on again."

"And?"

"And nothing. Now hush!"

During the next hour, it was all Tessa could do to keep from laughing at her friend, who looked like she was about to burst with curiosity.

As soon as the service was over, Jileen grabbed Tessa by the hand and hurried her outside. "All right. Tell me everything! You went to the movies and . . . ?"

"And he followed me home and killed a couple of vampires."

Jileen blinked at her in openmouthed astonishment. "What is it with you and vampires?"

"I don't know, but it's getting kind of creepy, you know?"

"Dinescu is like your own personal Superman."

"You should have seen him. He was like . . . like . . . I don't know how to describe it. It was horrific and bloody, but he was amazing. He's a hunter, you know."

"He is? I thought he sold antiques."

Tessa shrugged. "He does. He said hunting's an avocation." She bit down on the inside corner of her lip, wondering if she should tell Jileen the rest.

"I know that look," Jileen said. "What aren't you telling me?"

"He said he wanted to make love to me."

"Just like that? I mean, you've only known him a few days."

"Look who's talking, Miss Falls in Love on the First Date."

"We're talking about *you*, not me."

"Last night, he said if he stayed any longer he was

going to take me in his arms and make love to me until the sun came up."

"That's so romantic! How was it?"

"Jilly, I just met the man a week ago, remember?"

Jileen sighed dramatically. "I wish Luke said things like that. He's a great guy, but he doesn't have a romantic thought in that handsome head of his. Isn't it odd, that we're both dating vampire hunters?" Glancing at her watch, she said, "Listen, I've got to go. My folks are expecting me for lunch. Do you wanna come? I know my mom would love to see you."

"Not this time," Tessa said, giving her friend a hug. "I'll see you for lunch at work tomorrow."

Jileen lifted one brow. "Are you going out with him again?"

"I don't know. He didn't say anything about another date. Say hi to your mom and dad for me."

At home, Tessa kicked off her heels, then changed into a pair of sweats. In the kitchen, she made a tuna salad sandwich and opened a can of soda. Moving into the living room, she plopped down on the sofa.

She loved Jileen's parents, but she needed some time alone to come to terms with the events of the last few days. Last night, every time she closed her eyes, she saw Andrei with blood on his hands, heard his deep, sexy voice saying he wanted her. He had saved her life and she was more grateful than words could express, but she couldn't stop thinking that he had killed three men right before her eyes, no matter that they were vampires trying to kill her. He was a hunter. How many vampires had he destroyed? Did she want to go to bed with a killer? Even one who had saved her life?

It was a question that haunted her for the rest of the day, whether she was watching TV, sending an e-mail off to her mother, or trying to read a book. Of course, she might be worrying for nothing, since he hadn't asked to see her again.

Tossing the book aside, she stared out the window as another, more troubling question niggled at her mind. Why were all these vampires coming after her?

And why now?

Was it just a coincidence that three vampires had tried to kill her in the last few days? She sure wanted to think so.

Suddenly exhausted, she rested her head on the back of the sofa and closed her eyes. . . .

And Andrei was there. Clad in ubiquitous black, his dark eyes aglow with desire, he wrapped her in his embrace and swept her away to a place where she had never been. He aroused her in ways she had never imagined, wooed her with whispered words of love, seduced her with his kisses, until she cried out for him to take her, only to turn away in horror when she saw the blood on his hands. . . .

She bolted upright, a long, shuddering sigh of relief escaping her lips.

It had only been a dream.

Deep in his lair, Andrei roused from his daytime rest. He had been dreaming, something he had not done in over seven hundred years.

Dreaming of Tessa.

Seducing Tessa.

Until she had seen the bloodstains on his hands . . . so much blood.

He stared into the silent darkness that enveloped him like a shroud.

Vampires didn't dream, so how was it possible that he was dreaming of her?

That he was dreaming at all?

And then he knew the answer.

It was the blood.

Tessa's blood.

Chapter Five

Luke Moran signaled the bartender for another drink, then went back to studying the horde in the Crypt. It was a big crowd for a Sunday evening. His buddy Gene had hinted that this was a favorite hunting ground for vampires. Luke could see why. The atmosphere was suitably creepy, the music dark and heavily sensual. Without exception, everyone in the place wore black—a color favored not only by rebellious teenagers but by the undead, as well. Many wore long capes and cloaks or sported other goth attire.

Heaving a sigh, Luke reached for his drink. He had been here for over an hour, but, to the best of his knowledge, there wasn't a bloodsucker anywhere in sight.

Vampire hunting had seemed like an easy way to make a few bucks. Find one of the creatures. Follow him to his lair. Take his head while he was trapped in sleep during the day, or snap a photo of the creature with a stake in its heart. Unfortunately, it wasn't as easy as it sounded. He had been on the job for about eight months and, thus far, he hadn't found a single vampire.

And yet, they were here somewhere. Five bodies drained of blood were proof of that. Of course, the vampire or vampires responsible might have left town. How would he know?

Might as well face it—he was a flop as a hunter. But then, like Gene said, the only good hunters were born that way. And Gene should know. He was one of the best. Luke could arm himself with strings of garlic and wooden stakes and gallons of holy water, but he didn't have his friend's instincts, and he never would.

Hell, maybe it was time for him to look for greener pastures . . . there was nothing to keep him in Cutter's Corner. Nothing but that sweet filly Jileen.

She was a pistol, that one. More fun than any chick he'd ever dated. Maybe it was time to give up this idea of being a vampire slayer, find a nice, steady nine-to-five job here in town, and settle down with that little spitfire.

Pleased with his decision, Luke drained his glass. He was on his way out the door, thinking he might just drop in on his lady fair, when he brushed shoulders with a man entering the club.

Like everyone in the Crypt, the newcomer was dressed all in black, but there was something about him . . . Luke couldn't put a name to it, but he knew— knew!—that he was looking at the genuine article.

A real, one-hundred-percent, dyed-in-the-wool bloodsucker.

Glancing over his shoulder, Luke watched the man make his way to the bar. And all the while, his mind screamed the question: *How did I know what he was?*

Chapter Six

Andrei paused just inside the Crypt entrance, his eyes narrowing as he turned to look at the fair-haired young man walking out the door. Tessa's scent, though faint, had clung to the man's skin. What was that man to Tessa? More importantly, what was the man to her?

Andrei's hands curled into claws as an unexpected surge of jealousy uncoiled inside him—along with a sudden urge to rip the man's head from his shoulders.

Hissing an oath, he forced himself to turn away, to move to the bar, to order a glass of wine.

After finding a seat, Andrei scanned the crowd. After so many years a vampire, he had learned to control his hunger. Since then, he had become rather particular about his prey. In centuries past, he had not been so choosy. Any prey, anytime—that had been his motto. But with age came a certain fastidiousness. Given a choice, he eschewed blood that was tainted by drugs or disease or tobacco. He preferred women, of course. They tended to be cleaner, prettier, and sweeter-smelling.

It took only moments to make his choice—a slightly

plump redhead with freckles across her nose and a crooked smile. It took little effort to compel her to his side. He introduced himself, bought her a gin and tonic, invited her to dance. Holding her close, he mesmerized her with a look, then bent his head to her neck. She smelled faintly of lavender soap. To anyone watching, it looked like he was kissing her, or perhaps whispering in her ear. When he finished, he walked her back to the bar, released her from his compulsion, and left the club.

A thought took him to Tessa's apartment.

She was in bed, asleep.

And dreaming.

Of him.

The knowledge pleased him beyond measure.

He would seek her out tomorrow.

The thought filled him with excitement and a sense of anticipation he hadn't felt since he was a young man in love for the first time, with his whole life—his whole mortal life—ahead of him.

He grunted softly. His future certainly hadn't turned out as planned. He had been born to a wealthy family, had expected to marry well and eventually take over the running of his family estates in Baia Mare. His father had chosen his future bride and while he didn't love Cosmina, she had been a comely wench, well endowed, with a sweet smile and a pleasant demeanor. His father had assured him that love might come, in time.

And then Andrei had met Katerina. He had been smitten with her from the moment he first saw her standing on the balcony of his cousin's country home. He had pestered his cousin for an introduction. Once made, Andrei had spent the rest of the evening at her side.

Katerina had been lovely but aloof, a woman secure in her own beauty. He had been charmed by her loveliness, seduced by her innocence—a purity that was at odds with the mystery in her slanted gray eyes.

By the end of the night, he had been hopelessly in love, ready to throw away his inheritance and his future for one night in her arms.

But she wanted more than a flirtation. She wanted marriage. And much, much more. It had taken almost a year to obtain his father's blessing, not to mention a sizable amount of money to appease Cosmina's irate family. But, in the end, Andrei had taken Katerina to be his wife.

And to his bed.

It was there that he learned the secret behind those mysterious eyes. His bride was neither as young nor as innocent as she appeared.

The love of his life was a vampire.

One night of heaven had quickly turned into a life of hell.

Katerina's driving ambition was to be queen of the castle and for that to happen, Andrei had to be king. Over time, she killed his parents and then she killed his three older brothers, cleverly making each death look like an illness or an accident.

Only when every other possible heir to the estate had been dispatched did he discover her treachery. Enraged, he had sought to destroy her. But he was no match for her preternatural powers. She mesmerized him, drained him of blood to the point of death, and turned him into a monster fit to rule at her side.

She had stolen his will, forced him to do despicable things that even now, hundreds of years later, filled him with revulsion.

It had taken him over a century to gain enough power to withstand her compulsion and be his own man again. Another century had passed before he felt strong enough to fight for his freedom. And another hundred years before he achieved it. Like wild beasts, they had fought tooth and nail. Her preternatural powers were stronger, but, in the end, it had been his greater physical strength that had made the difference. With Katerina momentarily defeated, he had fled her presence and never looked back.

He had not seen her since, though their blood exchange still bound them together.

And would until one of them no longer existed.

He shook the disquieting thought aside. Better to think of the morrow and the chance to see Tessa again.

Chapter Seven

Tessa shifted in her chair, wiggled her toes inside her shoes, shook her head, all in an effort to ward off the desire to lay her head on her desk and take a nap. She'd gone to bed early last night, only to toss and turn, her dreams quickly turning into nightmares filled with images of blood and death. Of vampires stalking her. Of bats and wolves attacking her.

The last dream had been the most horrifying of all. She had been running through a dark forest, fleeing an unseen terror. And then, from out of nowhere, Andrei had appeared. She had thrown herself into his arms, a sigh of relief escaping her lips, only to recoil in horror when his teeth had turned to fangs. Great black wings had sprouted from his back, wrapping around her, cocooning her in darkness until she couldn't breathe, couldn't see anything but a pair of hell-red eyes blazing into hers. Her own screams had awakened her.

She jumped when her cell phone rang.

"Tessa?"

His voice wrapped around her like soft black velvet.

"Andrei! Oh, hi." She blinked several times, startled to hear his voice when she had been thinking of him.

"I was wondering if you'd like to go to the theater tomorrow night? I've got tickets for *Hell's Hollow*."

Tessa felt her eyes widen in surprise. *Hell's Hollow* was a vampire love story, rumored to have been written by a vampire, although most people believed the real writer had spread that rumor to garner interest in his first musical production. "I'd love to."

"Terrific. Pick you up at seven?"

"I'll be ready. Thank you."

"Until then."

"Bye."

She was still smiling when Jileen stepped into her office.

"What are you looking so happy about?" Jilly asked. "Did you just get a raise or something?"

"Better! Andrei called and asked me for a date."

"Cool. Where are you going?"

"To see *Hell's Hollow*. Tomorrow night."

"Wow, on opening night! I've heard those tickets are practically impossible to get."

"I know. I can't wait to see it."

"So, are you ready for lunch?"

"Sure, but I'm so excited, I'm not sure I'll be able to eat a bite." Tessa closed the file she had been working on, grabbed her handbag, and followed Jileen to the elevators. "What are you in the mood for?"

"I've been hungry for one of Tommy's hamburgers and a chocolate shake. How about you?"

"Whatever."

"You're thinking about him, aren't you?" Jileen pushed the button for the main floor. "Not that I blame you. He is dreamy."

"He is that. To tell you the truth, I haven't been able

to think of anything else since we met. It's like . . . I
don't know . . ." She shook away the memory of her
nightmares.

"Like you're smitten?" Jilly suggested.

"I guess so."

Jileen nodded. "I saw it in your eyes the other night."

They walked the short distance to the café, put in
their order, and then found a small table near the front
window.

"Are you still seeing Luke?" Tessa asked.

A dreamy look spread over her friend's face. "Yes.
We have a date tonight."

"You're rather smitten yourself, aren't you?"

"You could say that. Luke called me last night and
said he'd been thinking about giving up on hunting
because he hadn't been able to find a single vampire.
He said the decision to quit had no sooner crossed his
mind when he saw a real one! He said he didn't know
how he knew the man was a vampire, but in his gut,
he knew the guy was the real deal."

"That's great," Tessa exclaimed. "I'm all for anyone
who can rid this town of vampires."

Tessa found it hard to concentrate on the job at
hand the rest of the day. All she could think of was
Andrei and their date tomorrow night. Jileen had
teased her unmercifully on the way home from work,
insisting Tessa was obsessed with Andrei.

Tessa couldn't argue with that. Sometimes she wondered what Andrei saw in her. Though they were about
the same age, he seemed far older, his mannerisms
tinged with an old world charm that was sadly missing
in most of the men she knew.

At home, she spent most of the night trying on one dress after another, finally deciding on an ice-blue sheath and matching heels she had worn to a wedding a few months ago.

Tessa hurried out of her office at the stroke of five on Tuesday. She was home eating dinner by six, in the shower by six fifteen, dressed and ready to go by ten minutes to seven.

With time to spare, she sat on the edge of the sofa to catch her breath. Heart pounding with anticipation, she drummed her fingertips on the end table.

She knew he was at the door even before he rang the bell.

She closed her eyes, striving for calm. Made her way to the foyer. Opened the door. And felt her breath catch in her throat when she saw Andrei standing there. He had always been gorgeous, but clad in a dark suit and long, black coat, he was devastatingly handsome.

His gaze moved over her. "Tessa, you are more lovely than ever."

"So are you."

He arched one brow. "You think me lovely?"

She nodded solemnly.

"Are you ready? Curtain goes up at five after eight."

"Just let me get my coat."

Tessa felt her eyes widen when she saw the car waiting at the curb. "This is yours?"

He shrugged as he opened the door for her. "Just a little something I picked up the other day."

Tessa nodded as she slid into the passenger seat. She didn't know much about cars, but she'd seen this one advertised on the tube just the other day. "It's an Aston Martin, isn't it?"

"Indeed. If it's good enough for Bond, it's good enough for me." He closed the door gently, then walked around to the driver's side and slid behind the wheel. He usually drove the Challenger, but he'd wanted to impress her.

"There must be a lot of money in selling antiques," Tessa murmured as he pulled away from the curb.

They reached the theater at seven thirty. Tessa wasn't surprised when Andrei opted for valet parking.

She glanced at the other patrons as Andrei reached for her hand. She had never been to an opening night before and suddenly felt like Cinderella before her fairy godmother came to her rescue. She was surrounded by women wearing Valentino and Dior, Versace and Donna Karan. Obviously they had traveled here from the big city to the north. Few in Cutter's Corner, including Tessa, could afford to shell out seven thousand dollars for a gown by Oscar de la Renta. Of course, in his Armani suit and long, black coat, Andrei fit right in.

She forgot all about her clothes when she recognized several movie stars. Hard to believe that some of Hollywood's elites had made the trip to Cutter's Corner to see a play written by an unknown playwright. And then she frowned. What if some of them were vampires? With a huff of exasperation, she put the thought from her mind as Andrei escorted her into the theater.

Not only had Andrei scored tickets on opening night, but their seats were center orchestra.

"How did you get such great seats?" Tessa asked.

"I know the producer."

Tessa felt a rush of excitement as the lights dimmed and the crowd fell silent. A moment later, the heroine began to sing the first number. She had a beautiful voice, the notes as pure and clear as crystal.

Tessa leaned toward Andrei to whisper, "I've never heard anything like . . ." when there was an explosion in the wings, followed by a blinding flash of light. Screams sounded from backstage as the backdrop and the side curtains went up in flames.

Pandemonium erupted in the audience as several burning scraps of material landed in the aisles, setting the carpet runners on fire. Sparks flew through the air. The woman sitting in front of Tessa shrieked as an ember landed in her hair.

The stage manager shouted into a microphone, begging people to remain calm, but a second explosion sent him hurtling into the orchestra pit.

Rising, Andrei grasped Tessa's hand. There were few things on this earth that he feared, but fire was one of them. "We need to get the hell out of here. Now!"

Speechless with fright, Tessa glanced at the people around her, some seemingly frozen in fear, others pushing and shoving their way toward the exits. An elderly lady in a fur coat fainted in the aisle nearest them, blocking the way. Tessa gasped as several people jumped over her. Others vaulted over the seats behind them in their eagerness to flee the theater. She was surprised at how quickly the stink of smoke filled the air and stung her eyes.

There was no quick way out as people scrambled and pushed one another in their desperation to escape the flames, which had spread to the seats in the first three rows.

Andrei glanced at the flames. Dammit, they had to get out of there. He considered transporting the two of them to Tessa's place, but the use of his vampire powers would require an explanation, one he wasn't prepared to give.

Taking a deep breath, he exerted his preternatural influence on the people in front of them, ordering them to get the hell out of the way. Tessa was almost knocked to the floor several times, but Andrei kept her upright, putting his body between her and the mass of terrified people.

Fortunately, Tessa was so frightened, she didn't question the way a path magically opened in front of them.

Sirens wailed in the distance.

"What do you think happened?" Tessa asked, wiping her eyes as they emerged from the building.

"I think someone—mostly likely hunters—believed that the rumors of a vampire playwright were true."

"Seriously? You think they'd risk hurting hundreds of innocent people because of some silly rumor?"

"Fanatics do a lot of irrational things," he said grimly.

She couldn't argue with that.

Tugging on her hand, he led her away from the entrance.

"It's odd that the sprinklers didn't come on," Tessa remarked. Glancing over her shoulder, she saw that one side of the theater was now on fire.

In the light of the flames, she saw a man stagger out of a side door, gasped in horror when sparks from the building ignited the sleeve of his jacket. She let out a cry of alarm as he was suddenly engulfed in fire and then, in the blink of an eye, he dissolved into a pile of gray ash.

Swallowing the bile that rose in her throat, she tugged on Andrei's arm. "Did you see that?"

He nodded, a muscle tightening in his jaw as a gust of wind scattered the ashes. He had known Colin Dougherty for three hundred years. Colin had been a vampire, yes. But he had also been a kind man, one who had satisfied his thirst with blood obtained from a local blood bank rather than prey on mortals.

Had he been alone, Andrei would have gone back to the theater to see if he could find any trace of the hunter or hunters responsible. But there were other vampires in the vicinity; he couldn't leave Tessa standing on the sidewalk, alone and unprotected.

Tessa glanced at Andrei as he pulled out of the parking structure. He hadn't said a word since they'd escaped the theater. His jaw was set, his expression implacable.

She shifted in her seat. Time and again she had started to ask him what was wrong, only to swallow the words. Something told her she really didn't want to know what he was thinking.

She shuddered as a news flash interrupted the music on the radio to report on the fire. With a glance at Andrei, she switched it off. Tomorrow would be soon enough to hear the grisly details. She had seen enough carnage to give her nightmares for a year.

She breathed a sigh of relief when he pulled up in front of her building.

After turning off the engine, he turned to face her. "I'm sorry for this evening," he said quietly.

Tessa made a vague gesture with her hand. "The fire wasn't your fault."

He grunted softly, then opened his door. "Come, I'll walk you upstairs."

She was conscious of him standing behind her as she slid the key into the lock, her every sense attuned to his nearness. She wondered if he would kiss her good night, then felt a twinge of guilt for even thinking such a thing after what had happened at the theater.

Reaching inside, she switched on the light.

"Tessa."

Slowly, she turned to face him.

"The man who died," he said quietly. "He was a friend of mine."

"Oh! I'm so sorry." But even as she spoke the words, she remembered how quickly the flames had engulfed him, the way his body had turned to ash. And drifted away.

Andrei blew out a breath. "His name was Colin. He wrote the play." Another breath. "And he was a vampire. That's why he burned so quickly."

Tessa blinked at him. "You were friends with a vampire? But . . . I thought . . . you said you were a hunter."

"I knew him before he was turned," Andrei explained. "He was a good man. Devoted to his art and his music. He never hurt anyone."

"But if he was a vampire . . . ?"

"He never hunted humans. There was no reason for anyone to destroy him."

Tessa stared at him, not knowing what to say.

And suddenly, words didn't seem important. Standing on her tiptoes, she pressed a kiss to his cheek.

She gasped as his arms went around her, his mouth descending on hers, his tongue like a rapier as it dueled with her own. All thought left her as he pressed her body closer to his. And still closer. And it wasn't close enough. She had a crazy impulse to drag him into her apartment and rip off his clothes, to pull him down on the floor and beg him to make love to her all night long.

Her eyelids flew open as her mind filled with vivid images of herself doing that very thing. With a muffled cry, she took a step backward as other images played across her mind—frightening images from her nightmare of Andrei with fangs and eyes that glowed red in the dark.

He loosened his hold, but didn't release her.

"I . . . I . . ." She was breathing as if she'd just run a mile. Or twenty. She shook the unsettling memory of her nightmare away. What would he think if he could read her thoughts? No doubt he would think her foolish to be so upset by a bad dream.

A faint smile curved his lips. "Would it be all right if we tried again?"

She stared at him, her cheeks burning. Tried what again?

"Another date," he clarified. "Perhaps next week?"

She nodded, too flustered to speak.

He bowed over her hand. "I'll call you soon."

Tessa nodded again. She watched him descend the stairs, then went inside and closed and locked the door.

What if her nightmare was more than just a bad dream? What if it had been an omen of some kind? A warning? What if Andre really *was* a vampire? It would explain how he knew so much about them. How he knew so much about Colin.

* * *

After seeing Tessa safely home, Andrei drove back to the theater. He parked his car several blocks away.

Walking toward the entrance, he saw that the fire was out. Several foot cops patrolled the sidewalks around the building to make sure no one crossed the crime scene tape. The fire trucks were still in evidence. A number of curious folk stood across the street, watching the cleanup.

Andrei moved past the police, weaving in and out among the fire crew, unnoticed, thanks to what he liked to call a vampire veil, which hid him from sight when he didn't wish to be seen.

He prowled the inside of the theater, his senses probing the rubble for a clue, a scent, something—anything—that would tell him who had destroyed his friend. But, for once, his preternatural senses failed him. Then again, any trace of the killer's scent had likely been burned away by the fire or extinguished by the gallons of water that had been poured into the place.

Returning to his car, Andrei drove to the next town in search of prey, wondering, as he did so, if it had been a mistake to tell Tessa about Colin. Would it lead to questions best left unasked and unanswered?

He found his prey on a street corner waiting for a bus. A thought brought her into his car. He took her quickly and went on his way, leaving her with no memory of what had happened.

Back at home, he stood outside a moment, enjoying the quiet of the night. Then, drawn by an irresistible need to see Tessa, he walked to her apartment complex.

A thought took him to her front door. The sound of her deep, even breathing told him she was asleep. He had forgotten what mortal sleep was like. His rest was like death—until he met Tessa, there had been no dreams, no nightmares, only oblivion.

It took only moments to dissolve into mist, slip under the door, and float into her bedroom.

She slept on her side, her cheek pillowed on her hand. Her hair spread across her shoulders like skeins of fine gold silk, tempting his touch. Resuming his own form, he lifted several strands and let them sift through his fingers. Her hair was, indeed, like silk. An indrawn breath enveloped him in her unique scent.

He was suddenly desperate to hold her in his arms, to claim her lips with his, to explore every inch of her, from the crown of her head to the soles of her feet, and every delectable hill and valley in between.

Not since Katerina had he felt such an overwhelming physical desire for a woman, a need so strong that it was painful in its intensity.

It took every ounce of his considerable self-control—hard won in the last seven hundred years—to turn his back on her and leave the apartment.

A thought took him to his lair, located in the bowels of a three-story mansion that had been built over a hundred years ago. He had found the place quite by accident while passing through Cutter's Corner. A large sign in the front window had announced that the building was scheduled to be demolished. Andrei recalled paying a visit to the man in charge and offering to buy the place. The man had charged him twice what the property was worth, but after a little renovation and some major reconstruction in the basement, Andrei had a secure lair.

He had furnished the upper floors with antiques gathered over the years. And, as he'd told Tessa, he sold a few now and then to a select clientele—of other vampires. Most of them came looking for pieces to remind them of another time or another place, an inanimate object that harked back to a life or an era that no longer existed.

Now, standing in the center of the vast living room, he felt an overpowering sense of emptiness. How long since he'd had a friend to talk to, someone to share his life with? Occasionally, he had allied himself with other vampires—both male and female—but vampires tended to be solitary creatures, as untrusting of their own kind as they were of mortals. He had spent most of his long existence living alone in places like this—houses and buildings abandoned by mortals.

He lifted a brow. Maybe it was time to take another wife.

As long as it was Tessa. He had no trouble at all imagining her clad in a long white gown and veil.

Or in nothing at all.

So easy to imagine caressing her from head to toe . . . sipping the sweet red nectar that flowed through her veins.

In the morning, Tessa woke with a smile. Her dreams last night had been far more pleasant than the nightmares she'd been having. Last night, she had dreamed of becoming Andrei's wife, and while the reality of that was unlikely, at least in the near future, since she scarcely knew the man, it had nevertheless been wonderfully romantic. He, in a tux that emphasized his dark good looks, she in a long white gown and veil. Walking down the aisle, she had been blind to everyone but Andrei. . . .

Sitting up, she frowned. There had been more to the dream. Why couldn't she remember it?

Thoughts of last night's dream vanished when, over

breakfast, she turned on her iPad and brought up the morning paper. The fire at the theater headlined the news. How had she forgotten that dreadful ordeal? She read through the story, remembering all too clearly how quickly it had happened, how horrible it had been. The flames. The panic. The sheer terror of thinking she might die in the fire.

The article reported that the stage manager had sustained numerous injuries when he fell into the pit, the lead soprano had suffered minor burns, three people had been badly hurt in the rush to leave the theater, several others had also been injured. Andrei's friend Colin had been reported missing.

Tessa shivered. They would never find his body.

Her appetite gone, she pushed her plate away. If she lived to be a hundred, she would never forget the sight of that poor man being engulfed by flames, or how quickly he had been consumed, leaving nothing but ashes behind.

Tessa wasn't looking forward to lunch with Jileen. The last thing she wanted to do was discuss the grisly details of last night's fire.

Of course, it was the first thing Jilly mentioned.

"I heard about the fire on the news last night," she said, her eyes wide. "I tried to call you but . . ." She shrugged. "I guess your phone was off."

Tessa nodded. "I didn't think about turning it on until I got to work this morning."

"You obviously got out okay. I almost hate to ask how the rest of the evening went."

"He took me home. Neither one of us was in the mood to do much of anything else." She saw no need to mention kissing Andrei.

"Are you going to see him again?"

"I guess so. He said he'd call me."

"Why don't you call him? Luke and I are going dancing Friday night. You two should come with us."

"I don't know . . ."

"Come on, it's time our fellas met. Since they're both hunters, they should have a lot to talk about. Besides, it's Halloween. You don't want to sit home alone."

Tessa hurried home from work Friday night. Andrei had called her earlier in the week and when she mentioned going out with Jilly and Luke, he had agreed. At Jileen's suggestion, they had agreed to meet Jilly and Luke at the local cowboy bar.

Tessa decided on jeans, boots, and a western shirt, since the club had a casual western flair.

When Andrei arrived, she saw that he had been thinking along the same lines, although seeing him in black jeans, a black cowboy shirt, and boots, casual was not the word that came to mind.

Outside, he opened the door of a dark gray Challenger for her.

"Another car?" she asked, sliding into the passenger seat. "How many do you have?"

"Three." Rounding the front of the car, he climbed behind the wheel and the engine purred to life. "Hang on," he said, and hit the gas.

Jileen and Luke had already scored a table when Tessa and Andrei arrived. Tessa noted several couples in costume, no doubt going out to Halloween parties later.

Luke stood as they approached. Recognition flickered in his eyes when he saw Andrei. He swore under his breath, one hand diving inside his jacket as he put himself between Jileen and Andrei.

Eyes narrowed, Andrei said, "I wouldn't do that if I were you."

Jileen frowned.

"What's going on?" Tessa asked, glancing from Luke to Andrei and back again.

"Tessa! Get away from him!" Luke hissed. "He's a vampire!"

"Maybe we'd better take this outside," Andrei suggested, conscious of the stares of some of the other patrons.

"So you can kill me?" Luke shook his head. "I don't think so."

Andrei muttered an oath. Capturing Luke's gaze with his own, and then Jileen's, he said, "It's time to go."

Luke nodded, his movements wooden as he walked toward the door.

Jileen followed him.

Frowning, Tessa stared at Andrei. "What's going on?"

"I'll explain outside."

"Tell me now."

"Tessa," he growled, taking her by the arm, "this isn't the time or the place. Let's go."

She didn't want to leave. There was protection, of a sort, in being surrounded by people. But something in his tone compelled her to obey and the next thing she knew, they were all in Andrei's Challenger, heading out of the city.

Tessa glanced into the backseat. Jileen and Luke sat like zombies, not moving, not speaking. She faced forward again, her hands tightly folded in her lap. She was shaking and couldn't stop.

She slid a glance at Andrei. Could it be true, what Luke had said? Was Andrei a vampire?

He was *something*, she thought, remembering how he had mesmerized Jilly and Luke, the way his voice had compelled her to obey.

Fear spiked through her when he pulled off the highway onto a deserted side road. Mercy, did he intend to kill them all and dump their bodies out here?

He switched off the engine, then turned to look at her. "Is that what you think?" He shook his head. "If I intended to kill you, I wouldn't have bothered saving your life."

"The . . . then what are we doing out here?"

"Probably not the best choice of locations," he remarked, "but I wanted a place where we could be alone."

She stared at him, her eyes wide and afraid.

"Tessa, I'm not going to hurt you, or your friends."

"Is it true? What Luke said?"

He nodded. "I'm afraid so."

He was a vampire. She tried to wrap her mind around the enormity of it, felt a bubble of hysterical laughter rise in her throat. It had to be a joke. Of course, that was it! A Halloween prank and they were all in on it—Luke and Jilly and Andrei.

"Okay," she said, "you've had your fun at my expense. You can all stop pretending now." She glanced over her shoulder. Jileen and Luke stared straight ahead, unblinking. Unmoving.

"They're not pretending, Tessa. And neither am I."

"But . . . I saw you kill vampires."

"Better them than you. You have questions."

"Hundreds." So many, she didn't know where to start.

"Ask away."

"How long have you been a vampire?"

"Seven hundred years, more or less."

She blinked at him. "Seven. *Hundred*. Years."

He nodded.

"Why did you want to be a vampire?"

He snorted softly. "Believe me, I didn't."

She chewed on her thumbnail. Moments ago, she'd had hundreds of questions, but suddenly, she couldn't think of a single one. She was too busy trying to wrap her mind around the fact that he had been alive for seven hundred years. And then she frowned. How could he be a vampire? She had seen him during the day.

"Only fledglings and young vampires need to avoid the sun," he remarked. "Master vampires can day walk."

"How did you know what I was . . . ?" She frowned at him. "You read my mind, didn't you?"

He shrugged, as if it was no big deal. "It's a handy talent."

It took her a moment to digest that. A faint flush warmed her cheeks as she remembered the many times she had thought of making love to him when they were together. Had he read those thoughts, too?

Her cheeks grew hotter when he smiled faintly. He had!

"What are you going to do with Jilly and Luke?"

"I'm not sure. The easiest thing—the safest thing—would be to wipe the truth from their minds."

"You can do that?"

"If I have to."

"That's just wrong," Tessa said. "You have no right to play with their memories."

"Maybe not, but it's the best way to ensure their silence."

"Are you going to erase my memory, too?"

His gaze met hers, dark and intense. "Do I need to?"

She shook her head vigorously. "I won't tell anyone."

"I'll know if you do."

His words were mild, but Tessa sensed the unspoken threat behind them. At first, it frightened her, then it made her angry, and then she realized the warning stemmed from a deep sense of self-preservation.

"I need to talk to Luke and Jileen," he said. "Hopefully, they'll see things my way."

When she didn't say anything, he got out of the car, opened the back door, and called for Jilly and Luke to step outside. A word released them from his thrall.

Luke shook his head as if to clear it, his eyes widening when he saw Andrei. "What the hell!" he exclaimed. "What did you do to us?"

"Not what you intended to do to me," Andrei retorted.

"Where's Tessa?" Jileen asked.

"She's waiting in the car."

"Waiting for what?" Luke asked, his voice laced with suspicion.

"To see if you're going to be reasonable."

"About what?" Luke demanded.

"You know what I am. I know what you are, so you've got three options. You can give me your word, both of you, that you'll keep my secret."

Luke's eyes narrowed. "What are the other options?"

"I can wipe your memory or . . ." He flashed a hint of fang. "I can kill the two of you."

A wordless cry of fear and denial rose in Jileen's throat.

"It's your choice," Andrei said.

"Are you the one who's been killing the people in town?" Luke asked.

"No."

"Why should I believe you?"

"Why should I lie?"

Luke grunted. "Good point."

Andrei bared his fangs. "Two good points, actually. Both rather sharp."

Luke refused to be cowed. "So, if you're not killing our citizens, then who is?"

"I'm not the only vampire in town."

"Why . . . why are they coming here?" Jileen asked.

Andrei glanced at the car. "They're after Tessa."

"Tessa! Why?"

"There's something unique about her blood. I'm not sure what it is, but it's attracting vampires, the young ones, anyway. I've already destroyed a few of them."

"Does Tessa know they're after her?" Luke asked.

"Not yet."

"Might be a good idea to let her know, don't you think?" Luke muttered dryly.

"I'll tell her later. Back to you two. Can I trust you to keep quiet about me?"

Luke reached for Jileen's hand and gave it a squeeze. "We'll keep your secret."

Jileen took a deep breath. "I want your promise that you won't hurt Tessa."

Andrei nodded. "You've got it."

"Can we go now?" Jileen asked, darting a glance at Andrei.

He grunted softly, then nodded. There was little doubt that she was anxious to get away from him as quickly as possible.

But then, considering how the evening had gone, he could hardly blame her.

Chapter Eight

Jileen practically jumped out of the backseat of the car when Andrei pulled up in front of her apartment. She murmured a quick good-bye to Tessa and ran up the stairs.

Luke followed her, conscious of Andrei's narrow-eyed gaze on his back the whole way. The man was a freakin' vampire!

Stepping into Jileen's apartment, Luke found her huddled on the sofa, a bright pink throw pillow clutched to her chest. Face pale, she was visibly shaking.

"Lock the door, Luke!"

He turned the dead bolt; then, sitting beside her, he took her in his arms. "Take it easy. He's gone."

"I knew there were vampires," she said, a quiver in her voice. "I knew you were a hunter. But . . ." She shook her head. "I guess knowing and seeing are two different things. You've got to kill him, Luke! It's the only way to protect Tessa."

Luke snorted. "I don't blame you for being worried about her safety. I mean, damn, that man has power! I could feel it crawling over my skin. Did you feel it?"

"All I felt was fear for our lives!"

"I don't think he means Tessa any harm. Hell, I think he's in love with her."

Jileen stared at him. "Love? What would a vampire know about love?"

"I don't know. Maybe nothing. But it's obvious he cares for her."

"What if he turns her into what he is?" She clutched his arm. "Luke, you've got to do something!"

"We promised to keep his secret, Jilly, remember?"

"I don't think a promise to a monster counts." She shook her head ruefully as she reached for her cell phone.

"What are you going to do?" Luke asked.

"What do you think? I'm calling Tess. I need to know she made it safely home."

Tessa huddled against the passenger door. *Andrei is a vampire.* The words echoed and re-echoed inside her mind as he drove her home.

Sliding a glance in his direction, she wondered how she hadn't seen it before. Now that she knew, it seemed obvious. No mortal male was that flawlessly handsome, that charming.

She tensed when he pulled up in front of her condo.

"Tessa."

"I've got to go."

"You need to listen to me. You're the reason so many vampires are coming here. There's a rumor that your blood is drawing them."

She shook her head in denial. "That's ridiculous."

"I wish it was. I got the story out of one of the fledglings before I killed him. Some gypsy woman who calls herself Madame Murga is spreading the rumor that your blood can enhance a new vampire's strength. And I believe it."

"Madame Murga?" Tessa frowned. It had been ten years since she and her cousin Lisa had gone to see the gypsy. "Why would she be saying such a thing? And why on earth would you or anyone else believe it?"

Eyes wide with disbelief, Tessa lifted a hand to her neck. "You . . . you didn't! Did you . . . ?"

He nodded. "Only a small taste."

It was the last straw. She bolted out of the car and raced up the stairs. Her hands were shaking so badly when she reached the landing, she couldn't get the key in the lock.

She let out a hoarse cry when Andrei suddenly appeared beside her. Taking the key from her, he unlocked the door, then dropped the key in her hand.

Heart pounding, she crossed the threshold and slammed the door in his face.

Andrei whistled softly as he returned to his car.

Unless she withdrew her former invitation, no lock could keep him out.

But she didn't know that. And he saw no reason to tell her.

Trembling uncontrollably, Tessa stood with her back pressed against the door.

Andrei was a vampire.

He had tasted her blood.

And that fortune-teller, Madame Murga . . . why on earth was she spreading such an outlandish rumor? Tessa didn't believe for a minute that it was her blood drawing vampires to Cutter's Corner.

She needed to get in touch with the fortune-teller and make her stop spreading that ridiculous lie. Because it couldn't be true. Could it?

She did a quick search on the Internet. There was only one Madame Murga listed. She had passed away in her sleep three weeks ago. Of natural causes? Or the result of another mysterious accident?

Tessa jumped when her cell phone rang, blew out a sigh of relief when she recognized Jileen's number.

"Tessa? Are you all right? Is he there?"

"I'm alone and I'm fine." She dropped down on the sofa and pulled an afghan over her. "Jilly, he drank my blood."

"What? Just now?"

"No. I'm not sure when. He said he only took a little, but that's how he knows that vampires are after me." She took a deep breath. "I don't want to believe him, but what if it's true?"

"I don't know, Tess. It's like a nightmare. Maybe we'll wake up in the morning and find out one of us is just having a really bad dream."

"I wish!"

"The only answer is to . . . you know . . ."

"Kill him? Jilly, he saved my life more than once. Without him, I'd be dead now."

"I don't know what the answer is, but having Andrei protect you from other vampires is kind of like hiring a wolf to protect a lamb from the pack. I'm just not sure you can trust him."

"You could be right."

"I know I am. Maybe Luke . . ."

"No! Luke's a great guy and all that. He might even turn out to be a great hunter when he's had more experience. But he's no match for a seven-hundred-year-old vampire. You know I'm right, don't you?"

Jilly's sigh of resignation was audible. "Try to get some sleep. I'll call you tomorrow."

Sleep, Tessa thought after disconnecting the call. She wasn't sure she would ever sleep again.

Tessa woke late in the morning. Feeling as if she'd hardly slept at all, she staggered into the kitchen and plugged in the coffeemaker, then went through the apartment and turned off the lights. It had been childish, perhaps, leaving all the lights burning, but, childish or not, there was no way she was going to sleep in the dark.

Last night had been a night she would never forget. After all, how many women discovered the man they were dating was a vampire?

And on Halloween, no less.

Vampire.

The word repeated itself in her mind as she showered and dressed. While she fixed breakfast. While she rinsed the dishes.

Vampire.

She had seen movies depicting the undead, read books, been attacked twice, and yet she really knew very little about what being a vampire entailed other than the obvious—they didn't grow old, they drank blood to survive, they were hard to kill.

She thought about Andrei—how could she not? He had held her in his arms. He had kissed her. He had tasted her blood.

Try as she might, she couldn't decide how she felt about him now. Logically, she knew she should hate him, avoid him. She should feel disgust because he had kissed her. Because she had eagerly and willingly kissed him back.

Why didn't she?

Because he was tall, dark, and handsome?

Because he made her feel beautiful, desirable?

Determined to banish him from her mind, she grabbed her earbuds, pumped up the volume, and plunged into housecleaning with a vengeance. Dishes, laundry, dusting, vacuuming. She even washed the windows and scrubbed the toilet, two jobs she loathed.

As long as she was busy, she managed to keep Andrei out of her thoughts, but the minute she started fixing dinner, his handsome face popped into her mind, his eyes dark and filled with mystery, his smile sensual. Damn the man!

She jumped when the phone rang, afraid it might be him.

Hoping it might be him.

She breathed a sigh of relief—or was it disappointment?—when she heard Jilly's voice. "Tess?"

"Hi."

"You okay, girl? You sound, I don't know, kind of disappointed."

"No. No, I was just . . . just going quietly insane. How are you?"

"I'm a nervous wreck. I asked Luke to spend the night last night because I was afraid to be home alone. Silly, I know, but . . ."

"Not any sillier than me, sleeping with all the lights on."

Jilly laughed softly. "We're a pair, aren't we? Has he called you?"

"No."

"What are you going to do if he wants another date?"

"I don't know."

"You don't want to see him again, do you?"

Tessa bit down on her lower lip. Seeing him could be dangerous. It might even be fatal, but . . .

"Tess?"

"Jilly, I know I shouldn't see him again, but I've never felt this way about anybody else."

"Think about what you're saying! He's a vampire, for crying out loud. You've got to end it now, while you still can."

"You're right. I know you're right. Anyway, he didn't say anything about seeing me again."

"You'll let me know if he calls, promise?"

"I promise. I'll see you Monday."

"I hope so," Jilly said. And ended the call.

Tessa sat at the table a moment, then went to her desk and fired up her laptop. A Google search turned up over forty thousand hits. According to Wikipedia, vampires were mythical creatures. Such entities—called by a variety of names—were known to have been recorded in almost every culture, going back as far as the ancient Greeks and Romans. Their tales of demons and spirits were thought to be the basis for modern-day vampires, although Bram Stoker was given credit for creating the quintessential vampire in his immortal character Count Dracula, the indisputable inspiration for numerous books, films, and TV shows.

Vampires could turn into mist, scale tall buildings like a spider, read minds, control the weather, move faster than the eye could follow. They didn't age, were never sick. And how cool would that be, she thought absently, never to have to worry about growing old and helpless.

The idea that she found anything about being a vampire appealing brought her up short. No one wanted to get old. No one looked forward to dying, but it was a fact of life. You were born, you grew up. If you were lucky, you lived a good long life, and then, to put it poetically, you "went the way of all the earth."

With a shake of her head, Tessa shut down her laptop. She had been scared before she started reading about vampires. Now she was just depressed.

Thinking to cheer herself up, she whipped up a hot fudge sundae and found her favorite comedy on Netflix.

She was just dozing off when someone knocked at the door.

Something—a tingle in the air, a sudden change in the atmosphere—told her Andrei was waiting outside.

She froze, hardly daring to breathe. If she didn't answer, maybe he'd think she wasn't home and go away.

Several seconds passed.

And then, just when she was certain he'd gone, he knocked again.

"I know you're home, Tessa," he said. "I can hear the rapid beat of your heart."

Scowling, she added "exceptional hearing" to the long list of vampire traits.

She took a deep breath in an effort to calm her racing heart. Then, her hand visibly shaking, she opened the door.

He looked as handsome, as desirable, as always. Damn him.

"Can we talk?"

Tessa took a step backward. "What is there to say?"

"Hey, it's your life. If you don't want my help, fine."

She chewed on a corner of her lower lip. Then, hoping she wasn't making a big mistake, she gestured for him to come inside. She didn't close the door.

"Worried about your reputation?" he asked dryly.

"Worried about my life," she retorted.

He grinned inwardly, thinking an open door was no protection at all.

"So," she said, perching on the edge of the sofa, "what did you want to talk about?"

"Can't you guess? I warned you before to stay inside after dark. It's still good advice. Unlike older vampires, fledglings can't go out in the sun. All the vampires who've been after you have been newly turned."

"If my blood is so wonderful, why are they trying so hard to kill me? I mean, no me, no blood."

"Because they haven't yet learned to control their hunger. Once fledglings start to feed, most are no longer rational."

"Maybe I should bottle my blood," she muttered. "I could probably make a small fortune."

"Or a large one," he said, amused by her wry sense of humor. "For fledglings the chance to enhance their power is too tempting to deny. It's a matter of survival when so many are destroyed by older vampires. As far as I can tell, your blood doesn't seem to hold the same allure for any of the ancient ones, and that's a good thing."

"How so?"

"Because I'm not the only one who can walk in the daylight." Reaching inside his jacket, Andrei withdrew four short, sharp, wooden stakes and offered them to her. "You might want to keep these handy. . . ." He paused when she recoiled. "You got a problem with these?"

She looked up at him, her face pale. "I just don't think I could drive one of those into someone's heart."

"No? You'd be surprised by what you can do when the necessity arises."

"Isn't it . . . messy?"

"No. That's only in the movies."

"Don't I need a . . . a mallet or something?"

Andrei shook his head. "Vampires are powerful, but our flesh is as vulnerable as yours." He dropped the stakes on the coffee table. "Any wooden stake will do, but those made of hickory or oak are the best. These are hickory."

Tessa stared at them as if he had dropped a quartet of rattlesnakes on the table.

"There are only a few effective ways to destroy a vampire—a wooden stake in the heart, fire, or beheading."

Tessa blinked at him, unable to believe she was having this conversation with Andrei. A little voice in the back of her mind whispered, *Vampire.* "Why are you telling me this?"

"I don't want anything to happen to you, and since you've made it pretty clear you don't want me around, I want you to know how to protect yourself."

"What about garlic? And silver?"

"Garlic stinks," he said, shrugging. "Pure silver burns, but it won't deter a hungry vampire."

His gaze, so intense, unnerved her. Was he waiting for her to say more? What more was there to say, except, "Thank you for the information. And the advice." She swallowed the urge to invite him to stay.

Andrei nodded curtly. "Take care of yourself," he murmured.

He was almost out the door when she called, "Andrei, wait."

He turned, one brow arched in question.

"Remember the fortune-teller? The one spreading those rumors about me?"

He nodded. "Madame Murga?"

"I looked her up on the Internet. I thought if I could find her I could ask her to stop talking about me. She died a few weeks ago."

Andrei grunted softly. "Natural causes?"

"I guess so. It said she passed away in her sleep."

"Somehow I doubt that. Be on your guard, Tessa," he warned again, and left without another word.

Tessa stared at the wooden stakes. Taking a deep breath, she picked one up. It was solid, heavier than it looked. Andrei had said she would be surprised by what she could do if necessary. She tried to imagine driving that short piece of wood into Andrei's heart. Swallowing the bile that rose in her throat, she dropped the stake as if it was on fire.

She shut the door, shot the dead bolt home, then collapsed on the sofa, wondering how her once mundane life had gotten so amazingly complicated.

And so dangerous.

Feeling the need for solace, Tessa rose early in the morning and went to church. And while she found the music soothing, concentrating on the sermon was impossible.

What was there about her blood that was any different from anyone else's? There was nothing remarkable about her parents. They were just ordinary Americans. Her father had a little Cherokee blood, her mother was English and German. Certainly nothing out of the ordinary there. To her knowledge, there were no witches in her family, no Druids. Or elves. "Or orcs," she muttered.

Maybe she needed to have a blood test . . . she dismissed the idea as soon as it occurred to her. She didn't like doctors or needles. And what were the odds—if there was something supernaturally weird about her blood—that a doctor would be able to diagnose it?

From out of the past, the words of the gypsy woman echoed in her mind. *"I see a man,"* the fortune-teller had said. *"He is old. Very old. He will come into your life in a moment of danger. He will watch over you and protect you. He will bring you death. And life."*

Andrei had brought death to those who attacked her.

"And life," Tessa muttered on her way home from church. "What the heck does that mean? And why was Madame Murga spreading rumors about my blood in the first place?" What had she hoped to gain?

"Tess, you're not making any sense." Jilly said, injecting a note of patience in her voice. "Slow down and start over. When did you see a gypsy? And why on earth didn't you take me with you?"

Tessa took a deep breath, her hand tightening on her cell phone. Thinking about Madame Murga on the way home from church had freaked her out. And when that happened, what was a girl to do but call her best friend and vent? "I saw the gypsy ten years ago."

"Ten years?" Jilly's frown was obvious in her voice. "You went to see a gypsy when you were, what? Fifteen? Wow, I never would have thought that."

"It wasn't my idea, believe me. My cousin Lisa talked me into it. She was only thirteen at the time, but she was fascinated by the occult."

"So, this gypsy told you an old man would come into your life and bring death and life? And you think she meant Andrei?"

"She said he'd come into my life *in a moment of danger* and that he would protect me. Doesn't that sound like Andrei?"

"Well, yeah, in a way, I guess it does."

"In a way? *In a way?* Jilly, he saved my life twice."

"So, you really believe that a gypsy foretold Andrei coming into your life?"

"I don't know. I always thought fortune-tellers were fakes, you know?"

"So, maybe this one was for real."

"She said he would bring death, which he did. I just have this freaky feeling about what the 'life' part might mean."

"Maybe she just meant that he'd save your life?"

"Maybe."

"But you're not convinced?"

"I don't know," Tessa admitted, reluctant to mention the fortune-teller's most recent prediction. "Maybe I'm just overreacting."

"Well, who could blame you?" Jilly said. "It isn't every day you almost fall in love with a vampire. That's bound to shake up your equilibrium. Have you seen him lately?"

"He was here last night. He left four stakes on my coffee table."

"That's an odd gift," Jilly said, laughing. "Most guys bring flowers, not dinner."

"*Wooden* stakes, Jilly, so I could defend myself if I'm attacked again, since he won't be around anymore."

"Oh." Jilly's concern came through loud and clear.

"Thanks for letting me bend your ear."

"No problem. That's what friends are for. Try not to worry, Tess. Just stay away from Dinescu, be sure to stay inside after dark, and I'm sure you'll be all right. Oh! And keep your windows closed and your door locked!"

"Yes, Mother."

"Do you want to come over and spend the evening with me and Luke?"

"Thanks for the offer, but I'm sure the two of you

would rather be alone. Don't worry about me. I'm not going anywhere. I'm going to do my hair and my nails and just veg out on the sofa. I'll see you at lunch tomorrow."

"All right. Night, Tess. Call me if you need me."

After ending the call, Tessa stared at her phone. Maybe she should have gone over to Jilly's for a while. Spending time with her and Luke would help take her mind off vampires and other things she didn't want to think about, like her attraction to Andrei and how much she missed him, even though she'd seen him just yesterday. His visit had been brief and not particularly pleasant. Even when they weren't together, he was always in her mind. When she was with him, she felt . . . alive.

She thought of her visit to Madame Murga again.

"He will bring you death," the fortune-teller had predicted. *"And life."*

Chapter Nine

Katerina Glinin paced the floor, her long skirts whispering in her wake. She glanced occasionally at the young male vampire who huddled on the stone flagging in front of the hearth, his arms folded over his head. As if that would save him.

She paused in front of him. "Ilia, look at me."

He did as bidden though obviously reluctant to meet her eyes.

Like a snake facing a rabbit, her gaze trapped his. "Tell me more about this woman whose blood enhances the strength of fledglings."

"I don't know any more, I swear it. All I know is what I've heard. Rumors, that's all. I've never seen her."

"Who told you these rumors?"

"Friends of mine. They told me they were going after her. I never heard from them again."

"Do you think she killed them?"

He snorted his disdain. "A mortal female?"

"Where does this mortal live?"

"Cutter's Corner. My friend didn't tell me her name when he called me."

"You may go."

He was gone before she finished speaking.

Brow furrowed, Katerina resumed her pacing. She had not been to America in decades. Perhaps it was time to visit again.

She smiled faintly, wondering if Andrei still made his home there.

Andrei. She had known many men, loved a few, used others only to cast them aside when they ceased to amuse her.

But Andrei Dinescu was the only man she had ever married.

Katerina chuckled softly. According to the vows they had exchanged, he was still her husband.

"To have and to hold," she murmured, thinking how surprised he would be to see her after such a long time. "Until death do us part."

Chapter Ten

Andrei prowled the dark streets, his thoughts as black as the night. He had found a woman like no other, a woman who made him feel alive again. Young again. And she wanted nothing to do with him. Not that he could blame her. Being a vampire, he had little to offer her. Certainly nothing she wanted. Or needed.

But he couldn't get Tessa out of his mind. It had been a week since he had last seen her—the longest week of his life.

Almost before he realized what he was doing, he was in front of her apartment building. Was she home?

He opened his senses, searching for her, felt a surge of relief when he had assured himself that she was safely inside.

A thought took him to the landing in front of her door. The strong, steady beat of her heart called to him, as did the warm, sweet scent of her blood. The fragrance of her hair, her skin. The memory of holding her in his arms. The alluring heat of her kisses.

"Tessa." Her name whispered past his lips. He wanted her, wanted her as he had never wanted another woman.

Even more compelling was his soul-deep need for her, a longing unlike any he had ever known.

Few things had surprised him since becoming a vampire, but he was totally astonished when the apartment door opened and Tessa stood there.

"Andrei."

"How did you know I was here?"

"I'm not sure." It wasn't quite the truth. She had felt his presence, and how weird was that? And yet there was no denying it. She'd been sitting on the sofa, trying to read the latest book by her favorite author, when something had told her he was there. "What are you doing here?"

He shook his head. "I was out walking and the next thing I knew, I was here. I've missed you, Tessa. You have no idea how much."

"I've missed you, too," she said, her throat clogged with emotion. "I tried not to. I told myself it would never work, but . . ." She looked up at him, her gaze drinking him in, her whole being yearning toward him.

"Tess."

The longing in his voice reached deep inside her, drawing her across the threshold and into his embrace. For a moment, she simply stood there, her cheek pressed against his chest, her arms around his waist. This was what home felt like, she thought. Warm, secure, and so right.

He held her tight, his chin resting lightly on the top of her head. He had no idea what he had done to deserve her trust, had been certain he would never hold her close again.

After a moment, Tessa lifted her head. "Maybe we should go inside." She tugged lightly on his hand and he followed her into the house, obligingly shut the door.

Tessa took a deep breath. Being alone in the house with Andrei suddenly made her feel as if someone had sucked all the air out of the room. She had missed him, but now that he was here, he seemed larger than life. His presence filled the room.

He was a vampire—incredibly old, incredibly strong and powerful. And yet, in the deepest parts of her heart and soul, she knew he would never hurt her.

The question now, she thought, was where did they go from here?

Andrei stroked her cheek with his fingertips, his touch featherlight, yet she felt it in every nerve and fiber of her body. "I guess that's up to you."

She reminded herself once again that he could read her mind. Why did she keep forgetting that?

Moving to the sofa, she motioned for him to join her. "I don't want to rush into anything, if you know what I mean."

"Hmm. I'm guessing that means you don't want to be intimate until we know each other better."

Cheeks flushing, Tessa nodded. "I've never had a casual affair and I don't intend to start now." The truth was, she'd never had an affair of any kind.

"That's very wise of you," he said, amusement evident in his tone.

"You're making fun of me."

"No, never. Just tell me what the rules are."

"There aren't any 'rules' exactly. Just certain boundaries I'm not willing to cross just yet."

Andrei nodded. "If I start to cross a line, just tell me to stop."

"You drank my blood."

He nodded again.

"That's crossing the line big-time."

"Would you deny me that pleasure?"

She glared at him. "It might be pleasurable for you. Not for me."

"How do you know?"

"What do you mean?"

"Let me show you." His fingertips caressed her neck, then came to rest just below her ear.

Tessa's heart skipped a beat. His fingers were cool against her skin, yet she suddenly felt warm all over.

"Do you trust me?" he asked quietly.

"I don't know. Should I?"

"I promise I won't hurt you, and I'll stop immediately if you tell me to."

Tessa stared at him. Who in their right mind invited a vampire to bite them? And what if he didn't stop? There was no knight in shining armor waiting to come to her rescue.

Leaning forward, he brushed a kiss across her lips. "Trust me, Tessa. Let me show you what pleasure is."

"You promise you'll stop if I don't like it?"

"On my word of honor."

Did vampires have honor? She searched his face. If they were going to have any kind of relationship, she had to be able to trust him.

Reading the answer in her eyes, he smiled as he drew her into his arms. "Relax. It won't hurt at all."

Was he kidding? How was she going to relax when he was going to . . . she gasped at the touch of his fangs against her skin, closed her eyes as warmth flooded her, curling deep inside of her, filling her with a rush of pleasure. All thought of resistance fled as she sagged in his arms, her whole being tingling with sensual awareness.

All too soon, he lifted his head. "Tessa?"

"Hmm?" Her eyelids fluttered open. "Why did you stop?"

He chuckled softly. "One of us has to know when to quit."

"How can anything so . . . so . . . I mean, letting you drink from me should be repugnant. I should be freaking out instead of wanting you to do it again."

"Did I not say you would like it?"

"Why didn't it hurt?"

"Because I didn't want it to."

She pondered that a moment. Then, with a sigh, she snuggled against his chest, wondering what Jilly would say when she learned her best friend had welcomed Andrei back into her life.

Tessa waited until lunch on Monday to break the news to Jileen, figuring that her friend wouldn't go ballistic in the middle of the cafeteria. As Tessa had expected, Jilly was horrified by the news.

"Are you crazy?' Jileen exclaimed. "Like, totally insane?"

"I guess so." Tessa sipped her latte, then picked up her sandwich.

"You must be, because, seriously, there's really no other explanation." Jileen glanced around the cafeteria, then leaned forward. "You need to be careful," she whispered. "Luke staked a vampire last night, but his companion got away."

Tessa dropped the sandwich back onto her plate, her appetite gone.

"I'm sorry," Jilly said. "I didn't mean to spoil your lunch, but I thought you should know. Luke's going to come by and drive you home tonight, then I'll bring him back here to pick up his car."

Tessa started to say that wouldn't be necessary, then changed her mind. Better safe than sorry. The last thing she wanted was to be driving home alone when there was a vampire in the area. "Thanks, Jilly."

Whenever Tessa had a quiet moment the rest of the day, she wondered if she should quit her job and move to a new town. Sometimes she thought that would be the smart thing to do. And yet, if vampires from all over believed her blood had some magic power, moving really wouldn't solve the problem. Sooner or later, they would find her again. Try as she might, she could find no permanent solution to the matter. Unless she could somehow get all new blood . . . She shuddered at the thought. Even if such a thing was feasible, there was no way to be certain that would work, either.

"Miss Blackburn?"

"What?" She looked up to see a deliveryman standing on the other side of her desk. "Yes. Can I help you?"

"These are for you."

"For me?" Rising, Tessa reached for the flowers—a beautiful bouquet of pink roses and pink and white lilies in a tall, crystal vase. "Thank you." When she reached for her purse, intending to tip the man, he waved her off.

"Already taken care of," he said, smiling. "Enjoy your day."

"Thank you." After placing the vase on the corner of her desk, she reached for the card, which she read aloud. "To let you know I'm thinking of you. " It was signed *A. D.*

Andrei.

How could she even think of leaving town when he was here? If anyone could protect her, it was Andrei. Luke might be a hunter, but he wasn't nearly as strong or powerful or as experienced as Andrei.

Jilly came by her office a few minutes before five. "Ready to go?"

"Yeah, just let me grab my bag."

"Nice flowers," Jilly remarked. "I'll bet I can guess who they're from."

"I'll bet you'd be right."

"Tess . . ."

"Not here," Tessa said as they made their way to the elevators. "We'll talk later at my place."

Luke was waiting for them on the main floor when the elevator doors opened.

And so was Andrei.

Jileen tugged on Tessa's arm. "What's *he* doing here?"

"I don't know." *But I'm really glad to see him.* When Andrei smiled, she knew he'd read her thoughts. Again.

Luke glanced at Jileen. "I thought you said she needed a ride home?"

"She does," Andrei said. "And I'm it."

"Tess, are you sure?" Jileen asked.

"I'm sure," she replied, moving to Andrei's side. "Thanks for coming, Luke, but I'm going with Andrei."

"Yeah, well, I hope you don't regret it."

"I'll be fine. See you tomorrow, Jilly."

Jilly nodded, her expression sour.

"Your friends are afraid for your safety," Andrei remarked as they left the building. "They don't trust me."

"Can you blame them?"

"All things considered? I guess not."

"It doesn't matter," Tessa said. "I trust you." Reaching into her handbag, she withdrew her keys and pressed them into his hand. "Thank you for the flowers."

"You're welcome." He opened the door for her, closed it gently, and went around to the driver's side.

She waited until they were on the road before saying,

"Jilly told me that Luke found two vampires last night. He staked one, but the other one got away."

"No, he didn't."

"What do you mean?"

Andrei slid a glance in her direction.

"You were there?"

"Luke destroyed the fledgling. His companion was older, not so easily taken. Had Luke pursued him, the vampire would have killed him."

"But . . ." Tessa frowned. "If the other vampire was older, why didn't he kill Luke?"

"We are not all indiscriminate killers, *dragostea mea.*"

"You've called me that before. What does it mean?"

He glanced at her, his gaze dark and intense, his voice quietly compelling. "My love."

My love. The words sent a shiver down Tessa's spine. But surely it was just an expression.

Andrei pulled over to the side of the road and killed the engine. "Is that what you think?"

"But . . . we've only known each other a short time."

He shrugged. "Time is irrelevant. I've waited an eternity for you."

"Andrei . . . I don't know what to say."

"You don't have to say anything. I know you care for me. I know you're attracted to me. Love may come, in time."

"And if it doesn't?" She turned to stare out the side window. He could read minds. Could he compel her to love him?

"Tessa." When she turned to face him, his fingers lightly stroked her cheek, then came to rest in the hollow of her throat. Her pulse beat against his fingertips, fluttering wildly like a bird in flight. "Why would I do that?"

"I don't know. Could you? Make me love you?"

"No. I can compel you to do whatever I desire. But I can't make you fall in love with me."

"You didn't answer my question."

"If you wish to be rid of me, you have only to say so."

"And you'll leave, just like that?"

He nodded. "I will pack up the shattered pieces of my broken heart and leave the city."

"I'm serious."

"So am I." His hand curled around her nape. "You said you weren't ready to be intimate," he murmured, "but how do you feel about making out with a very old vampire?"

"Here?" she asked, unable to keep the smile out of her voice. "Now?"

"Here." He pushed his seat back as far as it would go, then lifted her onto his lap so that she was facing him. "Now," he said, and covered her mouth with his.

Chapter Eleven

"I love him, I love him not . . ." Tessa glanced at the vase of red roses sitting on her desk across from the vase of pink ones. The red ones had arrived first thing in the morning. "My office is beginning to look like a florist shop." She burst into giggles as she plucked the last petal from the rose in her hand. "I love him."

She hadn't been able to stop smiling or stop thinking about Andrei since last night. Her boss, Mr. Ambrose, had cast several curious glances in her direction. Three of her coworkers had asked if she'd won the lottery.

If what she was feeling wasn't love, Tessa mused, dropping the denuded stem into the wastebasket beside her desk, it was darn close. Even though she knew it was impossible, she would have sworn she could still feel his lips on hers, his arms around her. Still hear his voice murmuring that she was beautiful, desirable.

That he loved her.

Sighing, she refocused her attention on the file in front of her, but her gaze kept straying to the time in the lower corner of her computer screen.

Barely noon. Hours to go until she would see Andrei again.

Jileen was even more upset than Tessa had expected. "I can't believe you let him take you home last night! What is it with you? Have you got a death wish or something?" Jilly added sugar substitute to her iced tea, then stirred it so vigorously it slopped over onto the table.

"I think having him around is the best thing ever," Tessa said, helping Jilly mop up the mess. "I haven't been attacked in days. I think word that he's protecting me is spreading."

Jileen shook her head. "You've lost it, haven't you?" Leaning forward, she tapped Tessa on the forehead with the end of her spoon. "Come back to the real world, Tess. And if, as you say, he's keeping the other vampi . . ." She glanced warily around the cafeteria. ". . . keeping the others away, I'm sure it's only because he wants you all to himself."

"Jilly, I appreciate your concern, really I do. But I've got to see where this thing with Andrei goes. I think I might be in love with him."

Jilly's look of horror would have been comical under other circumstances. "You're *in love* with him? A man you've known for what? Less than a month? A man who just happens to be a . . . you-know-what?" She sighed dramatically. "I give up."

"I have to trust my instincts," Tessa said. "And I know I can trust him."

"It's your life," Jilly said. "I just hope you know what you're doing."

* * *

When Tessa told Andrei about Jileen's reaction at home later that night, he wasn't the least bit surprised.

"She's worried about you. It's only natural. Think about it. She's dating a hunter. I'm a vampire. The enemy."

"She thinks you're driving the other vampires away because you want me all to yourself."

"Well," he drawled, pulling her into his arms, "she's partially right. I definitely want you all to myself."

Jileen's attitude toward Tessa was several degrees cooler at work the next day. She usually popped into Tessa's office a couple of times before noon, but not today.

As Tessa left her office, she wondered if Jilly would meet her for lunch.

In the cafeteria, she feared she might have lost her best friend when she didn't see Jilly at their customary table. Sighing, she went through the line, thinking, yet again, how complicated her life had become since she met Andrei. And how much she'd miss Jilly if they couldn't mend the rift between them.

She was halfway through her sandwich when Jilly slid into the chair across from her. "Sorry I'm late."

"I was afraid you weren't coming."

"I wasn't." Jilly picked up her fork and pushed the salad around on her plate. "But then I decided I wasn't going to let a man come between us. Even if that man is a . . . you know."

"I'm glad."

"Well, it's not just me. Luke thinks you're crazy to go out with him too."

Tessa laughed as the tension between them dissolved.

"Would we be tempting fate if we tried another double date?"

"I think maybe *you're* crazy," Tessa said.

Jilly blew out a heavy sigh. "It's probably not the best idea I've ever had, but . . ."

"Have you talked to Luke about it?"

"Not yet, but I will."

"Okay. I'll mention it to Andrei and see what he says."

Tessa brought up the subject when Andrei was taking his leave from her place later that night.

He lifted one brow in an expression that was becoming familiar. "You've got to be kidding."

Tessa shrugged. "It was just a thought."

"A surprising one, all things considered. But if it's what you want, I'm game to try one more time."

"You mean it?"

"I said it, didn't I?"

"Where should we go?" Tessa asked.

"I'll leave that up to you and your friend."

"Do you have many friends?"

He hesitated a moment before saying, "None still living."

Tessa found herself thinking about what Andrei had said while she changed into her pj's and climbed into bed. *None still living.* Did vampires make friends? Besides herself, who in their right mind would want to associate with one of the undead?

Assuming vampires made friends, she supposed they sought out others of their own kind. After all, it might be difficult to hang out with someone who was also prey.

She was still turning that over in her mind when her cell phone rang.

It was Jilly. "So, did you talk to Andrei?"

"Yes. He's willing to try again."

"Really? I'm surprised he agreed. Not just because of what happened last time, but, you know, it's just hard to imagine vampires dating."

"I know." Tessa plumped the pillow behind her head. "What did Luke say?"

"Well, after what happened on Halloween, he wasn't too thrilled at the idea of double-dating again."

"I can understand that," Tessa said, grinning. "I'm still surprised that you suggested it."

"Believe me, I'd rather you were going out with anyone else, but that's neither here nor there. Anyway, Luke said he'd go, if that was what I wanted."

"Then I guess the big question is, where and when?"

"Dinner and a movie Friday night?" Jilly suggested.

"Okay. See you tomorrow." Tessa ended the call, switched off the lights, and slid under the covers.

She was thinking about Andrei—when wasn't she?—when she felt his presence in the room, felt the bed sag as he sat on the edge. "What are you doing here?" she whispered.

"I was hoping for a good-night kiss."

"How did you get in?" Sitting up, she turned on the light. "The door was locked."

He arched one brow in amusement. "A lock? Seriously?"

"Oh, right." She leaned toward him. "Didn't you say something about a kiss?"

Desire darkened his eyes as he reached for her, his arm curling around her waist, drawing her up against him. "I'm not crossing the line, am I?" he asked, his voice a low growl.

"Not yet." She closed her eyes as his mouth covered hers. Heat spread through her like liquid fire, magnifying every touch, pooling deep inside her. His hand stroked up and down her back, delved into the hair at her nape as his tongue teased her lips, then dipped inside to duel with hers. She gasped his name, her hands clutching his shoulders, as the heat within her intensified.

Andrei lifted his head, his eyes dark with passion. And tinged with a faint hint of red.

Tessa stared at him. "Your eyes . . ."

He turned his head away.

"Are you all right?"

"Of course." He looked back at her, his face impassive.

And the red was gone. "Did I imagine that?"

He didn't have to ask what she meant. "No. It happens sometimes, when passion fuels my hunger." He ran his knuckles along her cheek. "I should go. I haven't fed yet, and you're far too tempting."

"I wouldn't mind letting you have a taste of me."

"Probably not a good idea at the moment," he said, rising, "but I'll be glad to take you up on it tomorrow night."

"I'll look forward to it."

Murmuring, "Sweet dreams, *dragostea mea*," Andrei kissed her on the forehead and then, in a swirl of sparkling, dark gray motes, he vanished from her sight.

Chapter Twelve

Katerina walked along Fifth Avenue. New York had long been one of her favorite cities. She loved the excitement, the theaters, the shops. Saks, Lord & Taylor, Bloomingdale's, Bergdorf Goodman. She had been known to spend hours browsing the stores, buying whatever caught her eye, occasionally snacking on a particularly appealing customer. Or clerk.

She had hoped to find Andrei in the city, but, alas, he had not been there recently.

No matter. She had done everything she wanted to do in the Big Apple. She had shopped her favorite stores, intrigued by the latest fashions. Who would have ever thought that ragged jeans would be all the rage? She had gone to the theater, amused by *Wicked*, charmed by *The Lion King*, mesmerized by the sad plight of *The Phantom of the Opera*. What a vampire the phantom would have made!

Her thoughts returned to Andrei. She would find him, wherever he was. The blood bond that bound them together was stronger and more reliable than any GPS in the world.

Tomorrow night, it would lead her unerringly toward him.

Chapter Thirteen

In the morning, over breakfast, Tessa thought about Andrei's late-night visit. In some ways, it had been a pleasant surprise.

In others, a bit troubling.

"I haven't fed yet, and you're far too tempting."

Those words were both flattering and frightening.

They lingered in the back of her mind all that day, and quickly jumped to the forefront when Andrei arrived just after dinner.

He frowned as he followed her into the living room. "Is something wrong?"

"No. Well, sort of." She sat on the sofa and he settled in beside her.

He took her hand in his. "What does 'sort of' entail?"

"I keep thinking about what you said last night."

"Ah. My hunger and my desire are tightly interwoven, but you have nothing to fear from me, Tessa. I'm strong enough to control my appetite."

"And your desire?"

"I'll go as far as you'll let me," he answered candidly.

His thumb stroked her palm. Odd, she thought, that such a light touch should arouse her own desire.

His gaze met hers. A faint smile curved his lips, making her think he knew exactly how his touch affected her.

"Does last night's offer still stand?" His voice was low, husky.

"Are you hungry? Or is it thirsty?"

"I've already fed." His gaze moved to the hollow of her throat. "But I still need dessert."

Tessa laughed in spite of herself. "Just remember that this is dessert and not a seven-course meal."

Her heartbeat quickened as he drew her into his arms. Her eyelids fluttered down as he kissed her gently, slowly, as if he had all the time in the world. Which he did, she thought languidly. She clung to him as he kissed and caressed her, felt a rush of anticipation at the touch of his fangs.

She sighed as pleasure spiraled through her. She wished she could tell Jilly how wonderful it was to let Andrei drink from her. But her friend would never understand, not in a million years.

She sighed with regret when Andrei lifted his head.

"Thank you, my sweet."

"Thank *you*."

Andrei kissed her lightly, then went into the kitchen. He returned moments later carrying two glasses of red wine.

"You need this." He handed her a glass, then resumed his seat. "Drink it all." He watched her closely, relieved when the color returned to her cheeks.

She drained the glass and set it aside, then snuggled against him.

Awash with guilt, Andrei put his arm around Tessa's shoulders. He had taken more than he should have, making him rethink his bold statement that he was strong enough to control his hunger. Because the temptation to drain her dry had been almost overwhelming.

Tessa had just shut down her computer for the weekend when Mr. Ambrose called her into his office.

"I know this is last-minute," he said, "but I need you to deliver this file to Smithfield and Bridges for Jack's signature. I'd do it myself, but I have an appointment with Markinson and I've already canceled twice."

"No problem," Tessa said.

"You'll have to wait while he signs it."

Tessa nodded. "Yes, sir."

It wasn't until she was outside that Tessa realized it would be dark before she reached home.

Not to worry, she told herself as she pulled out of the parking lot. She had one of Andrei's wooden stakes in the glove compartment.

Tessa was thumbing through a magazine in Smithfield's waiting room when Andrei sent her a text, informing her that he was hunting but he would be there on time for their double date.

Hunting. She tried not to think what that entailed as she drove home twenty minutes later, but couldn't put the thought out of her mind. Did his victims feel the same sense of sensual euphoria that she did when he bit her? Did he prey on both men and women? She grimaced. Children? Did all blood taste the same? Why was hers so different from everyone else's?

She was still pondering that when she parked her car in her assigned place. The overhead light had burned out, leaving the condo parking area in total darkness. Taking a deep breath, Tessa opened the glove compartment. Better safe than sorry, she mused as she located the stake.

If she hurried, she would have just enough time to shower and change clothes before Andrei arrived. With that thought in mind, she stepped out of the car.

And shrieked when a hand closed over her forearm in a grip like iron. Time seemed to stop. She heard a ferocious growl, like that of a wild animal. Even in the darkness, she could see his fangs, sharp and white, the glittering red glow of his eyes.

He meant to kill her.

The thought spurred her to action.

Hardly aware of what she was doing, she drove the hickory stake into her attacker's chest.

With a hiss of pained surprise, he released her and staggered a few steps backward. His fangs gleamed in the bright glare of the headlights of an incoming car.

She had missed his heart.

With a wordless cry, he ripped the stake from his chest and tossed it aside.

Teeth bared, hands like claws, he lunged toward her.

A scream rose in Tessa's throat but before it found release, Andrei was there. She knew what he was going to do and she turned away, her hand covering her mouth. But there was no way to shut out the vampire's hoarse scream as his heart was ripped from his chest.

The scent of blood wafted through the air.

"Tessa?" She flinched when she felt Andrei's hand on her shoulder. "Tess?"

"I'm . . . all . . . right." Suddenly cold all over, she wrapped her arms around her middle.

"Go inside. I'll take care of this."

She nodded, her movements leaden as she picked

up her handbag. On legs that were none too steady, she made her way up the stairs and into her apartment. Feeling numb, she closed and locked the door; then, shaking from head to foot, she dropped to the floor as the strength drained out of her.

She had almost killed a man, even though he wasn't really a man anymore, but a vampire.

A monster.

Had he been a fledgling, like the others? What did Andrei do with the bodies? Did he bury them? Burn them? Or just dump them where they would never be found?

She choked back the bile rising in her throat. She had told Andrei she didn't think she could drive a stake into anybody's chest. But, as he had predicted, it was amazing what you were capable of when your life was in jeopardy. One thing was certain. She needed to work on her aim for the next time, because Andrei might not be there to save her.

She practically jumped out of her skin when someone knocked at the door.

"Tessa?"

She sagged in relief when she heard Andrei's voice. With one hand braced against the jamb, she gained her feet and let him in.

His gaze moved over her, missing nothing, before he drew her gently into his embrace. "That was close." Too damn close, he thought.

She nodded; then, resting her head against his chest, she wrapped her arms around his waist. His nearness calmed her, chasing away the worst vestiges of the night's horror.

One thing was certain: First thing in the morning, she was going to look into taking a self-defense class at the Y.

Chapter Fourteen

Andrei stayed with Tessa until she fell asleep.

As he slid behind the wheel of his car, he chuckled softly. *Self-defense lessons, indeed.* He was far better qualified to teach her how to defend herself. Perhaps he would mention it tomorrow night.

He had called Jilly earlier to let her know Tessa had decided to postpone their double date, which was understandable. She was still badly shaken. He hadn't gone into the details of why with Jilly. He had decided to leave that to Tessa, who could relate as much or as little of her ordeal as she saw fit.

He was about to pull away from the curb when an apparition from the past appeared in front of the car.

Katerina!

What the hell was she doing here?

Between one breath and the next, she was in the seat beside him.

"Good evening, my husband," she purred. "You don't look happy to see me."

"How perceptive of you."

She glanced up at the apartment building. "Is this your hunting ground? Not very glamorous."

"No."

Her nostrils flared, and then she raked her perfectly manicured fingernails down his arm, tearing through shirt and skin. "You should know better than to lie to me. I can smell prey on you."

"You asked if I hunt here. I don't."

"Then who is the woman?"

"An acquaintance. What brings you here?"

"Curiosity."

"Indeed?"

"I was told there's a female in this town with the most remarkable blood."

"Who told you that?" So she didn't yet know it was Tessa. Thank the Lord for favors great and small.

"One of my fledglings. Apparently only the very young are drawn to this female. It made me curious, so I decided to come and see this enigma for myself. And then I thought, as long as I was in the States, I would pay a visit to my husband."

Andrei clenched his hands on the wheel. That was twice she had called him "husband." It did not bode well.

"I need to feed," he said curtly.

"Wonderful! It's been centuries since we hunted together."

He would have informed her she wasn't welcome to join him, but at the moment he was willing to do whatever it took to put some distance between Tessa and Katerina.

"We're driving?" she asked as he made a U-turn. "Seriously?"

"I like to drive."

With an exaggerated sigh that clearly meant she was

humoring him, Katerina settled back in her seat. "Why are you holed up in this backwater town?"

"I got tired of big cities."

"After I find the female, we should go to New York."

"We?" He slid a glance in her direction. "There is no 'we.'"

"But Andrei, how can you say that? We're still legally married."

He swore under his breath. Wasn't there a statute of limitations or an expiration date on ancient wedding vows? If not, there should be. "What game are you playing now?"

"No games," she replied, batting her eyelashes at him. "I just got tired of wandering around alone and thought it would be fun to spend time with you."

"Yeah? Well, think again."

"Andrei, you're hurting my feelings."

He snorted. "Are those the same feelings you had when you slaughtered my family and made me a slave?"

She stared at him, eyes narrowed ominously.

He tightened his hold on the wheel. What the hell was he doing? Antagonizing her would gain him nothing. Tamping down his anger, he muttered, "I'm just surprised to see you, that's all." He felt her gaze on him, studying him like he was a bug under a microscope. It wasn't a pleasant feeling. "What makes you think this female you're looking for is here?"

"I know that she is. And now you too are here. I have to wonder if it is merely coincidence."

He grunted softly as he parked the car, then went around to open the door for her.

Katerina usually hunted among the rich and famous, but every now and then she had liked hunting in the slums. With that in mind, he had brought her to the worst part of the city, a place inhabited by drug addicts and transients, people who were down and out and wouldn't be missed.

People for whom death would be a blessing.

Because, even after all these years, Katerina still enjoyed killing those she preyed upon.

Chapter Fifteen

Jilly stared at Tessa, the hot fudge sundae in front of her forgotten. Since their double date had been canceled, she and Tessa had decided to meet for lunch at the local ice-cream shop and then take in an early movie.

"I . . ." Jilly shook her head. "I don't know what to say. You must have been totally freaked out. I don't even want to think about what would have happened if Andrei hadn't showed up. I guess I was wrong to want you to stay away from him."

Tessa nodded. Thinking about what had happened last night still sickened her. The memory had haunted her dreams. She'd had a horrible nightmare. In it, the vampire who had attacked her had risen from the grave and chased her through dark streets until he caught her. . . . She shook the memory from her mind. But for Andrei, the other vampire would have fed on her. She shuddered. Perhaps he would have killed her.

"I think you're right about taking some self-defense classes. Maybe I'll go with you."

"I thought it was a good idea, but now I don't know.

Vampires are so strong and quick, I'm not sure it would help much," Tessa said. "Still, I have to do something! I thought about moving, but what good would that do? Sooner or later, they'll find me. I have to be prepared."

"I can't believe I'm saying this, but maybe you should go stay with Andrei for a while?"

"He's never suggested that."

"Well, maybe *you* should. I can't imagine any place safer."

"Me either." Or more dangerous, Tessa thought. But for an entirely different reason. Every time Andrei held her, kissed her, caressed her, it was harder to resist him. Harder to deny her own desire and not surrender to the attraction that sizzled between them.

Since it was still light outside, Tessa decided to make a quick stop at the grocery store on the way home from the movies. She reasoned it would only take a minute to pick up a quart of milk and a ready-made salad. And she should be safe enough, since fledglings couldn't be out until after dark. Inevitably, she bought more than she intended.

She was loading her bags into the trunk when a woman approached her. Long, brown hair fell over her shoulders. Her complexion was clear and flawlessly beautiful. Straight brows framed dark gray eyes that missed nothing as she drew closer.

"Who are you?" the woman asked.

"Excuse me?"

"It's a simple question. Who are you? What are you to Andrei?"

"Who are *you*?"

The woman's smile was cold. "I'm his wife."

Tessa took a step backward. "Wife!"

"He's never mentioned me?"

"No. What do you want?"

"You've been with him. Your scent was on his clothing when I saw him last night." Animosity poured off the woman, so intense it was almost palpable.

Tessa swallowed hard, her heart pounding, her mind racing. Married! Andrei was married. Why hadn't he told her? Why hadn't it ever occurred to her to ask?

The woman took a step forward. "Stay away from him."

"No problem," Tessa said, forcing a note of calm into her voice.

The woman smiled, displaying shiny white fangs. "Smart girl."

A vampire. Tessa shivered. Why was she not surprised?

She stood there, feeling naked and vulnerable under the woman's malevolent gaze, sagged against the car door when, with a wave of her hand, Andrei's wife disappeared from sight.

Feeling sick to her stomach, Tessa opened the car door and sank onto the seat. For a moment, she sat there, hands clenched on the steering wheel, shaking from head to foot.

Wife.

He had a wife.

She blinked rapidly, refusing to cry.

He was a cheat and a liar. He didn't deserve her tears.

But they came anyway.

Tessa saw Andrei waiting on the landing outside her apartment when she got home. Knowing she would have to face him sooner or later, she gathered her bags, then took a deep breath.

He watched her, eyes narrowing, as she climbed the stairs toward him.

"What are you doing here?" she asked as she unlocked the door. "Shouldn't you be at home? With your *wife*?"

For once, she had caught him totally off guard. "What are you talking about?"

"I met her today. She warned me to stay away from you."

Andrei uttered several words Tessa didn't understand, but cussing sounded pretty much the same in any language.

She held up a staying hand when he started to follow her inside. "You're not welcome here anymore."

"Tessa, listen . . ."

"I'm through listening to you."

"Dammit, Tessa." His hands curled into fists. "Just listen!"

"You can say whatever you have to from out there." After setting her bags on the floor, she folded her arms over her chest. "Well? I'm waiting."

"I should have told you about Katerina, but I never thought she'd come looking for me. Or for you. I haven't seen her in centuries."

"Centuries?"

He nodded.

"But you are married?"

"Technically, I guess so."

Was he being honest with her now? Maybe she was being a fool, but this was a story she had to hear.

With a sigh, she stepped back. "Maybe you'd better come inside and explain. Just let me put these things away."

* * *

When she returned to the living room, Tessa found Andrei standing in front of the window, staring out.

He didn't turn around. "I was engaged to another woman when I met Katerina. I didn't know she was a vampire, only that she was the most beautiful, mysterious woman I had ever met. I broke my engagement and married her. Only then did I discover that Katerina had married me because she coveted my home and the title that went with it."

"Did you . . ." She hesitated a moment. "Did you have children?"

"No. Vampires are unable to reproduce."

Tessa decided that was probably a good thing, considering what he'd told her so far.

"Over the course of the next two years, she killed all the members of my family. No one ever suspected her, thanks in part to her deceit and in part to her ability to make people believe anything she told them. I didn't learn of her treachery until all my elder brothers had been killed, leaving me the only surviving heir."

"Oh, Andrei, I'm so sorry."

"She mesmerized the servants so they wouldn't ask questions when one of the maids turned up dead, drained of blood. She turned me against my will, compelled me to do things—despicable things that haunt me to this day. It took me a hundred years to gain enough strength to resist her compulsions, and another two centuries to escape her."

Tessa stared at his back, her heart aching for his pain.

And still he didn't face her.

She hesitated a moment, then slid her arms around his waist.

With a hoarse cry, he turned and gathered her into his arms. For several moments, he held her close.

"Why is she here now? What does she want?"

"She heard about you, about your blood, I mean."

"What? How is that possible?"

"Some fledgling told her. It piqued her interest and she decided to come to the States and see if she could find the woman with the mysterious blood. I'm not sure what her interest is. Curiosity? Boredom? Who the hell knows why Katerina does what she does. Anyway, she decided as long as she was here, she might as well spend some time with me."

"She wants you to be her husband again, doesn't she?"

He was silent for several moments before saying, "I'm afraid so."

"And you agreed?"

Again, he hesitated. "Not exactly."

Slipping out of his embrace, Tessa backed up a step. "What, exactly?"

"I can't beat her in a fight," he said flatly. "She's too powerful. My only hope—*our* only hope—is to humor her. If I resist, it will only make her more determined. But if I play along, she'll soon get bored and go back home."

"Are you sure about that?"

He shook his head. "With Katerina, you can never be certain of anything. But I don't know what else I can do."

"Where does that leave me? Leave us?"

"I'm not sure." Katerina was ancient, the most powerful vampire he knew. To make her angry was to invite not only her wrath, but Tessa's destruction. And possibly his own. "But if there's one thing I've learned, it's that her threats are rarely empty."

Remembering the icy tone of Katerina's voice, the menace in her eyes, Tessa shivered.

"As strong as she is, she can't enter your house uninvited."

"Why not? Why does that even keep vampires out?"

"Thresholds have power. They're meant to protect mortals from supernatural creatures. But the protection only extends to homes and other places of residence. You'll be safe at Jilly's, but not at work."

Suddenly chilled, Tessa drew his arms around her again.

"You need to learn to shield your mind. Even though Katerina can't force her way into your apartment, she has the power to compel you to go to her. If you feel her inside your head, you have to block her."

"How do I do that?"

"It's like building a wall around your thoughts. You build it brick by brick until you master the technique. In time, it will become second nature."

"You said supernatural creatures. Plural."

"Vampires aren't the only monsters out there. They're just the ones making the headlines these days."

Tessa closed her eyes. "I don't want to know about any others. I can't handle that right now."

Andrei brushed a kiss across the top of her head. "Are you ready to build that wall?"

Tessa was amazed at how easy it was to erect an imaginary barrier in her mind. She had thought it might take days—perhaps weeks—to accomplish, but it was surprisingly simple.

Even Andrei was impressed. "You're a natural," he remarked when she shut him out of her thoughts.

Tessa smiled, pleased by his praise, and then frowned.

Sometimes it was nice, having him know what she was thinking, like when she wanted him to hold her, kiss her . . . She gasped when he drew her into his arms. "I thought you couldn't read my mind?"

"You have to maintain control and not let yourself be distracted. Those sexy thoughts of yours brought the walls down," he said with a wicked grin. "And I'm only too happy to hold you," he murmured, lightly stroking her back. "And kiss you whenever you want."

Her eyelids fluttered down as his mouth moved seductively over hers.

"And do whatever else might please you."

Tessa was about to ask for more when she felt the prick of his fangs at her throat. Startled, she tried to pull away, but he held her in a grip of iron. He drank quickly, then sealed the wounds in her neck.

"Lock the door after me. I'll call you when I can."

And with no other explanation, he vanished from her sight.

Katerina's eyes were as cold as clouds in winter. "You've been with her."

It wasn't a question.

"I was hungry."

She lifted her head, nostrils flaring, searching for the scent of fresh blood. "Perhaps we should go back. She smells delicious."

"I don't share prey in my own city. Not even for you." Thwarting her was a risk, but letting her drink from Tessa was a bigger one. Thus far, Katerina hadn't made the connection between Tessa and the female she was searching for, and he hoped to keep it that way.

"You told me she wasn't prey."

He shrugged. "I take a drink every now and then."

"But you won't share," Katerina said, pouting. "Selfish as always, I see. Some things never change. Shall we go?"

Hunting with Katerina was a unique experience, by turns horrifying and amusing. Though she no longer needed to feed every day or even every week, she was a glutton with a playful streak who loved the hunt.

As they stalked the streets of a distant city, she made a game of it—challenging him to see which of them could find the tallest prey, the fattest, the drunkest, the oldest, the youngest.

He played the game because rejecting her was never wise. But he refused to kill his prey. In the old days, to his everlasting regret, she had compelled him to do so, but she no longer had that power over him.

"Don't you miss it?" she asked as they left the scene of their last hunt. "The thrill of drinking it all? Absorbing every memory, every hope? Every drop? Listening to their heartbeat slowing, slowing, until they take their last breath? The power of it?"

"No."

"You've always been a disappointment," she muttered. "Stubborn. Honorable to a fault. I should have known you wouldn't change." She sighed dramatically. "I should have turned your brother Danil instead. He would have made a much better vampire. But you were the more handsome. And a better lover."

"You seduced Danil?"

"Of course."

"And Kolya? And Rolan?"

She shrugged. "How else was I to decide?"

Shocked by this revelation, Andrei stared at her. To his chagrin, a part of him couldn't help being pleased that she had found him better in bed than his brothers.

And then he sobered. Had she preferred one of the others, he would have died long ago.

They walked another block before she came to an abrupt halt. Andrei took another step and then he too came to a stop as he caught the scent of vampire on the evening breeze.

"Anyone you know?" Katerina asked.

Andrei shook his head, all his senses on high alert as the other vampire stepped out of the shadows. Of medium height, he had lank, brown hair and glittering gray eyes under shaggy brows.

"I am the master of this city." The vampire's malevolent gaze darted from Katerina to Andrei and back again. "You are not welcome here."

"That's not very friendly," Katerina remarked.

"Neither is hunting in territory that isn't yours."

Andrei moved to one side as Katerina and the stranger squared off. The air pulsed with supernatural power as they took stock of each other in what Andrei often thought of as a paranormal test of strength. Between men, it would have been humorously called a pissing contest, but that hardly seemed fitting in the current situation.

He had no doubt that Katerina was the stronger of the two.

A moment later, he was proven right when Katerina's power drove the other vampire several steps backward and then to his knees.

"I trust you won't mind if we continue to hunt in your territory," she drawled, her voice honey-sweet and threatening at the same time.

The master of the city inclined his head. "Please. Be my guests."

Smirking, Katerina swept past him; then, as he lunged

after her, she turned on her heel and ripped out his heart.

She looked at Andrei as she tossed the bloody organ aside, then knelt to wipe her hands on the dead vampire's coat.

Face impassive, Andrei met her gaze.

And then they resumed the hunt.

Chapter Sixteen

"Jilly? It's Tessa. I need someone to talk to."

"Is something wrong?"

"You could say that."

"How about if we get together after church?" Jilly asked. "Or maybe you don't want to wait that long?"

"The sooner, the better."

"Well, why don't you come over now? I'll put the coffee on."

"Thanks, girlfriend. You're the best."

"Right," Jilly said, chuckling. "See you soon."

"I'll be there as soon as I get dressed."

It was a bleary-eyed Jileen who opened the door twenty minutes later. "Let's talk in the kitchen," she said, stifling a yawn. "What's this all about?"

"Just when you think things can't get worse," Tessa muttered, taking a chair at the table by the window.

"They do," Jilly said, finishing her thought. "What happened?"

"He has a wife."

Suddenly wide awake, Jilly blinked at her. "He's married?" She shook her head. "A married vampire. Well, that takes the cake."

"He hasn't seen her in centuries."

"Centuries? Good Lord. Don't tell me, she's a vampire too?"

Tessa nodded.

Jilly filled two cups with coffee, then dropped into the chair on the other side of the table. "So, why did she show up now?"

"She's looking for me. But she doesn't know it's me she's looking for."

"For you? Why? Oh, the blood thing." Jilly shook her head. "I can't imagine why yours is different from anyone else's."

"Me either. But that's only part of it."

"There's more?" Jilly sipped her coffee.

"Andrei said that, since she's here, she wants to take up where they left off."

"Oh, that's not good, is it?" Jilly frowned. "Why doesn't he just tell her to go to hell?"

"Apparently that's not an option. She's very old, older even than he is, and very powerful."

"And?"

"He's worried about what she might do to me."

"Oh, crap."

"That's not the only troubling thing he said."

"I don't think I want to hear any more." Jilly dropped two English muffins in the toaster. "Okay, tell me."

"He said vampires aren't the only supernatural creatures that are more than myth."

"*Oh, there's* good news," Jilly said dryly. "Did he say what other scary creatures are running around?"

"He didn't elaborate."

"Well, I wouldn't mind if one of them was Thor." Rising, Jilly set butter, jelly, honey, and peanut butter on the table, along with a couple of knives and two plates. She spread peanut butter and jelly on her muffin.

Tessa opted for butter and honey. "You know, a couple of months ago my life was ordinary. Dull, even."

"Did Andrei say how long his missus was staying?" Jilly asked, resuming her seat.

"No. But apparently she bores easily and he's hoping she'll soon tire of small-town life and go home."

"Let's hope." Jilly refilled her coffee cup. "What are you going to do now?"

"I don't know. I haven't talked to Andrei since last night."

"Well, I'm sure he'll call you when he can."

"I guess. One thing for sure, staying with him now is out of the question."

"No kidding."

Tessa sipped her coffee, thinking how glad she was to have a friend like Jilly, someone she could talk to, confide in.

Someone who could keep a secret.

Tessa was extraordinarily busy at work Monday morning, for which she was grateful, because it didn't give her much time to think about Andrei or his centuries-old wife. Still, in those rare moments when she had a few minutes to spare, she found herself constantly wondering if she should stop seeing Andrei—at least until Katerina was no longer a threat.

When she wasn't worrying about that, Tessa's mind filled with images of Andrei and Katerina wrapped in each other's arms. Andrei was a passionate man. Katerina was beautiful and she was his wife. He professed to hate her for what she had done to his family—to him.

But he was a man, and men had been known to make love to women for whom they had no affection.

She was clearing her desk of the day's work when her cell phone rang. "Hello?"

"How was your day, *dragostea mea?*" His voice was like liquid honey, warm and sweet.

"It was all right. I'm almost afraid to ask about yours."

"It would be better if I was with you."

"Are you and Katerina playing house?" She grimaced as soon as the words left her mouth. That was the last thing she wanted to know.

"So far we're just hunting companions. Listen, I can't talk long. I asked Luke to drive you home. I'm not sure our seeing each other is a good idea as long as Katerina is here. But if she's with me, she won't be looking for you. And you shouldn't be in any danger as long as you're inside before dark. I'll call you when I can."

Tessa glanced around to make sure no one was in earshot before whispering, "Did you find out why she wants my blood?"

But he had already disconnected the call.

Tessa didn't know who was more nervous on the drive home—Luke, Jilly, or herself. She found herself constantly looking out the windows, jumping every time the car hit a bump.

She didn't argue when Luke insisted on walking her upstairs to her apartment. Not wanting to be left alone, Jilly went with them.

After unlocking the door, Tessa switched on the porch light. "I'll be all right now." Reaching inside, she flipped the switch that turned on the lamps in the living room. "You two be careful going home."

"We'll be fine," Luke said. "Nobody's after us."

"I'll call you tomorrow," Jilly said.

Nodding, Tessa shut the door and shot the dead bolt home. It was, she thought, going to be a long, lonely night.

As Andrei expected, Katerina was ready to go hunting as soon as the sun went down. Tonight, she wasn't in the mood to play. In less than an hour, she drained two men and a woman. When she chose a teenage girl for her fourth victim, Andrei had no choice but to intervene. Knowing he was risking his sire's wrath, he pulled the girl from Katerina's grasp and wrapped a protective arm around her.

"Not this one," he said.

Fangs bared, eyes burning with rage, Katerina glared at him. "What do you think you're doing?"

"I won't let you kill her."

Katerina loosed an unladylike snort. "You think you can stop me?"

"I don't know."

"You're a fool if you try."

"Maybe. But I'm not a killer. Not anymore."

Katerina charged toward him in a blur of movement, so fast he barely had time to push the girl behind him before his sire's fangs ripped into his throat.

The pain was excruciating.

With his strength rapidly draining out of him, Andrei grabbed the girl's arm, focused all his energy on Tessa, and willed himself and the kid to her apartment.

Tessa was about to go to bed when she heard a faint knock at the door. Fear spiked through her. Andrei wouldn't knock. Had Katerina found her? Walls, Tessa thought as panic speared through her. She had to build walls.

Hardly daring to breathe, she drew the curtain away from the window and peered outside.

A teenage girl stood on the landing, her face deathly pale in the glow of the porch light, her brown eyes wide with fright.

"Tessa?" The girl knocked on the door again, harder this time. "Tessa? Are you in there?"

"Who are you? What are you doing here?"

"A man brought me. He's bleeding. He said you'd take us in."

A man? Bleeding? Andrei?

With a stake clutched in one hand, Tessa unlocked the door, gasped when she saw Andrei slumped against the railing. "Help me get him inside."

Between the two of them, they managed to drag him into the living room. Tessa immediately closed and bolted the door.

Kneeling on the floor beside Andrei, she grabbed the dish towel she had left on the coffee table and pressed it against the ugly wound in his throat. The cloth, once white, immediately turned dark red. "What happened?"

Face pale, voice trembling, the girl said, "You probably won't believe this, I can't believe it myself, but a vampire wanted to feed on me." She jerked her chin toward Andrei. "When he tried to protect me, she attacked him."

"She?"

The girl nodded. And then, as if she were a puppet and someone had suddenly cut the strings, she dropped to the floor. Arms wrapped around her waist, she rocked back and forth while tears streamed down her cheeks.

"You're safe now," Tessa said, sitting back on her heels. "What's your name?"

"Bailey. Is he going to be all right?"

"I don't know." Tessa bit down on her lower lip, wondering what she should do. Vampires were supposed to heal quickly, but when she lifted the towel, the wound was still raw and red. Still bleeding profusely. "Andrei?" She stroked his cheek. "Andrei, wake up."

He blinked once. Twice. "Tessa?"

"I'm here."

He looked up at her, his body tense, hands clenched at his sides. "Take care of the girl. Don't let Katerina have her."

Tessa glanced at Bailey, who was perched on the edge of the sofa, watching everything through eyes wide with disbelief.

"Don't worry, I'll look after her," Tessa assured him. "But . . . why aren't you healing?"

"Katerina bit me."

Tessa frowned. "I don't understand."

"The bite of a master vampire can be deadly to us."

A chill ran down Tessa's spine. "Deadly?"

He nodded.

"What can I do?"

"Nothing. I need her blood to heal."

"Then call her."

"No!"

"Then take my blood. It won't hurt you. Maybe it'll help."

His tormented gaze searched hers. Only Katerina's ancient blood could save him, but if he was going to die, what better way to go than with the taste of Tessa's blood on his tongue, her scent surrounding him?

He reached for her hand. Kissed her palm. Then bit into her wrist.

Tessa moaned softly, surprised by the sting of his fangs. His bite had never hurt before.

Eyes closed, Andrei drank slowly. Each drop sang in his veins. Warm. Sweet. It moved through him, reviving him. Strengthening him. Healing him.

Tempting him to take it all.

When he dared take no more, he sealed the wound in her wrist, then released her hand.

Feeling a little light-headed, Tessa took a deep breath before lifting the towel from his neck. The bleeding slowed. Stopped. The ragged edges of the ugly bite knit together even as she watched.

Shaking her head, Tessa looked at the drops of dark crimson smeared across her wrist. What kind of blood did she have, that it could cure a vampire's wound? A wound that should have been fatal? Was Madame Murga's prediction true after all?

Meeting Andrei's gaze, she read the same question in his eyes.

Tessa sat beside Andrei, his hand clasped in hers. For all that his wound appeared to be healed, he remained lying on the floor, unmoving, his face pale, eyes closed. Tiny lines of pain bracketed his mouth. Her blood might have healed his external injury, Tessa mused, but what if Katerina's bite had affected him internally? Psychologically?

Tessa frowned. It seemed odd that Katerina's bite would have such a devastating effect on him when she had been the one to turn him into a vampire in the first place.

Not knowing what else to do, Tessa covered Andrei with the afghan she kept over the back of the sofa, then went into the bathroom to wash the blood from her hands and arm.

When she returned to the living room, the girl stood shivering in front of the window, looking out.

"Bailey, would you like to take a hot shower? I have some pj's you can wear."

The girl turned to face her. "You want me to stay here?"

"Do you have anywhere else to go?"

"No, but . . ."

"Well, then," Tessa said briskly, "while you're showering, I'll fix you something to eat. It's a little late for dinner. Breakfast, maybe?"

"Thank you."

"The bathroom's in there," Tessa said, pointing the way. "Take as long as you like."

Brow furrowed, Tessa stared after the girl. Was Bailey a runaway? An orphan? She was wan and thin and obviously scared. But then, who could blame her for being frightened after what she had been through tonight?

With a last glance at Andrei, who appeared to be asleep—did vampires sleep?—Tessa went into the kitchen and rummaged around in the fridge.

She had several slices of bacon, scrambled eggs, and toast waiting by the time her houseguest finished showering.

Tessa looked up when Bailey padded into the kitchen, her long, brown hair wrapped in a towel.

"Sit down," Tessa invited, smiling. "Would you like something to drink? Juice? Milk? Or maybe some coffee?"

"Milk, please."

Tessa poured a glass for Bailey and a cup of coffee for herself before taking a seat.

Bailey ate ravenously.

Tessa sipped her coffee slowly, surreptitiously studying the girl. Her jeans and T-shirt were faded and worn. There was a dark bruise on her left arm, a faint scar on her cheek. A dozen questions about her guest chased themselves through Tessa's mind. Finally, she settled on the most innocuous one. "Do you live near here?"

"No."

"Is there anyone you want me to call?"

"No."

"You don't have to tell me if you'd rather not, but are you in some kind of trouble?"

Bailey looked up, her expression bleak. "I ran away from my foster parents."

There was a wealth of information in those few words and in the fear lurking in Bailey's eyes.

"How old are you?"

"Sixteen." Bailey swallowed the last of her breakfast, then drained the glass.

"Would you like something else? I have some cookies. They're store-bought, but not too bad."

"Yes, please."

Tessa smiled as she carried the cookie jar to the table. "You'll need more milk to wash those down." As she refilled Bailey's glass, the look of gratitude in the girl's eyes nearly brought tears to Tessa's own.

Bailey quickly put away half a dozen cookies, then sat back in her chair, her expression troubled. "He really is a vampire, isn't he?"

"Yes."

"I've heard about them on the news, but . . ." She

shook her head. "It's just so hard to believe they're real. That he's one of them."

Tell me about it, Tessa thought. Aloud, she said, "You don't have to be afraid of Andrei. He won't hurt you."

"I'm not afraid of him. But the other one . . ." Bailey shuddered. "She was going to kill me."

"You're safe now."

"I don't think I'll ever feel safe again."

"I know the feeling," Tessa muttered. "But she can't come in here uninvited. You must be tired. Why don't you go to bed?"

"You won't tell anyone I'm here? You won't call the police?"

"No, I promise."

"Do you want me to help you with the dishes?"

"No, thank you. Go get some rest. We'll talk more in the morning."

With a nod, Bailey left the room.

Tessa sat there for several minutes. Deciding the dishes could wait, she stacked them in the sink, then went into the living room to check on Andrei.

Only he wasn't there.

Bailey sat on the edge of the bed, her hands clasped in her lap, trying to process everything that had happened that night.

She had been attacked by a vampire.

Another vampire had been injured saving her. Was he Tessa's boyfriend? Her husband? She grimaced at the thought of anyone marrying a vampire, even one that was totally hot.

Did he live here?

Every instinct she possessed told her she should wait until Tessa went to bed and then run away just as fast as she could. And yet, where would she go? She couldn't go back to the foster home. If Mr. Fischer touched her one more time, she was afraid she might kill him.

She didn't want to live on the streets, begging for handouts. Or worse, sell her body for food and a place to stay. She had no real friends. The Fischers had insisted she come straight home from school to do her chores. Chores, she thought glumly. She did everything her foster mother should have done except sleep with her foster father. And she would rather starve to death in the gutter than let him put his fat, dirty hands on her again.

Maybe the best thing to do for now was stay here. She was clean and warm. No one would molest her here. No one knew what she was. The bed was soft. Her stomach was full for the first time in days.

Suddenly overcome with weariness, she crawled under the covers and closed her eyes.

Tessa wandered aimlessly through her apartment, too keyed up to sleep. Where had Andrei gone? Would he come back tonight? Where was Katerina? Who was Bailey?

Padding quietly down the hallway, Tessa peered into the guest bedroom. The girl had left the bedside lamp burning. Asleep, she looked even younger and more vulnerable than she had first appeared. Tessa started to turn the light off, then thought better of it. Maybe the girl was afraid of the dark.

Well, who could blame her? She'd had quite a fright tonight. And who knew what she had endured with her foster parents? Not all of them were kind to the kids they took in, she thought, recalling the ugly bruise on Bailey's arm. Tessa shook her head. She had heard far too many stories about foster kids being abused, locked in cellars or closets for days at a time, molested, beaten. Killed.

Tessa knew she should call the authorities. Just because Bailey had run away didn't mean her foster parents mistreated her. Teenagers were often rebellious. But Tessa couldn't forget the fear and mistrust she had seen shadowing the girl's eyes.

With a sigh, Tessa closed the door and tiptoed down the hall to her own room. Pets weren't allowed in her complex, she thought as she slipped into her nightgown. But, for now, she was harboring a lost lamb.

Chapter Seventeen

Head lifted, nostrils flared, Andrei paused on the sidewalk in his pursuit of prey. At first, he detected nothing out of the ordinary. And then he bit back a curse. "Katerina. What the hell are you doing here?"

"Wondering why you're still alive."

"Come to finish the job, have you?"

Head tilted to one side, she studied him through eyes as sharp and keen as a two-edged sword. "You should be dead." She took a step closer.

He flinched when she ran her fingertips along the side of his neck.

Katerina inhaled sharply. "That woman, the one you were with the other night. I can smell her blood on you. Tell me, husband. What is she to you?"

"One of many. None of whom I'm willing to share."

"She saved you, didn't she?"

"A mere mortal?" He snorted. "How could she?"

"You tell me."

"There's nothing to tell."

Eyes narrowed ominously, Katerina studied him a moment.

Andrei could feel her power crawling over him. It

was not a pleasant feeling, but different from other times he remembered.

"I rented a house," she said at length. "I expect you to move in with me tonight."

"After what you did?" Andrei tapped the bite mark on his neck. Unlike other wounds, this one had left an ugly scar. "Hell, no."

"Maybe I'm not making myself clear," she said, biting off each word. "Either you do as I say, willingly, or you will find yourself in need of some new private stock."

If it had been any other vampire, Andrei would have dismissed the threat out of hand. But Katerina was incredibly old and powerful, able to walk in the daylight. She couldn't enter Tessa's house uninvited, but neither could Tessa remain behind her locked door day and night until Katerina had either made good on her threat or decided to go back home.

"Fine," he said. "I'll play your game for three months, and then I want you out of my town and out of my life."

She lifted one shoulder in what he hoped was a gesture of acceptance.

"And remember, no hunting in my territory. No mysterious deaths, no bodies drained of blood, or the deal is off."

"Whatever. I'll expect you later."

He nodded. It was only after Katerina had gone that he realized there was something different about her. Something had changed.

Or was the change in him?

Chapter Eighteen

Bailey wandered through Tessa's apartment, pausing at the bookshelf to peruse the titles of the paperbacks and DVDs. She had seen most of the movies. She picked up several books before she found one that sounded interesting. After pulling a soda from the fridge, she curled up on the sofa.

Before leaving for work, Tessa had given Bailey twenty-five dollars "mad money" in case she wanted to go out to lunch or a movie, admonishing Bailey to be extra careful, reminding her that Katerina could walk in daylight.

Bailey opened the book, then closed it again, wondering if she should tell Tessa the truth, or if her new friend was better off not knowing. Bailey had never had any fear of the dark or of the creatures that lurked in the shadows. Until last night, she had been confident of her ability to protect herself, but all that had changed when she ran into a pair of genuine, dyed-in-the wool vampires. Fear had left her frozen, unable to fight or flee.

But they would never take her by surprise again.

Because—whether friend or foe—she had their scents now.

Chapter Nineteen

Tessa jumped every time the phone rang, always expecting it to be Andrei or Bailey, but it never was. She didn't know whether to be relieved when she didn't hear from either one of them, or worried.

Unable to concentrate on the file in front of her, she chewed on her thumbnail. She hadn't seen or heard from Andrei since Monday, couldn't help worrying about him. Vampire or not, he was hanging out with a woman he had once found irresistible, a woman who was older and more powerful than he was.

A woman who had tried to kill him. Had Katerina tried again? And succeeded? She banished the horrible thought from her mind.

And then there was Bailey, a girl who was, for all intents and purposes, a complete stranger. She couldn't help wondering what Bailey was doing. For all she knew, the girl could be lying about being a runaway foster child. Maybe she was a professional thief. She could be older and more worldly-wise than she looked. Maybe she had concocted that story about being a runaway so people like Tessa would feel sorry for her and take her in. Then, the first time she was left alone, she robbed them. Maybe . . .

Exasperated by her wild imaginings, Tessa took the elevator down to the cafeteria for a blueberry muffin and a cup of coffee.

She was staring into her empty cup when Andrei slid into the chair across from her. He looked incredibly handsome in a pair of faded jeans and a dark blue shirt. Just seeing him lifted her spirits.

Reaching across the table, he took her hand in his. "Are you all right?"

"I am now."

"I sensed something was bothering you. Do you want to talk about it?"

"I was worrying about you."

"Me? Whatever for?"

"I hadn't heard from you . . . I was afraid you were . . . that she . . ."

"No one's ever worried about me before."

"She tried to kill you!" Tessa exclaimed. "How can I not worry? Where is she, anyway?"

"Resting." He squeezed her hand. "I miss you."

"I miss you, too." She pressed her lips together to keep from asking the question that was ever present in the back of her mind.

"Tessa, don't ask."

"I won't." Her gaze searched his, as if she might find the answer there, even though she kept telling herself she didn't want to know.

Andrei blew out a sigh. "I'm not sure how much longer I can hold her off. But whatever happens with Katerina, you must believe it has nothing to do with my feelings for you."

Tessa nodded. "Has she said any more about me?"

"No. I'm trying to find a way to ask what she wants with the woman the fledgling described without arousing her suspicions about you."

"Is she suspicious?"

"I don't think so. I stopped by your place earlier to check in on Bailey."

"How's she doing?"

"There's something about her . . ."

"I knew it! She isn't what she seems, is she?"

"Not exactly."

Something in his tone sent a chill down her spine. "What do you mean?"

"I didn't notice it last night, what with everything else that was going on, but today . . . you remember I told you vampires aren't the only supernatural creatures?"

Tessa nodded. "Is she a vampire, too?"

"No. She's a shape-shifter." At her blank expression, he said, "You've heard of werewolves, right?"

"So, they're real too? Good heavens, please tell me I'm not harboring a werewolf under my roof!"

"No. She's a were-panther." Andrei gave her hand another squeeze. "She's not like a werewolf. She won't go crazy when the moon is full."

"But she can turn into a panther? Like, a real panther?"

"When she wants to. I don't think she's done it in a long time. If ever."

"Jilly will never believe this," Tessa muttered. "Not in a million years."

"I've got to go. Walk me out?"

Alone in the elevator, Andrei stopped the car between floors. Tessa's heart thudded against her ribs when he pulled her into his arms. She forgot about

Katerina, about were-panthers, about everything but the man whose gaze burned into hers. Though his kiss was gentle, she felt his power wash over her, the tightly leashed strength of the arms that held her tight. Tighter. His tongue stroked hers, inflaming her senses.

She moaned in protest when he lifted his head.

One last kiss, and he was gone.

Head reeling, lips still tingling from his kisses, Tessa returned to her office to find Jilly waiting for her.

"Where have you been? I was about to leave you a note." Jilly frowned. "Are you coming down with something? You look a little flushed."

"I was with Andrei."

"Oh, well, that explains it. Listen, I can't meet for lunch today. I forgot, I've got a dental appointment."

"Okay, call you later. I've got a *lot* to tell you."

"Uh-oh. Is it good news or bad?"

"I haven't decided yet," Tessa replied as her phone rang. "Gotta go."

Tessa drove home slowly. Was Bailey still there? Should she mention the shape-shifter thing?

After parking in her space, Tessa sat in the car, reluctant—and a little apprehensive—about facing her houseguest. Vampires. Were-panthers. What next?

She glanced around, making sure she was alone before she got out of the car and ran up the stairs.

Inside, she locked the door, then dropped her handbag on the sofa, and kicked off her heels.

She found Bailey in the kitchen stirring a pot of spaghetti sauce.

"Hi." Tessa gestured at the pot. "Smells good."

"Thanks. I hope you don't mind."

"Not at all. How was your day?"

"Quiet." Bailey filled a pan with water, set it on the stove, and turned on the burner.

"Well, that's good, I guess." Needing something to do, Tessa began to set the table.

"Andrei stopped by while you were at work," Bailey said.

"Yes, he told me."

"Oh. What else did he say?"

Trying to decide how to answer, Tessa laid the silverware.

"He told you, didn't he?" Bailey said.

"Yes."

"Do you want me to leave?"

"No. No, of course not. It's just . . ." Tessa pulled one of the chairs from the table and sat down. "It just came as a . . . a surprise, that's all."

"You're scared of me now."

"No, I'm not."

"I can smell your fear."

Tessa blew out a sigh. Andrei could read her mind. Bailey could sense her emotions . . . good grief, could the girl read her thoughts too?

"I'm not really afraid of you, exactly," Tessa said, choosing her words carefully. "It's just that, until a few weeks ago, I never knew vampires were real, and now . . . well, it takes some getting used to, that's all."

"It took some getting used to for me, too."

"What do you mean?"

Bailey turned the fire down low on the sauce, then sat across from Tessa. "I didn't know about the supernatural part of me until I turned sixteen. It freaked me out." She shook her head. "One night I was just like everybody else and the next I had this amazing, scary power."

"Have you met any other . . . ah, people like you?"

"No. Maybe there aren't any."

"Well, there must have been at least one or two others, or you wouldn't be here," Tessa said, grinning. "And there are probably a few more. Maybe Andrei could help you find them, if that's what you want."

"It's something to think about," Bailey remarked. Pushing away from the table, she went to the stove to add a package of spaghetti to the boiling water.

She was quiet during dinner.

Tessa glanced at her from time to time, wondering again what being a shape-shifter entailed. Were there rituals? Rules? Did were-panthers hunt prey, like vampires? That was a scary thought and she shied away from the question, thinking she didn't want to know the answer. But even as she sought to ignore it, she remembered Andrei telling her there were werewolves, too. Were were-panthers ferocious killers like the werewolves portrayed in books and movies? How closely related were werewolves and were-panthers?

Her appetite gone, Tessa carried her dishes to the sink and rinsed them off, then covered the leftover spaghetti sauce and put it in the fridge.

"I can finish cleaning up," Bailey offered.

"Great, thanks. I'm going to go get into something more comfortable." Tessa paused a moment. "Listen, we need to get you a couple of changes of clothes, some shoes, maybe a jacket and a pair of boots. Why don't you go online and see if you can find anything you like? Just make a note of colors and sizes and I'll order it later."

"I can't ask you to do that!"

"You didn't ask," Tessa said with a wink. "I want to do it."

In her room, Tessa changed into a T-shirt and a pair

of sweats, then called Jileen, who didn't bother with hello.

"So, what's the news?" Jilly asked.

"Are you sitting down?"

"I am now."

"Andrei rescued a girl from Katerina's clutches last night. Saved her life."

"Go on."

"Her name's Bailey. She's only sixteen and since he couldn't very well take her home, he brought her here." She didn't tell Jileen that Katerina had almost killed Andrei, or that her blood had somehow saved him.

"Is that the good news?"

"Just listen. It turns out Bailey ran away from a foster home. It sounds like she's run away from more than one. Anyway, not only is she a runaway teen, she's a . . ."

"A what?"

Tessa sighed. Might as well just spit it out. "A shape-shifter."

In the silence that followed, Tessa knew Jilly was trying to decide if she was joking or not.

"It's true," Tessa said. Then, taking a page from Jilly's playbook, she sighed dramatically. "So now I've got a runaway teenage were-panther on my hands."

And if there were werewolves and were-panthers, were there also were-lions and tigers and bears?

Oh, my.

Chapter Twenty

Andrei stood in the shadows under a tree, arms crossed over his chest, impatiently waiting for Katerina to stop playing with her food. She had been teasing and tormenting the poor man for the better part of thirty minutes.

A sharp cry of pain and denial told him the unfortunate man's suffering was approaching a cruel end.

Andrei was looking forward to going home when Katerina turned away from her victim. Striding toward Andrei, she threw her arms around his neck and kissed him. It was all he could do to keep from recoiling as her tongue—still heavily coated with her victim's blood—plunged into his mouth.

With an oath, he shoved her aside. "What the hell, woman!"

She glared at him, her eyes red and glowing in the darkness.

Andrei spat the man's blood from his mouth.

"I want you," Katerina said. "I'm your wife. You're my husband. I command you to fulfill your husbandly duties."

"Command me? Command me!" he exclaimed, his

voice rising with his anger. "You're lucky I don't take your head off."

She snorted. "As if you could."

"Don't tempt me," he muttered, even as he wondered if he had the strength necessary to defeat her. He would have tried right then, but he was afraid of what the consequences might be for Tessa if he failed. In the past, he'd had only himself to worry about. But Tessa had changed that.

Lips compressed, eyes still red with fury, Katerina glared at him—and then vanished from his sight.

"Shit!" Fear for Tessa swamped him. She was the best thing in his life, his only reason for existing. He couldn't lose her. Not now. Not ever.

A desperate thought took him to her apartment.

"Andrei!" Tessa blinked up at him. "What are you doing here?"

"Mind if I come in?"

"Of course not." She stepped back to allow him entrance, then closed and locked the door. "Is something wrong?"

Needing to hold her, he drew her into his arms. "I think I just made a big mistake and I'm afraid you're the one who might pay for it."

"What are you talking about?"

"Katerina. She wanted me to fulfill my 'husbandly' duty and I refused."

"Oh."

"I'm afraid she'll take her anger out on you."

Tessa shivered. She remembered all too clearly the woman's malevolent gaze—and razor-sharp fangs—as she warned Tessa to stay away from Andrei. "What are we going to do?"

"Unless you want to stay locked in your apartment indefinitely, there are only two options that I can think of—do what she wants or destroy her."

"Can you? Destroy her?"

"I don't know. Maybe."

If he tried and failed . . . Tessa wrapped her arms around his waist and held on tight. She didn't want to lose him. She didn't want to die. She didn't want him to make love to Katerina, either, although it wouldn't be love, she thought, just sex. But he would still be lying in Katerina's bed, holding her in his strong embrace. Her stomach roiled at the thought.

Andrei brushed a kiss across the top of her head. "I'll think of something."

She nodded. "Maybe, if you do what she wants, she'll go away."

And maybe she wouldn't.

"Okay if I spend the night here?" he asked.

That question, more than anything he had said, told her how worried he was for her safety.

It also took her mind off Katerina, at least for the moment. Should she offer him the sofa, or invite him to share her bed?

"The sofa will be fine," he remarked with a wry grin. "But I wouldn't say no to the other."

Tessa bit down on her lip, tempted more than she wanted to admit.

It didn't help when Andrei lowered his head and claimed her lips with his, sending a thrill of anticipation racing down her spine. Lordy, the man could kiss. His mouth moving over hers drove every other thought from her mind and she clung to him, her senses reeling as his tongue plundered her mouth.

"You don't play fair," she gasped when he lifted his head.

"Just trying to sway the jury," he replied with a wicked grin. "Is it working?"

"You said . . ."

"That I'd only go as far as you'd let me. That didn't mean I wouldn't try to change your mind."

"Andrei . . ."

"Okay, love, have it your way. The sofa it is. But I'm not giving up."

The sound of footsteps tiptoeing across the living room floor woke Andrei instantly. For a moment, his senses were on high alert. Then, realizing it was only Bailey heading for the kitchen, he relaxed.

"Sorry," she whispered. "I didn't mean to wake you."

Curious, Andrei followed the girl into the other room. "How did you know you woke me?"

"I heard the change in your breathing. Why?"

"So, your senses are enhanced, even in human form?"

She glanced at him over her shoulder. "I guess so."

"Your vision, too?" He braced one shoulder against the doorjamb, arms folded across his chest.

She nodded. "Funny, I never gave that any thought until you mentioned it." Opening the fridge, she pulled out a carton of orange juice and poured herself a glass. "Would you like a . . . no, I guess not," she said, grinning sheepishly. "Too bad Tessa doesn't keep a bag of blood handy for midnight snacks."

Andrei grimaced. "I wouldn't drink it if she did."

"No?"

He shook his head. "Tastes like plastic. I almost forgot. I bought you something." Reaching into his pocket, he withdrew a pink cell phone and handed it to her.

"For me?" She looked up at him, her eyes sparkling like a child's at Christmas.

"I figured you didn't have one. I've programmed all of our phone numbers in it so you can get in touch with us—and we can get in touch with you—if the need arises."

"Thank you so much." She tucked it into the pocket of her robe. "Tessa said maybe you could help me find other shifters."

"Probably." In his long life he had run into a shifter or two. "Why?"

"I was hoping I could find someone to teach me what I need to know."

"Like what?"

"I'm not sure. I've only had these new powers for a short time . . . I don't know what to expect."

He grunted softly. He'd had to learn how to use his vampire senses—his preternatural power—but he had assumed that shifters knew what to do instinctively, since they weren't made, but born that way. "What do you need to know?"

"How to shift when I want to. I've only done it once, and that was right after my sixteenth birthday. It just happened. I haven't been able to do it since."

"Have you tried concentrating? Picturing your other self in your mind?"

"Sort of."

"Do you want to try it now?"

She looked doubtful; then, putting her glass aside, she nodded. Closing her eyes, she clenched her hands, her face screwed up as she concentrated.

"You're trying too hard," Andrei said. "It's part of you, part of what you are. Embrace it. Reach for it."

Bailey opened her eyes, shook her arms, took a deep breath, and tried again.

Andrei watched in fascination as her body began to shift. One minute, a slender teenage girl stood in the middle of the kitchen. The next, a sleek black panther stood there amid a pile of tattered clothing, ears flicking back and forth, tail twitching.

He grinned, somewhat surprised that she hadn't thought to undress first. "Would you like to go hunting?" he asked.

When the big cat nodded, Andrei went into the living room and unlocked the door. "Wait for me on the landing."

He let the panther out, then double-locked the door. Going into Tessa's room, he spoke to her mind, assuring that she wouldn't wake up until morning. After kissing her on the forehead, he dissolved into mist and slipped under the front door.

Bailey the panther was waiting for him.

Resuming his own form, Andrei warded the entrance and the windows against intruders.

Convinced that Tessa would be safe in his absence, he transformed himself into a wolf and led the way out of town to a thick stand of timber that grew along a narrow stream. Rabbits and squirrels made their homes among the trees. If they were lucky, they might even find a deer.

Chapter Twenty-One

Katerina stood in the deep shadows, looking up at the apartment where Andrei's woman lived. What, exactly, was their relationship? That he drank from the woman was obvious. She had smelled the female's blood on him. Was that all the woman was to him? A source of fresh blood? Or was there more going on between them? Andrei was an attractive man. A stallion in bed. The woman was . . . pretty, she admitted reluctantly. Beautiful, even—for a mortal female.

She sniffed the air. And frowned when she caught the scent of the girl Andrei had taken from her. Why had he brought *her* here? Was she also prey?

She lifted her head as a vagrant breeze carried Andrei's scent.

He had passed by here only moments ago. The girl, too. Why had they gone off together?

And where were they now?

More importantly, why hadn't her bite destroyed him? Not that she regretted the fact that he was still alive. She wanted him in her bed and she intended to see him there, one way or another.

But that could wait.

Curious as to where Andrei and the girl had gone, she turned away from the apartment building and followed his scent down the dark streets toward a heavily wooded area located near the outskirts of town.

Andrei couldn't remember the last time he had changed into the wolf. It was an awesome sensation, feeling the cool earth beneath his paws, the play of muscle as he leaped over a fallen log, the myriad scents that assailed him—foliage and dung, a rabbit cowering in a hole, the stink of a carcass long dead.

He glanced at Bailey, running easily beside him. Her coat, as black as ink, seemed to shimmer in the moonlight. He could feel her joy, her exultation, as she raced through the night, free of restraint and fear.

A low growl rose in her throat as a jackrabbit bolted from its hiding place. A burst of speed, the snap of her jaws, and the rabbit hung limp in her mouth.

He sat back on his haunches as she quickly devoured the luckless creature, grinned a wolfish grin when she licked the blood from her muzzle and fur.

A noise, almost too faint for even the wolf's keen ears, drew Andrei's attention. Hackles raised, he moved to stand in front of Bailey as Katerina materialized out of the shadows.

In an instant, Andrei resumed his own form. "What the hell! What are you doing here?"

Katerina shrugged, her attention fixed on Bailey. "A shape-shifter? Did you know when you saved her?"

"No. What difference does it make?"

"None, perhaps." She licked her lips. "I've never had a shifter."

"And you're not having this one."

"You should have been a knight of the realm," Katerina mused, her voice thick with derision. "Always rescuing damsels in danger."

"I'll be taking her home now."

"Fine. I've decided we're leaving here tonight. Pack your things."

"Where are we going?"

"I'm not sure, but it doesn't seem as if the mortal I'm searching for is here, so I've decided to move on."

Andrei shook his head. "I'm not going anywhere."

"You may regret your decision."

"Is that a threat?"

Her eyes went red as she bared her fangs. "More like a promise."

"Dammit, Katerina . . ." he began.

But she was already gone.

"Bailey, we need to go."

He shifted to the wolf and they ran back to the apartment. As he had before, Andrei dissolved into mist and slipped under the crack below the door. Regaining his own form, he let Bailey in, then shot the dead bolt home. She immediately headed for her bedroom. No doubt to shift back to human form in private, he mused with a wry grin.

With Katerina's threat fresh in his mind, Andrei went to check on Tessa. She was sleeping peacefully. Bending, he brushed a kiss across her cheek before releasing her from his spell. Then, needing to hold her, he toed off his boots, slid under the covers, and drew her close, her back to his front.

With a small sigh of contentment, she snuggled against him, her fanny tightly pressed against his groin.

It was torture of the sweetest kind.

Chapter Twenty-Two

Tessa woke with a smile as she recalled the dream she'd had last night. A wonderful dream. In it, Andrei had made slow, sweet love to her, his voice husky with desire as he whispered love words in her ear, his hands masterful as he caressed her, arousing her to heights she had never imagined. And then he had slept beside her all night long. It had been so real, she could still feel the urgency of his kisses. . . .

Turning her head, she stared at the pillow beside hers, her eyes widening when she noticed there was a slight indentation, as if someone had been there recently.

Had her dream been more than a dream?

Slipping out of bed, she showered and dressed, then went into the kitchen.

Bailey was at the stove, frying bacon.

"You're going to spoil me," Tessa remarked as she poured herself a cup of coffee.

"Well, it's the least I can do since I can't pay for my room and board."

Tessa pulled a loaf of bread from the cupboard. "You don't owe me anything. Would you like some toast?"

"Yes, please."

Someone had taught the girl manners, Tessa mused. And how to cook and clean. "What are you going to do today?" she asked as she popped four slices of bread into the toaster.

"I don't know." Bailey turned the bacon. "Is there anything I can do around here? Change the sheets? Wash the windows? Scrub the floors?" Earlier, she had picked up the tattered remnants of her nightgown and robe. Next time she shifted, she had to remember to undress first. She frowned, wondering why Andrei's clothes shifted with him and hers didn't.

"Did your foster parents expect you to do all that?" Tessa asked.

"All that and more." Bailey cracked four eggs in a bowl, stirred them with a whisk. "Mow the yard. Wash the car. Take out the trash." She dumped the eggs in a frying pan. "They never did anything."

"Didn't they give you any free time to spend with your friends?" Tessa buttered the toast, then put two slices on each of the saucers Bailey had taken from the cupboard.

"I didn't really have any friends. I wasn't allowed to stay after school or go out on dates or anything." She dished up the bacon and eggs and carried both plates to the table.

"That's terrible." Tessa shook her head. "What are you going to do about school?"

"I don't know. I can't go back. They'll find me if I do."

That was probably true, Tessa thought. They ate in silence for several minutes. More than once, she caught

Bailey watching her as if she wanted to say something but each time, the girl seemed to change her mind.

Tessa glanced at the clock. "I've got to get ready to go."

"Are you sure you should?"

"What do you mean?"

Bailey's gaze slid away from hers. "Last night . . ."

"Go on."

"Andrei took me hunting."

"Hunting? Whatever for?"

"Not people," Bailey said with a lopsided grin. "He helped me shift and asked if I wanted to go out. And I did. And it was wonderful." Her eyes sparkled with the memory. "It was only the second time I've shifted. The first time was scary, but this time . . . with Andrei, it was amazing." Her smile faded. "That awful woman followed us."

"Katerina?"

Bailey nodded. "She wanted Andrei to go away with her, but he refused. I think she means to hurt you. As soon as she was gone, we came right back here. He didn't leave until early this morning."

So, he *had* spent the night.

What else had he done? Maybe that dream hadn't been a dream after all. But that was impossible. Surely she would know if it had been real.

"Thanks for telling me," Tessa said, carrying her dish to the sink. "I'll be careful. Luke and Jilly are coming by to drive me to work in a few minutes. You be careful too. Don't open the door for anyone except Andrei."

"He's really hot, isn't he?" Bailey murmured, a dreamy expression in her eyes.

Tessa shook her head. First an ancient vampire. Now a teenage shape-shifter. What next?

In her office, Tessa found it almost impossible to concentrate on the business at hand. Time and again, she found herself staring out the window, her thoughts chaotic. Andrei had spent the night in her bed. Katerina was a constant threat. Bailey seemed to be developing a crush on Andrei. But then, who could blame her? He was gorgeous and sexy as hell.

At lunch, she listened halfheartedly as Jilly went on and on about her growing relationship with Luke Moran and how much she loved him.

Tessa looked up when Jileen reached across the table and shook her arm. "You haven't heard a word I said, have you?"

"Of course I have."

"What did I just say?"

Tessa stared at her blankly.

"I knew it."

"I'm sorry."

"I was asking about your plans for Thanksgiving. It's next week, you know."

"Is it?"

"All right, 'fess up," Jilly said, her brow furrowing with concern. "What's bothering you? I mean, besides the obvious, of course."

Shoulders sagging, Tessa said, "I feel like I'm going quietly insane. I'm in love with a . . . you know . . . who's being stalked by his wife. My roommate is not entirely normal. I can't even drive to work alone because monsters are trying to get me. And now I think . . . never mind."

"Hey, you can't stop now!"

"Andrei spent the night in my bed. He was gone this morning, but . . ."

Jilly's eyebrows shot up into her hairline. "What?"

Tessa nodded. "I'm wondering if he . . . if he took advantage of me while I was asleep."

"Oh, my. What makes you think that?"

"I thought I dreamed it all, but it was so real. I mean, he wasn't in bed with me when I fell asleep."

"Did you ask him?"

Tessa shook her head. "I haven't seen or talked to him since."

"Well, if you'd been raped while you slept, there'd be some . . . well . . . evidence."

"I know. There wasn't any. But it was so real. Maybe vampires can do it without your even being aware it happened. I mean, he could have made me forget."

"I'm sure it was just an erotic dream, no matter how vivid it was."

"I guess so," Tessa said. "But enough about me. When you called about meeting for lunch, you said you had news to share."

Jilly leaned forward, her eyes bright with excitement. "I think Luke's going to ask me to marry him."

"Seriously?"

"I know we haven't known each other very long, but I'm head-over-heels in love with the guy."

"Have you thought it through? You know, what it would mean, being married to a hunter?"

"Lots of men have dangerous jobs. Cops. Those guys who go deep-sea fishing for a living. Firefighters." Jilly shrugged. "I can't let worrying about the future ruin the present."

It was, Tessa thought, excellent advice.

* * *

Tessa sat in the backseat of Luke's car. She was wondering how Bailey had spent the day when there was a thump on the roof, as if someone—or something—had landed on it. Her heart skipped a beat, then sank to the pit of her stomach as a fist smashed through the driver's-side window and grabbed the wheel.

Everything that happened next seemed to happen in slow motion.

Luke swore when he lost control of the car.

Jilly let out a shriek as the vehicle skidded wildly across the roadway toward Tessa's apartment building.

Tessa crossed her arms in front of her face as the car spun around and crashed into one of the trees that lined the parkway on the other side of the street.

She was going to die.

It was her last conscious thought before she pitched into a deep black void.

Pain.

Voices.

Sirens wailing in the distance.

As if from far away, she heard someone frantically calling her name, over and over again.

In spite of the pain that splintered through her, she fought her way through cobwebs of oblivion toward his voice, knowing if she remained in the peaceful darkness, she would never see him again.

"Tessa."

She opened her eyes, blinking against the light. "Andrei?"

His hand grasped hers. "Stay with me, love."

"Stay." She tried to smile but it was beyond her.

* * *

Ignoring the medics who insisted he couldn't ride to the hospital with Tessa, Andrei climbed into the ambulance, holding her hand all the while.

He knew immediately that being so close to her was a mistake. She was covered in blood from a multitude of cuts. She had hit her head against the window and sustained a nasty laceration when the car careened sideways into a tree. Blood leaked from the bandage swathed around her head.

"Jilly?" Tessa tugged on his hand. "Where's Jilly?"

"She's in the ambulance behind us," Andrei said.

"Is she . . . ?"

"She'll be fine. Luke, too." They were both pretty banged up. Jileen had a sprained wrist and possibly a concussion from where her head had hit the passenger window. Luke had a number of bruises, a broken nose, and probably a fractured rib or two. They were lucky, he thought as the ambulance pulled into the hospital parking lot. It could have been a lot worse.

He stayed by Tessa's side until they wheeled her into the examination room. Stepping into the hallway, he called Bailey and told her what had happened.

And then he returned to the scene of the accident.

Cloaking his presence from the police officers who were still on the scene, Andrei walked around the car. The scent of vampire was strong. He was about to track the man when Katerina strolled toward him.

Nostrils flared, she lifted her head and sniffed the air. "Fee fi fo fum, I smell the blood of an Englishman. No," she corrected with a throaty chuckle. "A fledgling."

Andrei nodded curtly. "I was just about to go after him."

"No need. He's already dead."

"You killed him?"

"Yes." She ran her bright red fingernails down his chest. "But not before he told me something very interesting."

Tension coiled like a serpent in Andrei's gut. He knew what was coming.

"Very interesting, indeed," she purred, her voice deepening to an angry growl as she curled her hand around his throat. "It seems one of the women who was in this car is the very female I've been searching for." Her fingernails dug into his skin. "Can you guess which one?"

For Andrei, the world and everything in it fell away. There was only his sire—his very angry sire—staring into his eyes, her own blazing like the flames of an unforgiving Hell.

"Why didn't you tell me?"

"You know why." He hissed the words, barely able to speak. She couldn't choke the life out of him. He didn't need to breathe. But, angry as she was, she could easily separate his head from his body.

"Indeed." Her fury enveloped him, sizzling through the very fiber of his being. He had looked death in the face on several occasions, but never had it seemed more imminent than now, at the hands of his maker.

Tessa. He had failed her. With his destruction, she would be at Katerina's mercy. Her only other protection was Luke, but he was no match for Katerina. Sooner or later, she would catch Tessa alone.

Andrei? Where are you?

Tess?

What's happening? You're in pain. I can feel it.

Nothing for you to worry about. Be careful. She knows who you are.

Katerina stared at him, her eyes narrowed. "What are you doing?"

"Doing?" He grimaced. "Mostly choking."

"Something's different." Her expression turned to one of curiosity, and then confusion.

Andrei felt it too, but he wasn't sure what it was. He had the strangest feeling that he could easily free himself from her grasp. Before he could put that belief to the test, a deep-throated growl sounded from the shadows. A moment later, a black panther sprang into view, yellow eyes glowing, teeth bared in a feral snarl.

Katerina's reaction was surprising and immediate. One minute her hand was wrapped around his throat. The next, she was gone in a shimmering cloud of blood-colored motes.

Andrei rubbed his throat as Bailey trotted up to him, her lips peeled back in a catlike grin. "You've got great timing, kid." Turning his head to the side, he removed his long, black coat and held it out in front of him while she shifted to human form. "What are you doing here?"

"Tessa was worried about you," she said, wrapping his coat around her nakedness.

"Is she okay?"

Bailey nodded. "Scared for you."

"I was a little scared myself," he admitted. "She's afraid of you."

"Katerina? Why?"

"I don't know. I've never known her to be afraid of anything. But you worry her. Come on, let's go see Tess."

* * *

It was late when Andrei and Bailey arrived at the hospital. They had made a side trip to Tessa's condo so Bailey could get dressed. Now, walking down the wide, puke-green corridor, Andrei's nostrils filled with the tantalizing scent of blood—some contaminated, some freshly spilled. The stink of fear and death and hopelessness lingered in the air.

He paused outside Tessa's room before opening the door and stepping inside. She was asleep, her face almost as pale as the pillow beneath her head, her breathing slow and shallow. But her heartbeat was steady and strong.

A nurse paused in the act of making notes on a chart when they entered the room.

"How is she?" Andrei asked.

"Are you family?"

"No. Is she going to be all right?"

"I'm sorry. I can't give you that information," the nurse said, hanging the chart on the foot of the bed.

"Yes, you can," Andrei said, his gaze holding the woman's.

"Doctor said she's going to be fine. There's no concussion, although the cut in her head required several stitches. She also has a couple of bruised ribs. If there are no complications, she should be able to go home in a day or two, although it will take six weeks or so for the bruising to heal."

Andrei nodded. "Thank you, Nurse. You can go now."

With a tentative smile, she blinked at him and left the room.

"What did you do to her?" Bailey asked.

"Just a little mind trick," Andrei said, moving toward the bed. "Why don't you wait for me in the hall?"

Bailey frowned at him. "Why? What are you going to do?"

"I'm going to give Tessa some of my blood. It will speed the healing process. Now, go outside."

"I want to watch."

He regarded her a moment, then shrugged. Lifting his arm, he bit into his wrist, parted Tessa's lips, and let a few drops of his blood fall onto her tongue.

When he judged she'd had enough, he sealed the wound in his arm.

"What now?" Bailey asked.

"She'll wake in the morning feeling much better. Stay here and keep an eye on her," he said, moving toward the door. "I need to find Luke and Jileen."

Katerina stalked the dark streets, her fury as black as the night. Things were not going as planned. She had not expected Andrei to be happy to see her, at least not at first, but she had been confident of her ability to win his affection, if not his love. She had wooed and won him centuries ago. But he was no longer young and innocent.

No longer enamored of her beauty.

No longer weak. Or easily manipulated.

How could she have forgotten how it had been back then? Over time, he had gained in strength and power, until he was able to resist her compulsions completely. Until he was able to leave her, something she would never have thought possible.

She had never loved him.

She didn't love him now.

But he was hers. And she intended to have him, one way or the other.

Only one thing stood in her way.

The other woman. Tessa. She was the one the fledglings talked about. Katerina had overheard them whispering about her in the local vampire hangout from time to time, though she had not known then that it was Tessa. There were, even now, half a dozen fledglings in the town, just waiting for a chance to get close to her, to taste her. The woman's blood was purported to strengthen a fledgling's supernatural power.

But it was only rumor, of course, started by some gypsy, because none who had gotten close to Tessa had survived to tell the tale.

She paused in her contemplation to feed from a homeless man who stumbled across her path.

After leaving the body behind a trash can, she continued on her way. There was something about the woman's blood. Something extraordinary. Katerina knew that for a fact.

Because her bite should have destroyed Andrei. Instead, he was stronger than ever. Had the woman's blood done that? What if the rumor was wrong? What if it wasn't fledglings who got stronger, but ancients?

Chapter Twenty-Three

In the morning, Tessa woke feeling as good as new. Her doctor was amazed that she didn't have any lingering soreness from the accident, that it was no longer painful for her to breathe. When he removed the bandage to check her stitches, he informed her that the laceration in her head had healed completely, leaving no scar.

Mystified, he agreed to let her go home the next day.

She was fretting at having to spend another night in the hospital when Andrei and Bailey entered the room, laden with take-out sacks from a local hamburger stand, a big bouquet of flowers, and a large white teddy bear.

Andrei handed her the teddy bear, his gaze moving over her, missing nothing. "How are you feeling?"

"I'm fine, really. The doctor said I can go home tomorrow. He just wants to run a couple of tests."

Bailey looked at Andrei as she placed the bags and the flowers on the tray, her eyes wide.

"What is it?" Tessa asked. "What's wrong?"

"Nothing." Andrei took her hand in his and gave it a squeeze. "I gave you a little of my blood last night, that's all."

"Oh! But . . . won't they . . . ?"

He shook his head. "They won't find anything out of the ordinary."

"So, what happened last night?" Tessa asked. "You were hurting."

"Nothing I couldn't handle, thanks to Bailey," he said, smiling at the girl.

Bailey flushed at the compliment. "You two probably want to be alone," she mumbled. "I think I'll go look at the babies in the nursery."

When they were alone, Tessa tugged on his arm. "So, what did happen last night? It was Katerina, wasn't it?"

"Yeah."

"Where is she now?"

"I don't know. She took off. She was afraid of Bailey, at least in her panther form."

"I don't believe it. Bailey's just a kid."

He twitched his shoulder in a shrug. "She might be a helpless teenager in her own skin, but as the panther . . . she's something else."

"I think she's got a crush on you," Tessa remarked.

Andrei snorted. "Whatever gave you that idea?"

"Just the way she looks at you, all doe-eyed," she said dryly. "Have you seen Jilly and Luke?"

"Not since last night."

Tessa's eyes widened. "Did you . . . ?"

"Yeah."

"Katerina's never going to give up, is she?"

"Probably not, but something's changed."

"What do you mean?"

"I'm not sure. Here." He pulled a burger out of the sack and handed it to her. "There's a malt and fries in there too," he said, when her stomach growled. "After all that's happened, you need to keep your strength up."

* * *

Bailey and Andrei stayed with Tessa until visiting hours were over; then Andrei transported Bailey back to the condo with strict orders to stay inside and keep the doors and windows locked.

Once he had her promise, he returned to the hospital. Every time he sensed a doctor or nurse approaching Tessa's room, he dissolved into mist until they were gone.

Tessa found it all rather amusing.

"Laugh if you want," he said, resuming his place in the chair beside her bed, "but I'm not leaving you here alone. Hospital thresholds have no power."

"Obviously, or you couldn't be here."

"Exactly. Why don't you get some rest?"

"I'm not tired. I feel great. Tell me about your past."

"What do you want to know?"

"What did you do after you got away from Katerina?"

"I left the country."

"What happened to your lands and your estate?"

"I don't know. I never went back. I wandered the earth, a vagabond with no home and no family, afraid to make friends for fear they might discover what I was. People were very superstitious back then. Vampires were blamed for everything—sickness, death, sour milk, a bad harvest. A lot of innocent people were accused of being vampires—or witches—and killed."

"In all those years, you never loved anyone? Never let anyone get close?"

He shook his head. "Don't get me wrong. I didn't live like a monk. I may be a vampire, but I'm still a man, with a man's needs, but those were easily met without entanglements, if you know what I mean."

"Yes," she said dryly, "I do." She could only imagine

how many women there had been in his long life. Even
at one a year, the number was staggering.

"One a year?" he asked, one brow arched in wry
amusement.

Tessa stuck her tongue out at him, mildly annoyed
because he was reading her mind again, but it wasn't
worth mentioning. "Doesn't it seem odd that Katerina
would come looking for you after all this time?"

"It's you she came looking for," he reminded her. "I
was an afterthought." Rising, he moved casually to the
window and drew the curtains.

"Why did you do that?" Tessa asked. "I like looking
at the lights across the way."

Resuming his seat, he said, "Because she's here."

"Here? Where? We're three flights up." Tessa sat up,
her gaze darting around the room. "What is she doing?
Hovering outside the window like a bat?"

"More like the angel of death."

Tessa sank back on the pillows. "Thank goodness
Luke and Jileen were able to go home this morning.
Did I tell you Luke's decided to stay at Jilly's house
until we've resolved the Katerina problem? They'll be
safe, won't they?"

"As long as they stay inside."

"That shouldn't be a problem. Jilly said they're both
taking a couple of sick days."

Andrei nodded. Rising, he pushed a lock of hair
behind her ear, then brushed a kiss across her lips. "It's
late. Get some sleep."

"Is she still out there?"

"No." Lowering the head of the bed, he removed
one of the pillows and tossed it on the chair. "Don't
worry. I won't leave you."

"I love you," she murmured, her eyelids fluttering
down. "You're so good to . . ."

He stroked her cheek as sleep claimed her, vowing that no one—vampire or mortal—would ever hurt her again.

In the morning, Luke and Jilly drove Tessa home. They stopped on the way to pick up doughnuts, pastries, and half a gallon of milk.

In the kitchen, Tessa placed the doughnuts on a plate and filled three glasses. "Make yourselves at home," she said. "I'm going to go see if Bailey's awake."

Tessa knocked softly on the girl's door. When there was no answer, she peeked inside. Bailey lay curled up on her side, one hand resting beneath her cheek, one foot peeking out of the covers. She looked incredibly young and innocent. No one, looking at her, would ever guess that when provoked, she morphed into a black panther.

Backing out of the room, Tessa closed the door and went to join Luke and Jilly.

"Is she okay?" Jilly asked.

"Yeah, she's asleep. She had a late night."

Jilly nodded as she helped herself to a chocolate éclair. "This has been some weekend."

"It certainly didn't go the way I planned, that's for sure," Tessa said.

"I can't believe we all walked away from that accident with nothing more to show for it than a couple of bruises." Luke shook his head in disbelief. "My car was totaled."

"Yes," Tessa said, smothering a grin, "it's a miracle." And its name was Andrei. He had not only given Tessa his blood, but her friends as well, though they didn't know it.

"What are you looking so smug about?" Luke asked.

"Who, me?" Tessa asked innocently. "Nothing."

"Okay, spill it," Jilly said, licking chocolate frosting from her lips. "I know that look."

"Are you sure you want me to tell you?" Tessa asked. "You might not like the answer."

Jilly and Luke exchanged glances.

"We want to know," Luke decided, his voice grim.

"Andrei gave both of you some of his blood while you were in the hospital. That's why you healed so quickly."

"His blood?" Jilly asked, eyes wide with alarm. "I have *Andrei's* blood in me?"

"Relax," Tessa said. "It's just a little."

"Vampire blood." Luke shook his head. "I can't have vampire blood in me. I'm a hunter!"

"Would you rather be black and blue and in pain?" Tessa asked irritably. "He did you both a favor."

"You're right," Jilly said, reaching for another éclair. "It's just so . . . I mean . . ." Her eyes widened. "I guess he gave you some too."

Tessa nodded.

"Where is he now?" Luke asked.

"I don't know. He spent the night in my hospital room. I haven't seen him since then."

"They let him stay with you, even though he's not family?" Jilly asked.

"They didn't know he was there, silly."

"Oh, right."

"Well," Luke said, slapping his hands on his thighs. "I need to get to work."

"You got a job?" Tessa asked.

"I'm a hunter, remember? There was an article in the paper this morning. They found a body drained of blood behind Monk's Café."

"How do you find vampires, anyway?" Tessa asked.

"It's kind of hit and miss," Luke admitted, pushing away from the table. "Mainly, they like to hide in deserted buildings or abandoned houses. I reckon this is another one looking for you. Fledglings don't have a lot of experience and sometimes they're pretty easy to find."

"What do you do when you find one? Do you just drive a stake in its heart?"

"This is a very grisly discussion for so early in the morning," Jilly remarked, grimacing.

"Sorry," Tessa said.

"I'll be back later. Jilly, why don't you stay here?" Luke suggested. "I'll feel better if the two of you are together."

Jilly looked at Tessa, who shrugged. "It's fine by me."

"Okay, then." Luke kissed Jilly on the cheek. "I'll call you guys later."

Jilly stared after him. "I hate it when he goes hunting. What if the vampire isn't a fledgling? What if he's old, like Andrei? What if . . . ?"

Tessa covered her friend's hand with her own. "Hey, aren't you the one who said worrying about the future would ruin the present? Besides, you can't think like that. You'll drive yourself insane. Anyway, he's got some of Andrei's blood now. Maybe it'll make him stronger somehow."

"Maybe." Shoulders slumped, Jilly reached for a buttermilk doughnut. "I'm going to be as fat as a pig," she muttered. "When he's gone, all I do is eat."

"I won't let that happen," Tessa said, replacing the doughnut in Jileen's hand with a large green apple from the bowl in the center of the table.

"An apple?" Jilly exclaimed. "Seriously?"

"Much better for you." Tessa looked up as Bailey,

still wearing her pj's, entered the kitchen. "Morning, sleepyhead."

"Morning," Bailey mumbled. "Oh, doughnuts! Can I have one?"

"Take them both," Tessa said, slanting a grin at Jilly. "I'm doing an intervention."

Tessa glanced out the window. She, Jilly, and Bailey had spent the morning giving each other manicures and pedicures, then passed a couple of hours playing canasta, trying to pretend that everything was all right.

But Jilly constantly glanced at the clock and checked her phone for messages.

Bailey prowled through the house from time to time, checking doors and windows.

Tessa couldn't help fretting because Andrei hadn't called or come over. She told herself there was nothing to worry about. Katerina couldn't enter the condo uninvited. Andrei and Luke could—she hoped—take care of themselves.

In an effort to distract herself and the others, Tessa put the latest Hemsworth DVD into the player but, for once, even Thor couldn't take her mind off her worries.

When the movie was over, Tessa went to the window.

It would be dark in an hour or two.

And there was still no word from Luke.

Or Andrei.

Chapter Twenty-Four

Luke found the vampire he was looking for sleeping under the desk in the office of a gas station that had been out of business for several years. Someone—the vampire, perhaps—had tacked black cloth over the broken windows.

Heart pounding with anticipation and trepidation, Luke stared at the creature. At rest, it looked pretty much like any other human male, except that its skin was papery dry and fish-belly white and there was dried blood caked on its lips.

Luke pulled his cell phone from his jacket pocket and snapped a photo. He refused to consider the fact that his victim had once been human, that he'd likely had a family, people who loved him. Maybe someone he loved. Whether he had been turned by choice or by force, it didn't matter. He was a monster now, a killer.

Luke frowned as a little voice in the back of his head whispered that he, too, was a killer. "But not of innocents," he muttered, hoping to ease his conscience.

Jaw clenched, he pulled a stake from the back pocket of his jeans. He hesitated a moment. Vampires, at least the young ones, were trapped in the deathlike sleep of their kind from dawn to dusk. Was it truly like death? Were they able to feel pain?

Thrusting the disquieting thought aside, he drove the stake into the vampire's heart. It slid in, as smooth as a hot knife through butter. There was very little blood.

With the deed done, Luke took a second photo of the creature, focusing on the stake and the vampire's face as proof that he had destroyed it.

Blowing out a sigh, he tore the black cloth from the windows.

The vampire turned to ash the minute the sun's light touched him.

Vampire hunting might be dangerous as hell, Luke mused, tucking his phone into the back pocket of his jeans, but, thanks to the town's generous bounty, he was making money.

He was heading for his car when he felt it, a shift in the atmosphere that caused the hairs on his arms to stand at attention.

He had felt that same sensation before, a warning that a vampire was nearby. And since it was daylight, it had to be one of the old ones. Adrenaline spiked through him as he ran to his car, jerked open the door, and slid behind the wheel. Thank goodness for keyless ignitions, he thought, as he hit the start button and stomped on the gas.

He felt a surge of relief. Damn, that had been close.

He didn't slow down until he pulled into a condo parking place.

He had just switched off the ignition when someone ripped the driver's-side door off its hinges and he found himself staring into a pair of hell-red eyes.

Acting instinctively, he grabbed the stake on the

passenger seat and lunged out of the car, his stake angling for her chest.

But she was too fast for him. The stake missed her heart and sank into her belly instead.

She let out a horrific shriek and vanished from his sight.

Legs trembling, his clothes spattered with dark red vampire blood, Luke scrambled up the stairs to Tessa's apartment.

She opened the door immediately. "Merciful heavens!" she exclaimed. "What happened?"

He darted past her and slammed the door. "I think I just had a close encounter with Katerina."

Tessa felt the blood drain from her face. "She's here?"

"Not anymore."

"Did I hear Luke?" Jilly ran out of the kitchen, only to come to an abrupt halt when she saw the blood splattered across his shirtfront. "Are you hurt?"

"I'm fine, honey. It's not my blood."

He'd barely finished speaking when she threw herself into his arms.

He hugged her tightly.

Tessa gave them a few moments before asking, "Luke, have you seen Andrei?"

"No, I thought he'd be here."

Tessa shook her head. Where could he be?

Andrei wiped his hands on the sides of his jeans. He had spent the day trailing Katerina from town to town, disposing of the bodies she had left in her wake. Only one kill had been made in Cutter's Corner, for which he was grateful. The last thing they needed were a lot of bodies drained of blood and a lot of hysterical citizens.

Fortunately, as far as he could tell, the corpse in town had been that of a transient and not likely to be missed.

It was after midnight by the time he buried the last body and willed himself to Tessa's condo.

He hadn't expected her to still be awake, but she opened the door even before he knocked.

Sighing, he stepped inside and after locking the door behind him, he wrapped her in his arms. He had waited all day for this moment.

Tessa looked up at him, her brow furrowed. "Are you all right?"

"I am now." After a day of burying Katerina's victims— most of whom had not died easily—holding Tessa was like a balm to his troubled soul. Katerina could be the poster girl for death and darkness, but Tessa radiated light and life, something that had been sorely missing from his existence until she came along.

Her gaze searched his. "Where were you?"

"Don't ask." He inhaled deeply, reveling in the clean sweet smell of her hair and skin. "How are you holding up?"

"I'm okay. We have two more houseguests." Bailey, Jilly, and Luke were all asleep in the guest room, with Bailey and Jileen sharing the bed and Luke sacked out on the floor.

Andrei nodded. "Oh? Why's that?"

Tessa explained briefly and he nodded again. He had caught Katerina's scent when he arrived. Even now, he could feel her mind probing his, seeking to get into his head. He felt her anger as he pushed her out and slammed the door.

"I was just getting ready for bed when I had a feeling you were here," Tessa remarked.

Andrei stroked her cheek, his eyes going hot as he drew her closer. "Shall I tuck you in?"

All thoughts of Katerina fled Tessa's mind as his mouth closed over hers. Nothing else mattered when he was holding her, kissing her. Her whole being responded to his touch, every nerve coming alive, every sensation heightened as his tongue found hers. Wanting to be closer, she leaned into him, her arms sliding around his neck as their kisses grew deeper and more intense.

Sweeping her into his arms, he carried her to the sofa, then stretched out on his back, carrying her with him, so that she lay sprawled across him, her legs tangled with his. His hands stroked her back as he rained kisses along the curve of her neck, her eyelids, the soft, sensitive place behind her ears.

She was lost, drowning in an ocean of sensation when, abruptly, he stopped. The next thing she knew, she was sitting on the sofa with him beside her.

A moment later, Bailey entered the room.

Tessa took a deep breath, certain her flaming cheeks would give them away.

Bailey stopped in the doorway, her gaze darting from Andrei to Tessa's flushed face and back again. "I'm . . . I'm sorry," she stammered, her own cheeks suddenly red. "I didn't mean to interrupt. I . . ."

"No harm done," Andrei said smoothly. "Tessa was just going to pour me a glass of wine."

Tessa smiled at Bailey. "Can I get you anything?" she asked, rising.

"No, thank you. I . . . Good night."

"Do you really want a glass of wine?" Tessa asked after Bailey retreated to her bedroom.

"No." Twining his fingers with hers, he drew her down beside him on the sofa again. "Your kisses are intoxicating enough."

"Flatterer."

He cupped her face in his palms. "You doubt me?" He kissed her, his touch as light as a butterfly, the pressure increasing slowly, building inside her like a volcano.

His hand curled around her nape as his tongue ravished her mouth.

Tessa groaned low in her throat as desire flooded her veins.

She gasped his name.

He kissed her until she thought she might go mad with wanting him.

"Tessa?" His voice whispered in her ear, low and husky.

Nodding, she closed her eyes. She moaned softly as the touch of his fangs sent a wave of sensual pleasure sweeping through her, carrying her away in a warm, red haze.

She came back to reality slowly, gradually becoming aware of his arm around her, his breath cool against her cheek, his hand lightly stroking her back.

She blinked at him, thinking nothing in the world could equal what she had just experienced.

"You think not?" he asked, his voice thick with amusement.

"I can't imagine anything better."

"Just say the word, *dragostea mea.* I will be more than happy to show you what you're missing."

"Andrei . . ."

"I'm a patient man," he said, his fingertips caressing her cheek. "Take as long as you need."

He would have her, he thought, whether he had to

wait a day, a week, or a year. Sooner or later, she would be his.

Tessa sipped her coffee, then glanced at Jilly, who sat across the kitchen table from her, nibbling on a sugar cookie. Earlier, they had gone to church; later, they had ordered pizza, salad, and breadsticks for lunch. Since no one had wanted to go out after dark, they had eaten the leftovers for dinner. Now, Bailey and Luke were in the living room watching Sunday night football.

"So, what are we going to do tomorrow?" Jilly asked.

Tessa frowned at her. "What do you mean?"

"If we're going to work, I need to go home and get a change of clothes."

"I'm not sure going to work is a good idea," Tessa said. And yet she was anxious to get out of the house. She was tired of feeling trapped in her own home. Tired of being afraid of Katerina. And yet, only an idiot wouldn't be afraid of the psycho vampire.

Tessa heaved a sigh of frustration. "I don't know what to do," she admitted. "If she was just a run-of-the-mill vampire who could only go out at night, it wouldn't be such a problem. But I keep asking myself what would happen if she showed up at the office and went on a rampage. A lot of innocent people could get hurt. Killed."

"I know, but . . . Has Andrei said anything?"

"No." At least nothing Tessa wanted to repeat. He had rested in bed beside her last night, his arm around her, his voice whispering love words in her ear, his nearness a constant temptation. When she'd finally drifted off to sleep, her dreams had been dark and erotic. Had he been in her bed this morning, she might have surrendered to the urges her dreams had aroused in her the night before. She told herself she was relieved he hadn't been there when she woke, but she was afraid she was lying to herself.

"Do you really think she'd follow us to work?" Jilly asked.

"I wouldn't put anything past that creature. She's evil."

"Maybe Andrei could go with us."

"Maybe. I know I'd feel a lot safer if he was there."

"Me too. Do you think there are other vampires like him? Vampires who don't go around wreaking havoc and killing everything in sight?"

"I have no idea. I'd like to think so, but maybe he's one of a kind."

Jilly ran her finger around the rim of her coffee cup, her expression pensive. "How many vampires do you suppose there are in the world? Hundreds? Thousands?"

"Thousands?" Tessa shook her head. "Merciful heavens, I hope not!"

There was a shimmer in the room and Andrei appeared. "Is this what you girls do all day? Fret about how many vampires are running around?" He kissed Tessa's cheek, then pulled another chair up to the table. "At best, there are a few hundred of us in the States, perhaps a thousand in the rest of the world. Tessa, can I talk to you alone?"

"Sure. We can go in my room."

Andrei nodded at Bailey and Luke as he followed Tessa into her bedroom and closed the door.

"What is it?" she asked anxiously. "What's wrong?"

Taking her by the hand, he led her to the bed. Sitting on the foot, he drew her down beside him. "I want to ask you something. Don't freak out, don't jump to conclusions," he admonished as her heart began to beat faster. "Just think about it, okay?"

She nodded.

"I've been doing a lot of thinking about this. About Katerina. I'm not sure I can defeat her in an all-out test of power. I barely escaped with my life the last time we fought. And then there are the fledglings. I sensed three of them resting nearby on my way here. They'll keep coming as long as they think your blood will strengthen them." He squeezed her hand. "We don't have many options. I can only protect you as best I can and hope that Katerina calls off her vendetta, or . . ."

Tessa went suddenly still. "Or?"

"I can bring you across, make you one of us."

She had known, somehow, that he would suggest this sooner or later. It still came as a shock. "How would that solve anything?"

"Because your blood would undergo a drastic change once you're one of us. Whatever it was that made me stronger would most likely be destroyed. Fledglings would no longer have any reason to come after you. And being turned by a master vampire will make you stronger than any fledgling, able to easily defeat any that come after you."

"Are you sure about that?"

He shrugged. "Nothing in life is certain. As for Katerina, she wants you for the same reason the fledglings do. Your blood."

Tessa stared at him. What if it was the only way? Would she rather be really dead? Or just undead? Feeling chilled to the bone, she wrapped her arms around her waist. "How do you make a vampire?"

"I would drain you to the point of death, then give you my blood, which would have mingled with yours."

"You'd drain me? To the point of death?" She

shuddered as horrific images of every vampire movie she had ever seen flashed across her mind. "What if you accidentally took too much? I'd be . . . dead."

"That won't happen."

"How can you be so sure? Have you ever done it before?"

"No."

"I'd be the first?" Somehow, she had assumed that, having lived for so many centuries, he would have made at least one other vampire.

"I never wanted to be a vampire. Why would I make one?"

"But you want to make me one?"

"I'm not sure we have any other options."

Tessa shook her head. "I don't know. I mean, once it's done, it's done, right? You can't undo it?" It wasn't like buying a dress. She couldn't decide she didn't like it and take it back.

"I'm afraid not," he said, grinning. "But who knows? You might like it."

Her eyes widened in disbelief. "Somehow I doubt that."

"It's not so bad." He ran his fingertips down her cheek and across her lower lip. "You'd never age. Never be sick. You would always be as young and beautiful as you are now. You would have incredible power and stamina."

Tessa looked at Andrei. Really looked at him. He was easily the most handsome man she had ever met. His skin was smooth and unlined. His hair thick and black. In ten years, a hundred, he would look the same. Men spent millions of dollars a year trying to maintain their health and vitality. Women spent millions on cosmetics guaranteed to reduce the signs of aging. But it was all money down the drain. No matter how she tried, how many vitamins she took, how much she exercised, she couldn't stop the years from passing, couldn't stop them from sapping her energy or leaving their mark on her face.

But Andrei could. All she had to do was let him make her a vampire. "Does it hurt?"

"No, love."

It was tempting, in a morbid sort of way. Tempting and scary. And gross. How could she drink his blood? True, she had tasted it, but a little taste was one thing. To turn her into a vampire, he would drink most of her blood and give it back to her. That was certainly more than a drop or two. She grimaced, sickened at the thought.

"The blood will be sweet to you, *dragostea mea.*"

"Seriously?"

"Once you're changed, you'll wonder why you ever thought the taste of blood would be repulsive."

"Was it that way for you?"

He nodded. The blood had been sweet. The hunger had been excruciating. But it wouldn't be that way for Tessa. He would teach her how to hunt, how to satisfy the craving without killing her prey. He was an old vampire. His blood was ancient, strong. She wouldn't need to hunt as often as other fledglings.

Tessa blew out a sigh. Try as she might, she simply couldn't picture herself as a vampire, stalking humans for their blood, living in darkness. Giving up all the things she loved. "There has to be another way."

Andrei sighed, then cocked his head to the side. "Luke and Jileen have decided to go back to her place and pick up a change of clothes."

"Maybe you should go with them," Tessa suggested. "I don't like to think of them going alone. But don't tell Luke it was my idea. I don't want him to think I doubt his hunter skills."

"Even though you do?"

Tessa nodded. "I'd just feel better knowing you're there to protect Jilly."

"All right, love. We'll be back soon."

Tessa lifted her face for his kiss. She smiled as she watched him walk away. She would have preferred to spend her time thinking about Andrei and how good he looked walking away, but his suggestion niggled at the back of her mind.

To be—or not to be—a vampire, that was the question.

With a sigh, she thrust it out of her mind. There was no way she was going to make a life-altering decision like that tonight.

And likely not for many nights to come.

Chapter Twenty-Five

Tessa was hunting for the TV remote when she heard a noise on the landing. Thinking it was Jilly and Luke, she started to unlock the door when something stayed her hand. She peered through the front window, but didn't see anything. She was about to write the sound off to her imagination when the door exploded inward, striking her shoulder and knocking her to the floor.

Hearing a gasp from behind her, she struggled to sit up. A glance showed Bailey standing in the hallway, wrapped in a towel, a trail of foamy soap bubbles melting on the floor behind her. She stared, wide-eyed, at the opening where the door had been.

Tessa's gaze darted toward the landing.

Three male vampires stood there, fangs bared, eyes blazing with anger and frustration because they couldn't cross the threshold.

Andrei! His name screamed in Tessa's mind.

"Tess, are you all right?" Bailey asked, her voice surprisingly steady.

"Yes. Don't look in their eyes. Guard your thoughts." Tessa frowned when she heard a growl. A quick glance showed that Bailey had shape-shifted. It was the first time Tessa had seen the girl in panther form. It was, she thought, an awesome—scary—sight.

It didn't seem to intimidate the vampires, who prowled back and forth in front of the doorway.

And then Andrei was there. Like a cleansing whirlwind, he broke the necks of the vampires before they knew what hit them. A moment later, Luke came thundering up the stairs, stake in hand. Face set, he drove the stake into the heart of the nearest vampire.

Tessa swallowed the bile rising in her throat. "Is that really necessary?"

"Broken necks aren't fatal," Luke said, his voice grim as he quickly dispatched the other two. There was surprisingly little blood as he struck the final, mortal blows. "It just slows them down."

A white-faced Jileen edged around the doorjamb into the living room. "I think I'm going to be sick," she murmured, and ran toward the bathroom.

Ignoring everyone else, Andrei knelt beside Tessa. "Are you all right?"

Gingerly, she massaged her shoulder. "Yes, I'm fine."

"What's wrong with your arm?"

"The door hit me."

If it had been her head . . . He clenched his hands. Damn Katerina! She was behind this. He had caught her scent on one of the vampires. "Tessa, did any of those fledglings bite you?"

"No."

"Have any others?"

She shook her head.

Andrei grunted softly. It was possible she could have been bitten without knowing it. Katerina could have taken her unawares, hypnotized her, and wiped the memory from her mind. But if anything like that had happened, he would have detected Katerina's scent on Tessa's clothing or skin.

What if he'd been wrong in his thinking? Tessa's blood had a certain zing to it. Madame Murga had said it would make new vampires stronger. But what if she had lied? What if the opposite was true? What if it destroyed them and the lie had cost the gypsy her life?

"Andrei?"

"I'd best have a look at your shoulder." He lifted the sleeve of her shirt. The skin wasn't broken, but her arm was badly bruised from her shoulder to her elbow. By tomorrow, it would be a lovely shade of black and blue. Lifting her in his arms, he held her close for a moment before carrying her to the sofa.

"I can walk, you know. It's my shoulder that's hurt, not my leg."

"Be quiet, love. I like holding you. Bailey, get some ice for Tessa's arm. Luke, get in here and guard the door while I dispose of the bodies."

With a growl, Bailey grabbed her towel in her teeth and padded behind the sofa. She emerged a moment later with the towel wrapped around her.

Andrei picked up the door and set it in place. "I won't be gone long. We'll fix the door when I get back."

It took a while for the three of them to settle down after everything that had happened.

Bailey decided she would sleep on the sofa so Jilly and Luke could have the bed. And some privacy.

Tessa and Jilly went into the kitchen. Luke remained in the living room, keeping an eye on the damaged front door.

"Remember when life was boring?" Jilly asked,

pouring herself another cup of coffee. "Remember when we didn't know vampires existed?"

"Seems like a long time ago," Tessa murmured. "I wish Andrei would get back here."

"I'm sure he's fine. You really do love him, don't you?" Jilly's voice held a note of wonder. "Even though he's, you know, not human?"

"Yeah, I really do."

"Assuming there comes a day when the vampire problem is resolved, do you see the two of you getting married? Settling down? What about kids? He probably can't have any, can he?"

"I don't have answers to any of your questions, Jilly. All I know is that I can't imagine my life without him."

Jilly shook her head. "You've got it bad, girlfriend. You're not going to do anything stupid, are you? I mean, you wouldn't let him turn you? Tell me you wouldn't."

Tessa stared into her cup.

"Tessa?"

"He suggested it earlier tonight. He said if I was a vampire, the fledglings would probably stop coming after me."

"Probably?"

"Well, there are no guarantees in life, you know," Tessa said, repeating what Andrei had said earlier.

"So you *are* thinking about it?"

"Sort of," Tessa said, choosing her words carefully. "I mean, it just seems like the easiest solution to everything."

She wouldn't have to worry about getting older when he never would. She wouldn't have to worry about getting sick and becoming a burden to him. On the other hand, she would have to give up so much— all her favorite foods. Her job. Being able to go for a walk on a sunny day, going to church on Easter morning. Getting a tan in the summer. And what about a family? Since vampires couldn't reproduce, she would never have children of her own. And what about her parents? What would they think?

"Would we still be able to be friends?" Jilly asked, her expression doubtful. "Or would you always be thinking about biting me?"

"I don't know about the biting part, but I hope we'll always be friends."

Jilly nodded, then smothered a yawn.

"It's late. Why don't you go to bed?" Tessa suggested.

"Will you be all right?"

"Yeah. I think I'll go wait for Andrei in my room."

"Okay."

Tessa bid Luke good night, hugged Bailey, then went into her room and closed the door. After changing into her nightgown, she brushed her teeth, then sat on the bed, her back against the headboard, wondering what was taking Andrei so long.

"You sent the three of them, didn't you?" Andrei glared at Katerina. She sat on an elegant Louis XV armchair upholstered in burgundy silk, her back rigid, her expression icy. He couldn't help thinking she looked every inch the queen she had always wanted to be. "Why?"

"My reasons are my own. I would have shared my thoughts with you, once upon a time. That time has passed. You are no longer welcome in my home. Begone."

Andrei stared at her, his eyes narrowed. "So, we're through with this charade?"

"I had hoped to rekindle the passion between us,"

she said, her tone glacial. "I've come to realize that is impossible."

"It always was," he retorted, his voice as frosty as her own. "One word of caution. Leave Tessa and her friends alone. If you harm any of them, I will hunt you down and I will destroy you."

Chin lifted defiantly, she glowered at him. "You may try." Her power filled the room, skittering over his skin like the fingers of doom.

Andrei smiled inwardly. She was not as indomitable as she would have him believe. In spite of her haughty expression and bold words, he had seen the barest hint of fear reflected in the depths of her eyes.

Andrei found Tessa in her room, staring off into space. She smiled when he appeared on the bed beside her.

"You were gone so long, I was beginning to worry," she said.

"No need."

"Where were you?"

"After I disposed of the bodies, I went to see Katerina."

"Oh."

"We're through."

Tessa stared at him wide-eyed. "Really? No more playing house?"

He nodded. "I guess she realized my heart wasn't in it. Listen," he said, taking her hands in his, "I want to try a little experiment tomorrow."

"What kind of experiment?"

"We've been going on the assumption that Madame Murga was right, and that your blood makes fledglings stronger, that it enhances their powers, because it added a little kick to mine."

"So?"

"Hell, what if she made it all up? What if she's wrong? What if it doesn't work the same on every vampire?" He paused, his brow furrowed. "What if it makes some stronger and weakens others?"

"What makes you think that?"

"I don't know. Just a hunch. We need to learn more about exactly what your blood can do."

"We know it healed you."

"Yes, but at first I didn't think your blood had any other effect on me. I'm starting to believe I was wrong. Katerina used to be a lot more powerful than I am. But that's not true anymore. I can feel the difference, and I think she can, too."

"So, this experiment? What does it entail?"

"I want to use you as bait to lure four or five fledglings. When I have them under control, I'll give a couple of them a little of your blood and see what happens."

"You want me to let them bite me?" Good grief, that was almost as revolting as the idea of letting him turn her.

"Of course not. I'll use a syringe to extract it and then have them drink it."

"I don't know . . ." Was there no end to this nightmare?

"It's up to you, of course," he said, squeezing her hands.

"How's that going to help keep other vampires away from me?"

"I need to see what kind of reaction they have to your blood. If it doesn't actually strengthen them, word that it failed will spread through the vampire population pretty fast."

"And if it does?"

He shrugged. "We'll see if we can come up with a Plan C."

And if not, she thought, they were back to Plan A—turning her into a vampire. Plan B was definitely the lesser of two evils.

"All right," Tessa agreed with a sigh. "I'll do it. When?"

"Tomorrow night."

Chapter Twenty-Six

When Tessa awoke in the morning, Andrei rested beside her. He had never stayed all night with her before. Always, in the past, he had been gone when she woke. For a moment, she lay there, studying him. In the movies, vampires always looked pale and dead at rest, but he looked the same as always—amazingly handsome and all too sexy. The sheet was pooled around his hips, offering a tantalizing glimpse of his broad shoulders and bare chest. Did he dream? If so, what did he dream of?

"What do you think?" His voice, as deep as ten feet down, slid over her senses like liquid heat, settling in the deepest part of her being.

"I *thought* you were asleep."

"I was." His lips twitched in a wicked grin. "Your lustful thoughts woke me."

"You stayed the night."

He gazed at her, one brow arched in inquiry. "Would you rather I had left?"

"No. Won't you kiss me good morning?"

"My pleasure." His hand curled around her nape, drawing her closer.

His kiss sent a shiver of delight down her spine. "I could get used to this."

"Then we should do it again," he murmured.

Desire unfolded inside her like a flower opening to the sun. He turned on his side, his arm drawing her closer so that her body was aligned intimately with his. She sucked in a deep breath when his hand slid under her sleep shirt to stroke her bare skin.

Andrei paused. "Do you want me to stop?"

"No," she said, her voice husky, "but I think we'd better."

"I was afraid you'd say that."

She grinned when her alarm went off. "Saved by the bell," she muttered as she rolled over to turn it off.

Andrei loosed a heavy sigh.

"I'm sorry," Tessa said, "but Jilly and I decided to go to work today. I was wondering if you'd be willing to spend the day in my office. You don't have to if you don't . . ."

He pulled her into his arms again and kissed her soundly. "I can't think of anything I'd rather do."

"I was hoping you'd say that."

She sat up, her eyes widening with feminine appreciation when—clad in nothing but a pair of black briefs—he rose and padded into the bathroom. She almost hated to see the door close behind him.

Moments later, the shower came on. She had no trouble at all imagining him in the stall, his broad chest and flat belly covered in soapy water.

With a shake of her head, she pulled on her robe and went to see about breakfast.

On her way into the kitchen, Tessa noted that the front door had been repaired. Jilly, Luke, and Bailey were already there—Bailey making waffles, Jilly pouring coffee. Luke sat at the table, the morning paper spread before him. Andrei appeared a few minutes later, his hair still damp from his shower.

"There was another killing last night," Luke remarked grimly. "Some homeless guy going through a Dumpster found the woman's body."

Tessa noticed that no one asked if the body had been drained of blood. Like everyone else, she assumed that, if Luke had mentioned it, it was a vampire kill.

"Luke, I want you to stay here with Bailey today," Andrei said. "I'm going to work with Tessa and Jileen. The fledglings won't be out and about until nightfall, but Katerina . . . You never can tell. I don't think she'd be stupid enough to try anything in a crowded workplace in broad daylight. But I wouldn't bet on it. And that's why I'll be there."

Tessa glanced at the fall decorations that adorned the lobby of Milo and Max. Pumpkins and sheaves of Indian corn made a colorful display on one of the tables. Life-size mannequins in Pilgrim garb flanked the entrance.

"Thanksgiving is Thursday, isn't it?" Tessa remarked as she followed Jilly through the revolving door.

"I think I mentioned that last week," Jilly reminded her as they headed toward the elevators.

"I know. It's just hard to think about celebrating the holidays when people are being found in Dumpsters, drained of blood."

"I know. You're right. I've just always loved Thanksgiving and Christmas. Maybe we could plan a small celebration for the four of us."

Tessa glanced over her shoulder at Andrei.

"The five of us," Jilly amended.

Andrei shook his head. "I don't want to ruin your holiday."

"Don't be silly," Tessa said. "You have to come. You're practically family."

"In that case," he said, smiling, "I'll bring the wine."

Sitting at her computer, Tessa tried not to think about the experiment Andrei had mentioned the night before, but she couldn't put it out of her mind. Tonight, he'd said. He wanted to do it tonight.

Change your mind?

It was disconcerting, hearing his voice when she couldn't see him. But she knew he was in her office. She could sense his presence, knew he was sitting in the chair across from her desk, even though no one could see him.

"No, I haven't," she whispered. "I'm just not looking forward to it."

You'll be fine.

"I know. Be quiet now. Mr. Ambrose is coming."

Somehow, she made it through the day and the drive home, and even managed to eat a little dinner.

Her heart was pounding like a bass drum when, hours later, Andrei drove them to the next town.

"Just walk down the street as if you're on your way home from a date or a late movie," he told her. "I'll be right behind you."

Tessa nodded. Nerves strung tight, she took a firm hold on her courage and strolled down the street, pausing now and then to glance into one of the store windows.

When she reached the end of the block, she crossed the street and started back the other way.

By the time she reached the point where they had left Andrei's car, she decided it had been a waste of time.

"Not at all," Andrei said, materializing beside her. "I've got five fledglings locked up at my place."

"Your place?"

He grinned at her. "Don't you want to see where I live?"

Tessa stared at the big, old house. The outside—a weathered gray—was in desperate need of a coat of paint, but the house itself looked sound. Funny, she had never noticed the place before. Had Andrei put some kind of spell on it to make it invisible to passersby?

She gasped when she stepped inside. The living room was large enough to hold her whole condo with space left over. The walls were papered in a navy-and-gray stripe, the floors polished wood. She wasn't much of a connoisseur of furniture but she would have bet her 401K that all the furnishings in the room were antiques. And gorgeous ones at that.

"Would you like to see the rest?" he asked.

She nodded, eyes wide with wonder as he took her through the rest of the house. Every room was furnished with exquisite antiques in a variety of woods—oak and walnut, cherry and ebony.

The kitchen was the only room not furnished. No table. No refrigerator or stove. No dishwasher or microwave. But then, he really didn't need any appliances.

In the library, Tessa noticed a small cherrywood secretary with a drop-down writing desk on one side and three glass-fronted shelves on the other. She fell in love with it immediately.

"You like it?" he asked.

"It's beautiful."

"It's yours."

"I'm sure I can't afford it," she said, remembering that he sold furniture for a living.

Drawing her into his arms, he kissed her lightly. "I'm sure you can."

"Where do you sleep?" Tessa asked. The bedrooms upstairs were furnished, but none of the beds—whether brass, sleigh, or Victorian—included a mattress. All the closets were empty.

"My lair is in the basement."

"Oh?"

He regarded her a moment, then took her by the hand and led her through a narrow door that had been painted to look like part of the wall. It opened onto an equally narrow staircase that led to the basement. Lights came on when they reached the bottom of the steps.

"Oh, Andrei, it's lovely."

And so it was. A thick burgundy-colored carpet covered the floor. A dozen paintings adorned the beige walls. A king-size bed with a walnut headboard and a matching wardrobe dominated the room. A comfortable-looking chair and footstool stood in one corner, a bookcase crammed with paperbacks in the other.

Andrei slid his arm around her waist. "I've never brought anyone else here."

The thought pleased her beyond measure.

"Now to business," he said.

"What? Oh." The vampires, she thought, shuddering.

"It won't take long."

"Where are they?"

Gesturing for her to follow, he led her back upstairs, through the kitchen, and out the rear entrance.

The backyard was large and empty save for what looked like a small storage shed. When he unlocked the door, she saw that it wasn't a shed, but a cage. Three men and two women huddled inside, their hands shackled to one of the bars over their heads.

"The restraints are made of silver," Andrei remarked. "It renders them powerless."

The vampires paid him no attention. As one, they stared, unblinking, at Tessa. One of the males hissed at her and she took an involuntary step backward. They all appeared to be in their early twenties or thirties. Just looking at them, so close, was frightening. There wasn't a doubt in her mind that, if it were possible, they would attack her without mercy. And yet she couldn't help feeling sorry for them. They had been turned in the prime of life, all hope of a normal future—of home and family—forever lost.

"Are you ready, Tess?" Andrei asked, pulling a syringe from his coat pocket.

"Not really."

"You don't have to do this."

She lifted her head defiantly. "Yes, I do." If this would stop these creatures from hunting her, it would be worth it. She removed her jacket, tried to roll up her shirtsleeve, but her hand was shaking so badly, she couldn't manage it.

Andrei did it for her. "Look at me," he said.

She felt his power move over her, a pleasant tingle; a moment later, the needle was filled with her blood. She hadn't felt a thing.

Andrei filled three shot glasses—pulled from another coat pocket—and offered them to two of the men and one of the women. "Drink."

They didn't hesitate.

The two who hadn't been given anything watched with blatant envy as the other three drained the glasses and licked the drops that were left.

"Why didn't you give it to all of them?" Tessa asked.

"We need witnesses."

"Oh, right. You mentioned that before. What if nothing . . . ?"

"Happens? I don't think that's going to be a problem," Andrei said as all three of the vampires went limp, held upright only by their restraints.

The other two vampires stared at them in horror.

"What happened?" the male demanded, face dark with anger. "You poisoned her blood, didn't you?"

Andrei shook his head. "You saw me draw it from the woman. I didn't alter it in any way. If you don't believe me, I'll let you drink from her directly."

Tessa stared at Andrei. Was he serious?

The vampire shook his head. "No way, man."

"What are you going to do with us?" the female asked.

"I'm going to let you go," Andrei said. "And you're going to spread the word that this woman's blood is deadly to all but the ancients. And I want you to tell the vampires here in town to leave. Tonight. If I find any of them here tomorrow, I'll destroy them. That includes the two of you." He glanced from one to the other. "Understood?"

Eyes wide and scared, they nodded.

"Tessa, go back to the house and lock the door. I'll join you in a moment."

She tried to walk away slowly, with dignity, but her feet wouldn't cooperate. She ran the whole way. And slammed the door behind her.

In the living room, she paced the floor while she tried to process what had just happened. She had killed three people. Instead of enhancing the fledglings' power, as she'd expected, her blood had killed them. She had killed them.

"Tessa?"

She whirled around to face him. "How could you?" she exclaimed. "How could you do that? You killed them. *I* killed them."

"We didn't know it would happen," he said quietly. "There was no other way to find out. On the bright side, Cutter's Corner should be vampire-free by tomorrow night."

"Except for you," Tessa said. "And Katerina."

"Do you want me to leave?"

She met his gaze. And then shook her head. Heaven help her, whatever he was, whatever he'd done, she didn't want to live without him.

Chapter Twenty-Seven

Over the course of the next two days, Tessa scoured every page of the *Cutter's Corner Gazette,* and every newspaper from the surrounding towns. To her relief, there were no reports of mysterious deaths. No missing persons. No bodies drained of blood.

Luke and Andrei had gone through the town street by street, checking all the known vampire hangouts and possible lairs.

"No sign of vamps, living or dead. It's time to celebrate!" Luke had declared when they returned. And then he frowned. "Hey, I'm out of a job! At least in this town."

Andrei had brought the most welcome news of all. There was no trace of Katerina.

As guilty as Tessa felt for causing the destruction of three vampires, she also experienced a profound surge of relief that Andrei's experiment appeared to have been a success.

Thrusting worries about vampires from their minds, Tessa and Jilly got together Wednesday evening to plan Thanksgiving dinner. They had the kitchen all to themselves since Luke had decided to go out and wander through the town, just to make sure there were no new vampires skulking about. Andrei had gone hunting. Bailey was in her bedroom, reading a book.

"Shall we go traditional?" Jilly asked. "Turkey, stuffing, sweet potatoes, cranberry sauce?"

"That's always good. Or we could have prime rib and mashed potatoes."

"Prime rib. Wow, that sounds even better."

"Maybe we should ask Luke what he wants."

"No way," Jilly said. "We're the ones doing all the cooking. We'll decide."

"All right," Tessa agreed, laughing. "So, what'll it be?"

"I had my taste buds all set for turkey until you mentioned prime rib. So, let's be nontraditional this year."

"Okay by me. Do you want to cook here, or at your place?"

"Here," Jilly said. "Your kitchen's bigger and so is your oven. What'll we have for dessert? Pumpkin pie?"

Tessa shrugged. "Tradition!" she sang in her best Tevye imitation.

"Well, how about hot fudge sundaes smothered in whipped cream and cherries?"

"Now you're talking my language! Okay, I'll buy the prime rib and seasoning and make cheesy potatoes, and you bring a vegetable and dessert. And some sodas. We'll plan to eat around, oh, four, I guess."

"Sounds good," Jilly said. "You know, it's been so long since I've stayed at my own house, I won't know what to do. You're probably glad to be rid of us."

Tessa laughed as she followed Jilly to the front door. "Don't be silly. I'm just glad the danger's passed and life is back to normal. See you tomorrow."

"Maybe we can catch a movie Friday afternoon."

"Okay. Night."

Still smiling, Tessa closed the door. It felt good to

think about mundane things, like Thanksgiving dinner, instead of worrying about vampires.

Sitting on the arm of the sofa, she took a deep breath. Three days without a hint of trouble. Finally, they could all come and go without always looking over their shoulders, or jumping at every unexpected noise and shadow.

Glancing at her watch, she saw that it was still early. Maybe she would go shopping tonight rather than waiting until morning.

She looked out the window, trying to decide if she wanted to put on her shoes and a jacket and head for the market, or just stay home and relax.

A sound from outside drew her attention. It was probably nothing, she told herself. Just the wind. Maybe her neighbor's tomcat prowling around. "Nothing to worry about," she said, her voice a bit too loud. "The vampires are gone."

She had almost convinced herself she was imagining things when a shadow passed in front of the window.

Jumping to her feet, Tessa closed the curtains, then checked to make sure the door was locked.

Shaking all over, she dropped onto the sofa. She told herself there was nothing out there, she was over-reacting. But to no avail. Grocery shopping could wait until tomorrow. Cowardly or not, she wasn't leaving the house until the sun was up.

Andrei listened intently to Tessa's description of what had happened. He hadn't noticed anything out of the ordinary when he returned to her condo, but he went outside to scout around anyway, just to reassure her.

Standing on the landing, he opened his preternatural senses. He was about to go back inside when he caught it. A faint scent reminiscent of Bailey after she shifted. He inhaled slowly, drawing in the scent. Definitely a shifter of some kind. Had Bailey lied when she'd said she didn't know any others of her kind? Or had this one been tracking her?

"Well?" Tessa asked anxiously. "Did you find anything?"

"Yes and no. I'm going to have a little talk with Bailey."

"What about?"

"I think there's another shifter in the neighborhood."

"Mind if I listen in?"

"Of course not. It's your house."

At Bailey's invitation, Andrei stepped into her bedroom.

Tessa waited by the door.

Sitting on the bed, a book in her lap, Bailey glanced from one to the other. "Is something wrong?"

Andrei shook his head. "Are you sure you don't know any other shape-shifters?"

"I'm sure," Bailey said, frowning. "Don't you believe me?"

"There was one here a little while ago."

"Here?" The girl's eyes widened in alarm. "How do you know?"

"I caught his scent a few minutes ago. It's very faint, but it's there."

"But how . . . who?" She shook her head. "Are they looking for me?"

"I don't know, but it seems logical. Any idea who it might be?"

"No." Laying the book aside, she wrapped her arms around her middle, the color draining from her face as she stared up at Andrei.

"Hey, there's nothing to be afraid of." Sitting on the edge of the bed, he put his arm around her shoulders. "I'm going to see if I can track whoever it is. Do you want to come along?"

She hesitated, then nodded.

"Put on a jacket. And boots, if you've got any. It's starting to rain."

"I'm going too," Tessa decided.

Andrei looked at her, one brow arched.

"It's all right, isn't it?"

He shrugged. "Sure, if you want."

With a nod, she went into her own room to don a pair of fur-lined boots and a warm jacket with a hood.

Returning to the living room, she found Bailey and Andrei waiting for her.

Tessa gestured at Andrei. "Don't you need a jacket, too?"

"The weather doesn't bother me. Come on."

He paused on the porch. The rain made it more difficult to locate the scent, but he found it after a moment's concentration. "Let's go."

Tessa and Bailey trailed Andrei down the stairs and across the street. He'd said the scent was weak, but he seemed to be following it easily enough, Tessa thought as he picked up the pace. She huddled into her jacket, wondering what had possessed her to go out in weather like this. She refused to believe she was jealous of a sixteen-year-old girl, but she didn't like the way Bailey looked at Andrei, as if he was her own personal knight in shining armor. And if she was being honest, it rankled that he was so protective of the girl. It shamed her to feel that way.

Tessa huffed a sigh of exasperation. She was being

ridiculous and she knew it. She should have just stayed home.

They were almost at the forested area near the edge of town when Bailey growled. Tessa stared at the girl. She had never heard a human make a sound like that in her life. And even as the thought crossed her mind, Bailey kicked off her boots, then dropped to her hands and knees. In the twinkling of an eye, the girl was gone and a black panther stood in the midst of a pile of shredded clothing. The cat stared into the darkness, ears and tail twitching.

As if that wasn't shocking enough, a moment later Andrei changed into a big black wolf.

Stunned by what she was seeing, Tessa held her breath as another panther materialized out of the darkness. It padded silently forward, yellow eyes glowing in the dark, until the two panthers were standing almost nose to nose.

One of them made a sort of purring sound and then they circled each other, first one way, then the other.

Tessa glanced at the wolf. He stood stiff-legged, hackles raised, watching the two cats.

Tessa chewed on her lower lip, wishing more than ever that she had just stayed home.

Abruptly, the larger panther darted into the forest and out of sight. After a moment, Bailey the panther ran after it.

Tessa felt a shiver in the air as Andrei regained his own form. "What just happened?" she asked.

"Apparently Bailey's found another shifter," Andrei said, gathering her ruined clothing. "Or he found her."

"Is she coming back?"

"I don't know."

"But . . . should we just let her go like that? She could be in danger."

"So could we," he said, taking her by the arm and guiding her back the way they'd come. "There are half a dozen other shifters lurking in the shadows near the trees."

Feeling exhilarated, Bailey ran after the big black panther. Never before had she shifted so easily or so quickly. She knew, somehow, that it was because of the other cat. His power had somehow enhanced her own. It had been the most incredible feeling in the world.

She ran tirelessly, effortlessly, following him through the forest and into the hills beyond. Scents and sensations flowed over her and through her. All her senses were heightened. She tasted fear on the wind as a rabbit scurried out of her way, its heart beating wildly. Gradually, the other panther slowed. When he stopped beside a small stream, so did she. When he dropped to his belly to lap at the water, she followed his lead. It was icy cold on her tongue.

Rising, he shook himself and suddenly a man stood before her. A beautiful man with short, brown hair and piercing green eyes. "I am Tristan."

She shifted to her human form with ease. "I'm Bailey." He was naked and so was she, yet she felt no shame, no embarrassment.

"You are one of us," he said, his voice and expression solemn.

Bailey grinned, thinking he was stating the obvious. She wondered how old he was. If she'd had to guess, she would have said no more than twenty, though she'd never been good at guessing things like that.

"You have no pack."

"Pack?"

"People to protect you. To teach you."

"I have Andrei."

"A vampire." Tristan snorted disdainfully. "What can *he* teach you?"

"He helped me as best he could," she said, springing to Andrei's defense.

"He cannot teach you what you need to know. If it is your wish, you may stay here, with us."

"Us?" She glanced around, eyes widening when six panthers of varying size padded into view.

"These are pack," he said. "Family."

Before he finished speaking, they had all shifted to human form—a middle-aged man and woman and three girls and a boy who looked like they were her age or a little younger.

All six nodded to her, their smiles friendly but curious. The woman pulled a large bag from under a deadfall and passed out hooded robes to everyone, including Bailey. It reminded her of the kind of robe worn by Obi-Wan Kenobi in *Star Wars*. She accepted it gratefully. She hadn't been embarrassed by her nudity in front of Tristan, but felt suddenly shy in the presence of the others.

Holding the robe close around her, she looked at Tristan. "How did you find me?"

"We have been watching you for a long time, waiting for you to grow up."

The thought should have frightened her. Instead, a little thrill of excitement shot through her. "Why?"

"Because you and I are destined to be life-mates."

Bailey backed up a step, then folded her arms over

her chest. "I'm only sixteen. I'm not ready to be anybody's 'life-mate.'"

"Of course you aren't. We just wanted to introduce ourselves to you, let you know you're not alone." He nodded at the man and the woman. "These are my parents, Thomas and Colette. My sisters, Mercy, Faith, and Charity. And my brother, Justin. You will meet the rest of the pack if you decide to join us."

"Pleased to meet you all," Bailey said. Then, looking at Tristan, she asked, "So, what happens now?"

"You may stay with us, or I will escort you back home."

"I think I want to go back to Tessa's."

"Very well. But first . . ." He motioned to the others and they came forward one by one to embrace her.

To Bailey's amazement, they each sniffed her for several seconds before letting her go. When the last girl backed away, Bailey looked askance at Tristan. "What was that all about?"

"So they will recognize you in either form. Come," he said, holding out his hand, "I will take you home."

Bailey was surprised again when he led her to a late-model Chevy. He held her door open for her before rounding the car and sliding behind the wheel. Bailey glanced out the window as he drove toward town, her emotions running rampant. One minute she was excited about what had just happened. The next, apprehensive. But, either way, she felt drawn to Tristan.

In some ways, she felt as if she had known him all her life.

As if she had been biding her time, waiting for him to find her.

* * *

Tessa sat on the sofa beside Andrei, listening intently as Bailey related her encounter with Tristan and his family.

"So, have you made a decision?" Tessa asked when Bailey fell silent.

"No." Bailey looked at Andrei. "What do you think I should do?"

"That's up to you. I'm not your father, but if I was, I'd tell you to get to know Tristan and his family better before you decide."

Bailey nodded, then glanced at Tessa. "What would you do?"

"I agree with Andrei. You're welcome to invite Tristan here, if you like. As for that 'life-mate' thing . . ." Tessa shook her head. "I don't know anything about were-panther lore," she said, smiling. "But it does sound romantic. Do you have a way to get in touch with him? Maybe you could invite him for Thanksgiving dinner tomorrow afternoon."

"Really?" Bailey asked.

"What better way to get to know him than to invite him to have dinner with your family?"

Chapter Twenty-Eight

Tessa grinned at Bailey as they set the table for dinner. It had been a hectic morning. The first order of business had been a quick trip to the market in search of the perfect prime rib. With that accomplished, she and Bailey had spent a hurried few minutes dusting and vacuuming and cleaning the bathroom before going to their own rooms to shower and dress for the day.

Tristan had given Bailey his cell phone number and she had called him last night to invite him to dinner. Tessa wasn't sure how she felt about having another shape-shifter in the house, but she kept her misgivings to herself.

Their guests were scheduled to arrive at four.

At three thirty, Tessa set out chips and dip and a vegetable platter. She checked to make sure there was plenty of ice, chilled the wine Andrei had dropped off the night before, checked the roast and the potatoes.

Luke and Jilly arrived a few minutes before four, Tristan shortly thereafter.

Bailey made the introductions.

Tessa smiled as she shook Tristan's hand. He was a handsome young man, almost as tall as Andrei, with short, dark brown hair and vivid green eyes. He was obviously ill at ease in a roomful of strangers, but he greeted each of them politely. Tessa noted that Bailey couldn't keep her eyes off him.

"Where's Andrei?" Jilly asked.

"I don't know. I haven't heard from him. Oh," she said, hurrying toward the front door, "he's here."

She felt her heart skip a beat as he swept her into his arms and kissed her. And kissed her again, his hands moving up and down her spine, then delving into her hair.

"I missed you," he murmured.

She gazed up at him, breathless, her other guests forgotten. "You should miss me more often."

"Darlin', I miss you every second we're apart." He smiled down at her, his eyes alight. "I have news but I'm not sure if it's good news or not."

"What is it?"

"I stopped by Katerina's place on my way here. There's still no sign of her. It looks like she packed up and left town."

"That sounds like good news to me!"

"If she's truly gone from Cutter's Corner, then it is. If she's still here . . . shielding her presence . . ." He shook his head. "It's easier to fight an enemy you can see."

"Well, let's not worry about her now," Tessa said, taking him by the hand. "For today, let's pretend she doesn't exist."

"All right, love."

Still holding her hand, Andrei exchanged greetings with Luke and Jilly, shook hands with Tristan, gave Bailey a one-armed hug. If he was surprised to see Tristan, he didn't let on.

A short time later, Tessa announced dinner was

ready and they sat down to eat. She glanced at Andrei, seated to her left. Was it uncomfortable for him to be here, she wondered, watching the rest of them enjoying the meal?

Catching her gaze, Andrei shook his head. Food had held no interest for him since he became a vampire. And yet . . . he stared at the thick slice of rare prime rib on Tessa's plate and felt his mouth water. As if watching himself from a distance, he picked up her knife, took the fork from her hand, cut a small piece of meat, and ate it. It seemed odd to consume something that wasn't liquid, odder still to have to chew before he swallowed. The meat was rare and tender and slid easily down his throat.

Tessa stared at him, as did everyone else at the table.

Shrugging, he helped himself to a slice from the platter in the center of the table. He might regret it later, he thought as he took another bite. But for now he was going to enjoy it. Later tonight, he would ponder how it was possible for him to consume mortal food.

The night had passed pleasantly enough, Tessa thought as she loaded the last of the dishes into the dishwasher. Jilly and Bailey had offered to help, but she had insisted on doing it after everyone had gone home. "It's a holiday," she'd said. "Let's not spend it in the kitchen."

Now, near midnight, she switched on the machine, turned off the light, and went into the living room, where Andrei waited for her. Jilly and Luke had gone home; Bailey had gone out with Tristan.

"It was fun, wasn't it?" Tessa remarked, curling up

on the sofa next to him. "At least after we all managed to relax."

He chuckled. The amount of preternatural power in the room had raised the hairs along Luke's arms. "I think Tristan will be good for Bailey."

"Do you really think they're destined to be life-mated?"

"I guess it's possible. I don't know much about the shifter community."

"But you knew they existed?"

"I've run across one now and then."

"Can I ask you something?"

"You know you can ask me anything."

"I thought you couldn't eat . . . you know . . . regular food. But you ate the roast. How did you manage it?"

"I have no idea. I don't even know where the urge came from. I haven't eaten solid food in centuries." His gaze moved to her throat. "I think it has something to do with your blood."

She lifted a hand to her neck. "What do you mean?"

"It's made me stronger in ways I can't explain. Perhaps that includes the ability to consume mortal food from time to time."

She stared at him, eyes wide.

He laughed softly. "It's pretty amazing. Who knows? Tomorrow night I might try a hamburger."

She didn't know if he was kidding or not. But there were more important things on her mind. "Do you really think Katerina is gone for good?"

"One can only hope." Andrei wrapped his arm around Tessa's shoulders and drew her closer. "Let's not talk about her now," he whispered, his voice husky with desire.

He gave her no time to respond. Lowering his head,

he kissed her, gently at first, then with greater intensity. Somehow, they were lying side by side on the sofa, their bodies pressed so intimately together Tessa couldn't tell where she ended and he began.

His hand slipped beneath her sweater, his skin cool against her heated flesh as he kissed her again and yet again, his tongue teasing hers in a dance as old as time. She couldn't think, could scarcely breathe. There was only Andrei, his mouth on hers, his hands caressing her until she thought she might die from wanting him.

She felt his fangs brush against the side of her neck, featherlight, a silent plea.

Gasping, "Yes," she clung to him as the only solid thing in a world suddenly spinning out of control.

She cried out in protest when he sat up, drawing her with him, straightening her sweater.

Tessa blinked up at Andrei, her whole body throbbing with desire. Before she could ask why he'd stopped, Bailey entered the condo.

The girl blushed to the roots of her hair. Stammering, "I'm sorry," she averted her face and bolted for her room.

The sound of her door slamming was very loud in the silence that followed.

With a sigh, Tessa ran a hand through her hair, then glanced at Andrei.

He traced her lower lip with his fingers. "And the fair maiden is saved by the bell yet again," he muttered dryly.

When Tessa woke Friday morning, the first thing she noticed was Andrei resting beside her. It was, she thought, starting to be a habit, and a dangerous one. They had indulged in some hot and heavy kissing last night before she'd managed to put on the brakes. She wondered how much longer she could play with fire before she got burned, or Andrei ran out of patience with her.

Propping herself up on one elbow, she spent a few moments admiring the strong lines of his face, the width of his shoulders.

"If you keep looking at me like that," he murmured, his voice deep and sleep-roughened, "I won't be responsible for what happens next."

Blushing from head to foot, Tessa jerked her gaze away, only then noticing the beautiful cherrywood secretary she had admired at Andrei's. Somehow, he had carried it into her bedroom during the night without her hearing a thing. She had planned to put it in the living room by the window, but it fit perfectly on the wall across from her bed.

"Andrei, you remembered."

"Of course." He stroked her cheek with his knuckles. "What would you like to do this morning?" he asked.

"I know what *you'd* like to do," she muttered.

"Are you reading *my* mind now?"

"That's not really necessary." She glanced at the sheet, and the visible evidence of his arousal beneath it.

Andrei chuckled, not the least bit embarrassed.

It was oh, so temping, Tessa thought, but something held her back. She wanted him desperately and yet, once they made love, she was committed. She couldn't share her body without sharing her heart. Once she crossed that line, there was no turning back. And as much as she wanted him, as much as she loved him . . . the word, *vampire*, slithered, unwanted, through the back of her mind.

She met his hooded gaze, her own tormented, his

filled with a look of such understanding and sadness that she quickly glanced away before he saw her tears.

"Tessa."

She shook her head, refusing to look at him.

"Tessa. It's okay. You have every right to be afraid to tie your life to mine. I don't blame you." He placed his hand on her back. "I just want you to be happy, the way you were before I turned your life upside down."

His hand fell away, though she could still feel his touch.

When she turned around, he was gone.

The tears came then, slowly building in intensity until she fell back on the mattress, sobbing. Why was life so complicated? Why couldn't she have fallen in love with some ordinary guy? She didn't want to live without Andrei, but she couldn't bring herself to have an affair with him. She wanted marriage and a family. A man who would come home from work at night and ask about her day. She wanted a marriage like the one her parents had—a solid relationship built on love and trust. Was that asking too much?

She cried until she had no tears left, then went into the bathroom to wash her face. She frowned at her reflection. If she went into the kitchen, her eyes all red and puffy, Bailey was going to know something was wrong.

Her heart skipped a beat when her cell phone rang. Was it Andrei? She ran into the bedroom and snatched it off the nightstand.

It was Jilly. "Hi!" she said exuberantly. "Are you sitting down?"

"No, why? What's wrong?"

"Luke asked me to marry him!"

Tessa dropped down on the edge of the bed.

"Tess? Are you there? Did you hear what I said?"

"That's wonderful, Jilly. I'm . . . I'm happy for you. For both of you."

"You don't sound very happy."

"I am, really." She forced a smile into her voice. "So, when's the big day?"

"Gosh, we haven't settled on a date yet, but we both want a small wedding. Just close friends and family. Nothing fancy. You'll be my maid of honor, won't you?"

"Of course."

"Thanks! I've got to go call my mom. I wanted to tell you first. Tell Bailey and Andrei, okay? I'll call you later!"

Of all the rotten timing, Tessa mused. Tossing her phone on the bed, she went to tell Bailey the happy news.

Andrei wandered the busy streets of Cutter's Corner. It was the day after Thanksgiving. Most of the businesses were still closed, although the movie theater and the specialty shops were crowded with people who had the day off.

He and Luke had swept the town before, searching for any vampires who had decided to stay but, having nothing better to do, Andrei had decided to look again. Thus far, it had been a waste of time.

If his preternatural senses were to be trusted, he was the only vampire left in town.

Perhaps it was time to move on.

He ducked into a restaurant, something he rarely did. He ordered a glass of the house chardonnay, which came with a small basket of bread and crackers. He had been a fool to think Tessa would be his. Oh, he could compel her to stay with him, to share his bed, he could even make her believe she loved him, but the idea held no appeal. It wouldn't be real, and more than anything, he wanted her, warm and willing. He didn't blame her for not wanting him. For being afraid of him, deny it though she might. Other than the desire that sizzled between them whenever they were together, they had little in common. And yet, he wanted her like no other woman he had ever known. Needed her in ways he didn't understand.

Without thinking about what he was doing, he buttered a slice of bread and took a bite. And then another. He frowned when he realized what he was doing. And then, angry without knowing why, he tossed a handful of bills on the table and left the restaurant.

He preyed on the first mortal that crossed his path. Only when he realized he was close to draining the woman did he free her from his thrall and send her on her way.

What the hell? How could he be hungry for both bread and blood? What the hell was happening to him?

"Married?" Bailey paused in the act of adding cheese to her sandwich. "Wow. I knew they liked each other, but didn't they just meet a little while ago?"

Tessa nodded. "It does seem a little sudden, but . . ." She shrugged. "They seem happy together."

"I guess."

"How are things going with you and Tristan?"

Bailey shrugged. "Oh, you know." She sliced a tomato. "He's really cool. I like being with him. I still don't know about that 'life-mate' thing, but I kind of like hanging out with the pack. I feel like I belong there, with them."

"Oh."

"I like it here with you, too," Bailey said quickly.

"Well, you know you're welcome to stay as long as you want." Tessa pulled a soda from the fridge, then sat at the table. "Was it really terrible in your foster home?"

"Yeah. They had three kids of their own, and two other foster kids. They made us eat last and wear their kids' hand-me-downs. Plus we had to do all the chores, and whenever they went out with their kids, they locked us in the basement."

"Bailey, maybe you should go to the police and report them."

"No! There was an older girl there—Kim—when I first arrived. She told the school principal that Mr. Fischer molested her. No one believed her. A lady from social services came to the house a few days later, but all she saw was what the Fischers wanted her to see. They gave us nicer clothes to wear and made sure we were all clean and had nice haircuts. Mr. and Mrs. Fischer were on their best behavior. They threw out all the booze and stocked the refrigerator with milk and good food. The social worker congratulated them on being such outstanding foster parents. A week later, Kim 'fell' down the basement steps and broke her neck."

"Bailey, that's terrible! We've got to do something." But what? They had no proof of any misconduct other than Bailey's word.

The girl nodded. "Mrs. Fischer isn't so bad, but she's afraid of her husband, just like the rest of us."

"Would you go back, if he wasn't there anymore?" Tessa asked.

"No. I'd rather stay here, with you, or with Tristan's pack."

Tessa stared out the window. There were all kinds of monsters in the world, she mused. She couldn't blame Mrs. Fischer or Bailey for being afraid to confront the man. If he'd killed once to protect himself, what was to stop him from doing so again?

But she knew someone who wouldn't be intimidated by the man.

If she ever saw him again.

Tessa wasn't sure how she did it, but she managed to get through the rest of the day, and when it was over, she congratulated herself because she'd only cried five or six hundred times. If only Andrei hadn't read her mind. If only he hadn't been so understanding. She loved him, she really did, but was love enough? They lived such different lives.

Jilly called early Saturday morning, insisting Tessa go with her to look at wedding dresses. "Even though we want a small wedding, I want a long white dress and veil."

So it was that Tessa found herself sitting in one of the dressing rooms at Maribel's Bridal Shoppe, admiring one gown after another, each more beautiful than the last.

"I don't know how I'll ever decide!" Jilly said, throwing her arms up in exasperation. "I love all of them! You should try one on."

"Me? Whatever for?"

Jilly cocked her head to one side, her eyes narrowing. "Okay, what happened?"

"I'm sure I don't know what you mean."

"I'm sure you do."

Blinking back tears, Tessa looked away.

"Oh, Tess, I'm sorry. Why didn't you tell me? If I'd known, I never would have dragged you in here, of all places."

"It's all right."

"No, it isn't. Let me change and we'll go to Tommy's for a burger and fries and you can tell me all about it."

Twenty minutes later, they were sitting in a booth at Tommy's.

"Nothing happened," Tessa said, dropping a straw into her soda. "Not really. We were in bed Friday morning—just talking," she clarified. "And I started thinking about Andrei being a vampire. I knew he wanted to make love to me, and I wanted him to, but I just couldn't. I mean, once we make love . . ."

Jilly's eyes grew wide with disbelief. "You haven't done the deed yet? Seriously?"

Tessa shook her head. "He read my mind. He said he didn't blame me for not wanting to commit, that he just wanted me to be happy. And then . . ." She fisted the tears from her eyes. "And then he just . . . left."

"Oh, girlfriend, I am so sorry. Is there anything I can do?"

"I don't know what it would be."

"I know how much you care for him," Jilly said, obviously choosing her words carefully. "But maybe it's for the best."

"That's what I keep telling myself." Pushing her plate aside, she said, "I'm sorry, but would you mind if we go home now?"

Chapter Twenty-Nine

Tessa waved as Jilly pulled out of the parking lot. She felt awful for asking Jilly to take her home, but she needed to be alone. Heavy-hearted, she climbed the stairs to her condo. It was here that she had first met Andrei. Here that he had saved her life. Maybe she should move.

Opening the door, she called Bailey's name, but there was no answer. In the kitchen, she found a note on the fridge saying that Bailey had gone to the movies with Tristan.

Feeling sorry for herself, Tessa filled a bowl with ice cream and hot fudge and curled up on the sofa. But for the first time in her life, even chocolate fudge brownie ice cream didn't make her feel better.

Jilly was engaged to Luke. Bailey seemed to be falling for Tristan. Her parents were off on a whirlwind second honeymoon.

And she was home alone with nothing to do and no one to keep her company.

Andrei? Where are you?

Where do you want me to be?

His voice moved through her, darker and sweeter

than the hot fudge in her dish, making her aching heart skip a beat. *Here. I want you here. With me.*

As if she had conjured him, he materialized in front of her. "Tessa."

She put the bowl aside very carefully. Stood on shaky legs. And moved into his arms. "Please don't ever leave me again," she whispered. "Promise me."

"Never, unless you send me away."

"I won't." She lifted her face for his kiss. "I won't."

His hand stroked her back as he lowered his head. As always, his kisses were intoxicating, always exciting, never the same twice. Worries fled her mind and there was only Andrei, his voice whispering love words as he nuzzled her ear, then kissed her again. And yet again.

"So, *dragostea mea*," Andrei said when they came up for air sometime later. "Where do we go from here?"

Tessa shook her head. "I don't know. I just know I can't lose you."

"You won't." He ran his knuckles down her cheek, then kissed the tip of her nose. "Even if I have to live like a monk for the rest of your life."

"Andrei, that wouldn't be fair to you."

"I can wait. I know how you feel. It's a big decision for you."

"Not for you, I guess."

"I love you, Tess. I just want you to be happy."

"You make me happy. But . . ."

He pressed his fingertips to her lips. "But I'm a vampire. I get it."

"Jilly and Luke are getting married." She regretted the words as soon as they were spoken.

"Is that what you want, Tess? Marriage?"

Yes! She bit down on her lip to keep the word from escaping.

He regarded her through unblinking eyes. When

she felt him probing the edges of her mind, she put up her walls, not wanting him to know what she was thinking. Feeling.

"This isn't the time for secrets between us," he remarked. "Most girls want to get married. There's nothing wrong with that. But I need to know who you have in mind."

Taking him by the hand, Tessa moved to the sofa, sat down, and tugged him down beside her. "You, of course. But . . ."

"But I'm a vampire," he said again. "And that complicates things."

She nodded. "It's not just what you do to survive. I can accept that. It's . . . well, look at you. You've lived hundreds of years and you still look young. What happens when I grow old and you don't?"

"I won't love you less."

"But how will *I* feel about *you?* What if I start to hate you? What if I suddenly decide I don't want to die and I ask you to turn me when I'm old and gray and you find yourself stuck with a fledgling wife who looks like your grandmother?"

"Tessa, stop. You can't live your life worrying about what might happen. Life is fragile, uncertain." He put his arm around her shoulders and drew her closer. "There are no guarantees either one of us will be here tomorrow. There's only today."

It was pretty much the same thing Jilly had once said.

Maybe it was time to listen.

In the days that followed, Andrei didn't pressure her one way or the other. He had promised her weeks ago not to try to take advantage of her, to wait until she was ready. And he kept his promise. Tessa didn't know if her indecision was harder on him, or herself. His longing was evident when she looked in his eyes. And when he held her close, well, there was no denying that he wanted her. Or that she wanted him. It was, she knew, only a matter of time before she surrendered to her own desires.

In the meantime, Jilly was getting married.

The girls at the office gave her a surprise shower after work on Friday.

Tessa met Jilly at the bridal shop the next afternoon. The happy couple had set the date for the following weekend and time was running out for Jilly to find a dress.

After trying on more than a dozen beautiful gowns, she finally narrowed it down to two.

"I just can't make up my mind!" Jilly exclaimed. "You decide."

"I like the one you had on before. It fits like it was made for you. And it accents all your curves."

"I think you're right. Let me try it on one more time."

Tessa sighed as Jilly ducked into the dressing room. For a moment, she pretended she was getting married, imagined herself in a long white gown, walking down the aisle on her father's arm . . . the thought brought her up short. What if she decided to spend the rest of her life with Andrei? How would she explain him to her parents? Would she even be able to tell them the truth? Perhaps Andrei wouldn't want them to know. Eventually, they would notice that he never looked any older, that he was never sick, that he rarely ate, or drank anything but red wine. Just thinking about all the complications and possible repercussions gave her a headache.

"So, are you sure about this one?" Jilly asked, emerging from the dressing room.

"What? Oh yes. Jilly, you look beautiful."

"Thank you. And thanks for coming with me. Let me change, and I'll take you out to lunch."

Tessa grabbed a towel as she stepped out of the shower, eager to spend the evening with Andrei, just the two of them. Bailey had gone out with Tristan. Again. The two were becoming inseparable. Tessa had a feeling that it wouldn't be long before Bailey decided to join Tristan's pack, whatever that entailed.

After donning a multicolored skirt and pale pink shirt, Tessa brushed her hair, took a last look in the mirror, and went into the living room. A moment later, Andrei appeared bearing a bottle of red wine and a box of dark chocolates.

His gaze moved over her, bringing a blush to her whole body. "You look lovely."

"So do you."

He kissed her cheek, handed her the candy, and carried the wine into the kitchen.

Tessa set the box on the coffee table, then followed him. In the last few days, their relationship had changed in subtle ways. They weren't living together, they weren't sleeping together, and yet he was no longer a guest in her home. He often spent the night in her bed, though he was usually gone in the morning.

He was at home in her kitchen. She smiled as he opened the wine and filled two goblets. "Cabernet sauvignon," he said, offering her one of the glasses. "From Chateau Montelena. One hundred fifty dollars a bottle."

"A hundred and fifty dollars? I can't wait to taste it." Returning to the living room, she sat on the sofa and sipped her wine.

"What do you think?" Taking the seat beside her, he stretched his legs out in front of him.

"Worth every penny!"

"How was your day, *dragostea mea*?"

"Almost as good as this wine. Jilly finally found a dress. I guess now I need to find one."

"You'll outshine the bride, no matter what you wear."

"I'm glad you think so." She set her goblet aside to unwrap the candy box. "So many choices," she murmured as she lifted the lid. After a moment, she reached for a fat dark chocolate truffle. "These are sooo good. Too bad you can't have one."

"Who says I can't?" He plucked one from the box and popped it into his mouth.

Tessa stared at him as a look of pure enjoyment spread across his face.

"Why so surprised?" he asked. "It's not the first time you've seen me eat."

"I know, but . . . it's just so . . ." She shrugged. Then smiled inwardly. She had worried that, if her parents met Andrei, they would wonder why he didn't eat much. Apparently that was one fear she could lay to rest.

Andrei draped one arm over the back of the sofa. "What's going on in that head of yours?"

"Oh, nothing much. I was thinking about us earlier, about introducing you to my parents and . . . you know, whether you'd want them to know what you are, and how they'd react and . . ."

"Does this mean we've reached the 'meet the parents' stage in our relationship?" he asked with a wry grin.

"Sort of."

"I see."

"Do you?"

He set his glass on the coffee table. And then he

kissed her, his lips lightly brushing hers, his tongue teasing her lower lip before dipping inside. Lifting his head, he gazed deeply into her eyes, and then he kissed her again. There was nothing light about this one, nothing tentative.

Pleasure curled in the pit of Tessa's belly as his arms enveloped her and his kisses grew longer and more intense. As always, she forgot everything but the wonder of being loved by this remarkable man, by the feeling that she was the most important thing in his life.

Lifting his head, he gazed into her eyes. "You are mine, *dragostea mea*," he said fervently. "Never doubt it for a minute."

Andrei's words played and replayed in Tessa's mind long after he had left to go hunting. It seemed he had taken the decision out of her hands, she thought. It hadn't been a question or a suggestion, but a statement of fact. The "I am woman, hear me roar" part of her wanted to be upset. How dare he? And yet the softer, more submissive part of her found it appealing on some level she found troubling. Then again, he wasn't an ordinary man. He was a vampire, with supernatural powers, not concerned with political correctness or women's lib. He was a man who loved her, who had sworn to protect her.

And right or wrong, for better or worse, she loved him just the way he was.

Bailey ran alongside Tristan, every sense alert as they tracked a deer along a narrow trail in the mountains behind the town. Each time she shifted, it became

easier, more natural. To think there had been a time
when she hated what she was. But no more. She rev-
eled in it now. She loved the power, the feel of earth
and leaves beneath her paws, the myriad smells that assailed her from every side. She loved the bond forming
between herself and Tristan. She looked forward to
being his life-mate, to joining with him, to becoming a
full-fledged member of the pack.

The pack. There was a bond between herself and
the others. When they ran together, she could hear
their thoughts, as they could hear hers. Sometimes they
all hunted together. But tonight, it was just the two of
them. Running side by side like twin shadows in the
darkness.

Tristan growled, the sound low and filled with excitement as the deer came into view. He looked at her
and she heard his voice in her mind, asking if she
wanted to make the kill. When she nodded, he fell
back and she darted forward. The kill was quick and
clean.

Since it was her kill, he sat back on his haunches, letting her consume the choicest parts before he took his
place beside her.

As she gorged on the soft, inner parts of the deer,
she couldn't help wondering what Mr. Fischer would
think if he could see her now.

The idea percolated in her mind. She thought of
Kim. She thought of all the times that horrible man
had molested her and the other girls. The times he had
hit his wife for being kind to her or one of the other
foster kids.

When they'd had their fill, Bailey and Tristan returned to the place where they had left their clothing.

Instead of putting on her jeans, shirt, and shoes,
Bailey pulled on her Jedi-like robe. For once, she was

going to put her fears aside. She was going to confront the monster and let him know if he ever hurt or molested another child, he would have her to contend with. And then she would show him what he'd be dealing with if he didn't heed her warning.

Tristan looked at her askance when she stepped into view. "What's up?"

She quickly told him what she intended to do.

"I'll be happy to drive you," Tristan said. "I just hope he puts up a fight, because I'd love to take him out. Are you ready to go?"

She nodded. "Before I lose my nerve."

The Fischer house looked the same as always. A single light burned in the living room window. Mr. Fischer liked to watch TV in the evening by himself, so Bailey knew everyone else had been sent to bed, including Mrs. Fischer.

She took a deep breath when Tristan parked the car.

"Are you sure about this?" he asked.

"Yes." Another deep breath, and she stepped out of the car, padded barefooted to the ugly brown front door. And rang the bell.

When Mr. Fischer answered the door, her courage almost deserted her, but then she sensed Tristan behind her. As long as he was there, she had nothing to fear.

"You!" Fischer exclaimed. "Where the hell have you been?" He reached for her with one beefy hand, no doubt intending to drag her inside and punish her for running off.

Bailey danced effortlessly out of his way. "I'm here to talk to you," she said, pleased that her voice was strong and steady.

"Talk?" He sneered. "What about?"

"I know what you did to Kim. If you ever molest or abuse another child, you'll answer to me."

He snorted his disdain. "What's a kid like you gonna do about it?"

"I'll show you."

Fischer's beady eyes grew wide when she stepped out of the robe to stand naked before him. Tristan stood behind her, blocking her from the view of passing cars.

"If you ever hurt another child—or strike Mrs. Fischer—I'll know about it. And I'll come after you."

"Yeah, I'm real scared," he said, unbuckling his belt. "Now get in here where you belong!"

He reached for her again.

In that instant, Bailey shifted. Ears laid back, she bared her fangs. A low growl rumbled deep in her throat.

Fischer gaped at her, eyes wide as dinner plates, mouth hanging open as he stumbled backward.

Bailey followed him inside, then backed him against a wall.

Tristan followed them, her robe in his hands.

Shifting back to human form, Bailey pulled on the robe. "If you ever touch another child, I'll tear you apart."

Fischer nodded. Face pale, brow beaded with sweat, he sank to his knees.

Bailey didn't wait for a reply. His fear was real. He believed every word she said. Of that, she had no doubt.

With a last warning look, she turned on her heel. Head high, back soldier-straight, she walked out of the house. She'd done it! And she hadn't been afraid at all!

"I'm proud of you," Tristan said when they were in his car driving home.

Bailey grinned. "I'm proud of me too." She had faced her worst fear. If she could stand up to Mr. Fischer without flinching, she could do anything.

Chapter Thirty

The next week passed by quickly. Another wedding shower for Jilly. Another day of shopping, this time for a bridesmaid's dress for Tessa. She bought the first one she tried on—a pale blue, floor-length silk with a dark blue sash. A small hat with a short veil and a pair of matching shoes completed her outfit. They had found a dress for Bailey as well.

The day of Jilly's wedding dawned bright and clear.

Tessa glanced over her shoulder as Andrei appeared in the doorway of her room.

"Ready to go, beautiful?" he asked.

It was all she could do not to swoon. Clad in a new black Armani suit that had been tailored just for him, a white silk shirt, and black boots polished to a high shine, the man was so devastatingly handsome he fairly took her breath away. "Yes, just let me grab my handbag."

Jilly had chosen to be married in a small chapel located in a shady glen. When Tessa arrived, the bride was pacing back and forth. Munching on a candy bar.

"Not too late to change your mind," Mr. Hix said, patting his daughter's arm.

"No, no, I'm not having second thoughts about Luke," Jilly said. "I don't know why I'm so nervous."

Tessa plucked the candy bar from Jilly's hand. "Brides are supposed to be jittery." She gave Jilly a hug, then handed her a Kleenex pulled from the box on a nearby table. "But not smeared with chocolate. You look lovely, by the way."

"Thanks. So do you. Is Luke here?"

"Yes," Tessa said. "I saw his new car out front. Very nice, by the way. Don't worry, girlfriend, you won't be alone at the altar."

Just then, the organist began to play the "Wedding March."

Tessa glanced over her shoulder as she took her place. "Just remember to breathe, Jilly. Here we go."

Tessa blinked tears from her eyes as Jilly and Luke exchanged their wedding vows. As they shared their first kiss, Tessa looked out at the guests, and saw Andrei watching her.

His gaze caught and held hers as, in her mind, she heard his voice. *Will you marry me, Tess?*

Happiness swelled in her breast, chasing away every doubt, every fear. *Yes. Oh, yes!*

His smile matched the one in her heart.

After the ceremony, Andrei took her aside while Jilly and Luke were busy with their guests. "You said yes." His gaze searched hers. "Did you mean it?"

Nodding, she murmured, "I love you, Andrei, for as long as I live."

Her words poured over him and through him like a warm summer breeze, chasing the cold from his heart and soul. Murmuring her name, he swept her into his arms, holding her as if he would never let her go.

She would have been content to stay there forever but, all too soon, Jilly was tugging on her arm. "Come on, the photographer wants to take some pictures in here, and then take a few in front of the church."

Andrei kissed Tessa on the cheek, thinking she looked more radiant than the bride. "Go on, love. I'll see you later."

After what seemed like hundreds of photos, the bridal party and guests went to the reception, which was being held at the Corner's Country Club, located not far from the chapel. Tessa was dying to tell Jilly about Andrei's proposal, but this was Jilly's night and she didn't want to say or do anything that would distract the bride from her own happiness.

The bride and groom did all the usual things—the first dance as man and wife, cutting the cake, tossing the garter and the bouquet.

For Tessa, the best part of the reception was dancing with Andrei. When she was in his arms, everything and everyone else melted away and it was just the two of them lost in a world of their own.

"You look like you swallowed the sun," Andrei remarked as he twirled her around the floor.

Tessa smiled at him. "I feel that way too. All warm and glowy inside."

He drew her closer, his gaze hot enough to melt steel.

Tessa felt herself blushing. "Andrei, stop looking at me like that."

"Like what?"

"Like you're going to seduce me right here in the middle of the dance floor."

"Would you like me to?"

She stared at him. Was he serious? Right here, right now, with everyone watching?

Leaning down, he whispered, "No one will see us."

She didn't doubt for a minute that he meant it. He was a master vampire, after all, possessed of amazing powers. Still, as intrigued as she was by the idea, she shook her head. "I don't think so."

He laughed softly. "Chicken."

"How would you do it? Just hypnotize everyone in the place?"

"More or less."

"You could really do that?"

"Want me to show you?"

"No. When we make love, I'd like it to be someplace more romantic than the floor of the country club."

"Just say the word. I'll take you anywhere you want to go."

The man was as incorrigible as he was desirable.

"It was a lovely wedding," Tessa remarked, slipping off her shoes.

Andrei sat on her bed, his back resting against the headboard, one knee bent. He had discarded his suit coat and boots. Now he watched her through heavy-lidded eyes as she stepped out of her dress. "Yes," he murmured, his gaze following her as she hung her gown in the closet. "Lovely."

With her back toward him, she asked, "Are you spending the night?"

"I think not."

"Oh?" She pulled on her robe before she turned to face him.

"I've been hungering for you all night," he said. "And not just for your body. I don't think staying is a good idea."

"Will I see you tomorrow?"

"Of course." He swung his legs over the edge of the bed, then stood. "Sweet dreams, love."

Although she very much wanted him to stay, she didn't try to change his mind. She could see the struggle in his eyes, knew he was keeping a tight rein on his hunger and his desire.

Hands clenched at his sides, he kissed her cheek, and then he was gone.

Theirs had better be a short engagement, she thought.

For his sake. And hers.

Tessa called her parents first thing Sunday morning to tell them the good news.

Her father was less than thrilled at the idea of his daughter being engaged to a man they had never met, one she had known such a short time, but he wished her well, then said gruffly, "Your mom wants to talk to you."

There was a muffled exchange and then her mother came on the line. "I'm sure he's a wonderful man," Alice Blackburn said, a smile in her voice. "What's his name? How old is he? Where did you meet?"

"I met Andrei outside my apartment." Tessa didn't mention that the first time she had seen him, he had saved her from a vampire attack, and deliberately ignored the question about his age. "He sells antiques. He's got some pieces I know you'll love," she said, hoping to divert her mother from more questions about Andrei. "Wait until you see the gorgeous glass-fronted secretary he gave me."

In the background, Tessa heard her father mutter, "Well, at least he's employed."

"Be quiet, Henry!"

Tessa grinned as her mother cleared her throat. "Have you set a date?"

"No. We haven't gotten that far. And, of course, we'll wait until you and Dad get home."

"Maybe you could send us a photo of the two of you?"

Tessa frowned. Uh-oh. Could you photograph a vampire?

"Tess?"

"Um, sure. Oh, Mom, I almost forgot the other news. Jilly got married last night."

"That's wonderful. Give her my best."

"I will. Listen, Mom, I've got to go or I'll be late for church. I just wanted to give you the good news."

"If you're happy, I'm happy," her mother said. "We can't wait to meet him."

Tessa ended the call, then fell back on the mattress, her arms outstretched. Thank goodness that was over!

Andrei was at the condo when Tessa and Bailey returned from church.

"How long have you been here?" Tessa toed off her heels and removed her coat before going into Andrei's arms.

"Just a few minutes," he said, giving her a hug. "How's it going, Bailey?"

"Fine. I hear you two are getting married."

"Yeah," he said, gazing into Tessa's eyes. "Unless she's changed her mind."

"No way, Mr. Dinescu," Tessa said. "You're mine now."

"Well, congratulations to both of you," Bailey said. "Tess, I'm going over to Tristan's for lunch, if that's okay."

"Hey, I'm not your mother," Tessa said, grinning. "But behave yourself and don't be too late."

"I wish you *were* my mom." Bailey glanced down at her shoes, her voice barely audible. "Do you think you could adopt me?"

"Are you serious?" Tessa asked. "Because if you are . . ." She looked at Andrei. "What do you think? Should we adopt a teenager?"

"It's up to you. But I'm not sure it's a good idea."

"Why not?" Tessa asked.

"Never mind," Bailey said quickly, and it was obvious, from her tone, that she was embarrassed for asking. And equally obvious that she thought Andrei didn't want her.

"Let me explain," he said. "I think it would be great for Tessa to adopt you. But it's not that easy. There's a lot of paperwork involved. The agency would have to investigate Tessa's background. I don't think that would be a problem. She doesn't have a police record. . . ."

Tessa poked him on the arm. "How do you know?"

He laughed softly. "How do you think?"

"Reading my mind again?" she asked. "Or checking the Internet?"

"As I was saying, you don't have a police record, you're an upstanding citizen, you've got a good-paying job."

"So, why isn't it a good idea?" Tessa glanced at Bailey, who looked like she was on the verge of tears.

"For one thing, they'd probably send Bailey back to the Fischers while the investigation was in progress."

Bailey shuddered. "No way! I'm never going back there. Not that they'd want me," she added, and quickly told them about the house call she and Tristan had made on Mr. Fischer. "I don't think he'll be mistreating anybody ever again."

"Good for you!" Tessa exclaimed.

"You know," Andrei said, "by the time they check into Tessa's background and do a credit check . . ." He shrugged. "The whole investigation might take a year or two. By then, Bailey will be married or an adult."

"I didn't think of that," Bailey exclaimed. "But you're probably right."

"And in the meantime," Tessa said, "you can stay here."

Tessa snuggled against Andrei. A fire burned in the hearth, casting rainbow colors on the two empty goblets on the coffee table. "It would have been nice to adopt Bailey, but not at the risk of having her sent back to the Fischers, or to some other foster home."

"Enough about Bailey," Andrei murmured. His fingers stroked her nape, sending little shivers of pleasure down her spine. "You haven't changed your mind about us, have you? No second thoughts?"

"No." She smiled up at him. "No second thoughts."

"Good." Reaching into his jacket pocket, he withdrew a small velvet box. "I thought we should make it official."

Tessa gasped when he lifted the lid. Inside, nestled against a bed of black velvet, lay the most exquisite diamond-and-platinum engagement ring she had ever seen. "Oh, Andrei," she murmured. "It's beautiful."

Lifting it from the box, he slid it on her finger.

"It must have cost a fortune." The center diamond was large and square, surrounded by a halo of fiery round diamonds.

"Nothing from Tiffany's comes cheap," he said, smiling. The center diamond was close to four carats. "I'm glad you like it."

"How did you know my size?"

"I measured your finger while you were sleeping, of course."

"I need to ask you a favor."

"Anything, love."

"My mom wants me to send her a photo of us. Is that possible?"

"I don't see why not, unless you're camera shy."

"I didn't know if vampires could be photographed."

"These days it's not a problem, more's the pity."

"What do you mean?"

"In days past, you couldn't capture our image on film. And if you did, it quickly disappeared. But these days, with digital technology . . ." He shrugged. "It was more advantageous when our likeness couldn't be captured."

"I'll just tell her no."

"No, it's fine. Where's your phone?" he asked with a grin. "This will be my first selfie. And be sure to get your ring in the photo. I want your folks to know you're marrying a man who can afford to take good care of you."

Eyes as wide as saucers, Jilly stared at Tessa's ring. "Girl, that is the most gorgeous thing I've ever seen. I had no idea Andrei was so dang rich."

"Me either." Tessa held up her hand, turning it

this way and that so that the diamonds reflected the cafeteria lights. Tessa had been surprised when Jilly called last night to say she would be at work in the morning. She and Luke had decided to postpone their honeymoon until spring so they could save enough money to go to Hawaii.

Tessa added sweetener to her iced tea. "I sent my folks a photo of me and Andrei. My dad wasn't too keen on my engagement to a 'stranger' until he saw the ring. Now he can't wait to meet his future son-in-law."

"When will your folks be home?"

"I don't know. Hopefully by Christmas."

"Have you and Andrei set a date?"

"No. I can't do that until I know when my mom and dad will be back. So, how's married life?"

"Wonderful! I mean, wonderful." Jilly leaned forward, her voice dropping to a whisper. "Making love to Luke was awesome before but it's different now. Better, somehow, because I know he's mine, that he really loves me."

"He loved you before."

"I know, but, well, a lot of people say a marriage license is just a piece of paper, but it's more than that. It's like a symbol of our love." Cheeks flushed, she said, "I don't know how to explain it, but I think you'll be glad you waited."

"I'm tired of waiting," Tessa said. "There've been so many times when we've almost done it and every time, I've pulled back. I think, deep down, I'm a little afraid."

"Of sex?"

Now it was Tessa's turn to whisper. "No. Of sex with a . . . you know."

"Oh. Do they do it different?"

Tessa stared at Jilly, then burst out laughing. And sobered again just as quickly. What if vampires *did* do it differently?

Chapter Thirty-One

Tessa pulled into her parking place and switched off the engine. She sat there a minute, listening to the rain pounding on the roof, and wished she had an umbrella.

After her earlier conversation with Jilly, she decided she needed to have a serious talk with Andrei. Until today, she had just assumed that vampires made love like everyone else on the planet, but maybe they didn't. How would she know? They hadn't been sexually intimate but as far as she could tell, he had all the right equipment in all the right places. She couldn't decide if discussing the subject with Andrei would be the silliest conversation she'd ever had, or the most embarrassing.

Taking a deep breath, she grabbed her handbag, stepped out of the car, and dashed up the stairs.

Tessa was fumbling with her key when an arm curled around her throat, cutting off her breath. She dropped her handbag, her fingernails digging into the arm around her neck, but to no avail. Her attacker had a grip like iron.

Her chest burned as she fought to draw air into her lungs.

Black spots danced before her eyes as her vision narrowed.

Darkness closed in around her.

And then swallowed her whole.

Bailey checked the clock on the stove. She had a meat loaf in the oven and she turned the heat down, covered the corn, and turned off the gas. She glanced at the clock again. Where was Tessa? She was usually home by now.

Going into the living room, she peered out the window. Seeing Tessa's car in the lot, she opened the door, expecting to see Tessa on the landing or coming up the stairs.

But she wasn't there.

Frowning, Bailey was about to go back inside when she saw Tessa's handbag near the railing. Fear sent an icy tingle down Bailey's spine as she grabbed the purse, quickly ducked inside, and bolted the door.

Tossing the bag on the sofa, she pulled her cell phone from her pocket and punched in Andrei's number.

He was at the door before she had time to say more than Tessa's name.

Bailey took a wary step backward when she saw his face. He stood on the landing, his face a mask of fury, but there was fear in his eyes as his gaze swept the area.

Bailey wanted to ask if he could tell what had happened, but she was afraid to speak. Power rolled off him in waves, making the hair on her arms and the back of her neck stand at attention.

"Have you talked to her?" he asked curtly.

"No. Can you tell . . . do you know . . . ?"

"A vampire's taken her."

"Is she . . . ?"

"I don't know." His hands curled over the banister, his fingers digging into the wood. He had no sense of her, which meant she was unconscious. Or . . . He slammed his fist on the rail, so hard it shattered. Bits of wood and dust drifted down to the parking lot. Dammit! He should have been there when she got off work, but he had gone hunting farther afield than usual and gotten tangled up with a hunter.

"What now?" Bailey asked, careful to keep out of his reach.

"I'm going after her."

"Do you want me to come with you?"

"No. Hold out your arm."

"What?"

"I'm going to drink a little of your blood and then you're going to drink a little of mine."

She stared at him, eyes wide. "Why?"

"It will forge a link between us so we can communicate mentally."

"Oh." Bailey held out her hand, palm up, pressed her lips together as he bit into her wrist. She was surprised when it didn't hurt. A moment later, he licked the wound. She watched, fascinated, as the shallow cut healed itself.

When he was done, he bit into his own wrist and held it out to her.

Bailey stared at the dark red blood. She had never tasted vampire blood. What if she developed a taste for it? Heaving a sigh, she licked the crimson drops from his arm.

"Stay here," he said. "I don't have to tell you to keep the door locked. Oh. You might want to call Luke and let him know there's another vampire in town, maybe more than one."

Bailey nodded. After locking the door, she went to the window. Lightning split the skies. In the bright flash of light, she saw that he was already gone.

Andrei cursed as the vampire's trail grew faint and then disappeared. He had expected as much, knowing that sooner or later, the vampire would will himself to his destination, leaving no trace behind.

But he had the culprit's scent. He would recognize it if he came upon it again.

Hands clenched, eyes narrowed, he stood in the rain, his senses reaching out for any indication that Tessa was still alive.

His mind sought hers but found no connection.

And still he stood there, heedless of the wind and the rain, waiting.

"Slow down," Luke said. "What did Dinescu tell you?"

Bailey paced the floor, too agitated to sit still. "All he told me is that a vampire has taken Tessa."

"Taken her where? Is she all right?"

"He doesn't know. He can't track her."

Luke muttered an oath.

"He wanted me to warn you that there might be more than one."

"Okay, thanks, kid. I'm going out to scout around. If I find out anything, I'll let you know."

Loaded for bear, Luke drove to the outskirts of town. Huddled inside his jacket with the hood pulled low against the rain, he searched the most likely vampire hidey-holes—a burned-out building, a deserted warehouse, an abandoned motor home. All were empty, with no indication that anyone or anything had inhabited them recently.

In his car again, he drove to a club that Andrei had once pointed out as a vampire hangout. Armed with a couple of stakes and a sawed-off shotgun, he entered the tavern.

There were perhaps a dozen men and women in the place, most in goth attire. They all watched him as he made his way toward the bar and ordered a glass of beer.

While waiting, he noticed a stack of papers on the end of the bar. Thinking it was advertising a concert in the area, he picked one up. Read it. And read it again. Holy hell! A million-dollar reward. For Tessa.

Luke glanced around and when he was certain no one was looking, he grabbed the flyers and shoved them inside his jacket.

Anxious to get in touch with Andrei, he quickly scanned the patrons. He had tried to explain to Jilly how he recognized vampires, but he just couldn't put it into words. It was just an indefinable feeling that had crawled down his spine the first time he had destroyed a vampire. It had taken him a while to realize what it was. What it meant.

But he knew now. It meant he was born to be a hunter.

Tessa woke with a groan. Her throat was sore. It hurt to swallow. When she tried to touch her neck, she discovered her hands were bound behind her back.

Fear threaded its way through her as she glanced

around. She was on a bed in a shabby motel room. Rain pounded on the tin roof. Lightning flashed behind the worn curtains.

Struggling to sit up, she realized her ankles were also bound.

Andrei!

Tessa! I'm coming.

Relief washed through her, only to be swept away when the door opened and a burly man lumbered into the room. A wide smile played over his lips when he looked at her.

"You'll die if you bite me!" she warned, scooting as far away from him as she could.

He snorted. "I don't want to bite you. I'm going to . . ." His eyes widened as he realized someone was behind him.

Tessa gagged as a stake suddenly burst through his chest.

The cavalry had arrived.

In moments, her hands and feet were free and she was in Andrei's arms.

He held her close a moment, his gaze scanning the room.

"He didn't want to bite me," she said, her whole body trembling. "Why did he bring me here?"

"I don't know." Andrei guided her to the bed and urged her to sit down. Kneeling beside the dead man, he searched the vampire's pockets, sat back on his heels when he found a folded sheet of paper tucked inside his jacket. After unfolding it, he read it quickly.

"What is it?" Tessa said, worried by the scowl on his face. "What does it say?"

"It's a wanted poster."

Tessa frowned. "You mean like, wanted dead or alive?"

He nodded curtly.

"Who's it for?" she asked, although she had a terrible premonition that she already knew the answer.

"Katerina has offered a sizable reward for your capture."

"Oh," she said weakly. "How much am I worth?"

"A cool million." Andrei cursed softly. When word of this got out, Cutter's Corner would be swarming with vampires and bounty hunters of every stripe. "Come on, let's get the hell out of here."

Lifting her in his arms, he transported them to his lair. He had just removed Tessa's shoes and tucked her into his bed when his cell phone rang.

He stepped out of the room to answer it.

"Andrei? It's Luke. You're not going to believe what I found in that goth hangout on Chatham Road."

"A wanted poster?"

"How'd you know?"

"I just took one off the vampire who had Tessa."

"Is she all right?"

"Yes. A little shaken up. We're at my place."

"She doesn't really have anything to worry about anymore, does she? I mean, if a vampire bites her, he'll die. Shoot," Luke said, laughing. "She's the ultimate weapon."

Andrei grunted softly. Luke was joking, but it suddenly occurred to him that Luke was right. It had taken only a few sips of Tessa's blood to destroy the vampires he'd held captive. Yet her blood had protected him from Katerina's bite. A bite that should have been fatal.

"Anything I can do on this end?" Luke asked.

"Just be careful. And check in on Bailey, will you? Make sure she's okay."

"I'll head over there now." Luke whistled softly. "A million bucks! Damn. I don't know who's handing out those flyers for Katerina, but you know when word spreads, this town will be crawling with bounty hunters and vampires."

Andrei's hand tightened on the phone. "Yeah."

There was only one way to put an end to this, he thought as he disconnected the call.

And that was to put an end to Katerina.

Chapter Thirty-Two

Katerina prowled Cutter's Corner, her rage growing with every step. Impossible as it seemed, Andrei and his friends had thwarted her at every turn. Like scared rabbits, Tessa, the were-panther, the hunter, and his woman were all safe inside their holes.

As for Andrei—the traitor!—try as she might, she couldn't find him. He had shut her out of his mind. Even more unbelievable, he had managed to block the blood link between them so that she could no longer track his whereabouts, something that had never happened before.

Something that should have been impossible.

She was his sire. It was her blood that had brought him back from the brink of death.

She cursed his name, her anger and frustration mounting with every passing moment.

It was the woman, she thought. Tessa. Something about her blood had transformed Andrei's, making him stronger, impervious to his sire's power over him.

How was it possible? If the woman's blood made Andrei stronger, Katerina mused, it should work for her as well. And if it did, she would again be dominant and he would again be at her mercy. And then she would destroy him for his infidelity.

She lifted her head, nostrils flaring at the scent of prey.

Rounding the corner, she saw a young man strolling toward her. He was tall and broad-shouldered, with dark brown hair and the muscular physique of an athlete.

Unleashing her preternatural power, she slowed as he drew near.

When he was an arm's length away, he stopped, his expression slightly puzzled. "Do I know you?" he asked, sounding as confused as he looked.

"No." She ran her nails over his chest. "But you will."

"What do you want?"

"You." She took a deep breath, inhaling his scent. He smelled so good. Young and healthy. And ripe for the taking. Her gaze trapped his, drawing him closer. She had thought to drain him dry but killing him suddenly seemed like a terrible waste. "What's your name?"

"Noah."

"I'm Katerina." She linked her arm with his, tugging him along as she continued on her way.

"Where are we going?"

"So many questions. You're not married, are you?"

"No." He glanced around, his expression troubled.

"Relax," she purred. "There's nothing to be afraid of. I'm going to give you a gift, a wonderful gift."

She hadn't turned anyone—male or female—in a very long time. Killing was so much more satisfying. But the thought of making a new vampire was suddenly appealing. Fledglings could be entertaining in so many delightful ways.

So eager to please their sires.

She would turn him tonight, she decided. And when he woke tomorrow, he would be hers, subject to her every command, her every whim. She knew instinctively that he would be easier to control than Andrei had ever been.

Noah would be a pleasant distraction until she found a way to rid the world of Andrei and his whore.

Chapter Thirty-Three

Tessa stared at the ceiling. All this fuss about her blood. Why was it different from everyone else's?

She'd had blood tests in the past. Doctors had never found anything out of the ordinary. So, what was it that made her blood so unique? So deadly?

It destroyed fledglings, but not Andrei. Why?

Why did it attract newly-made vampires, only to kill them?

Sitting up, she wrapped her arms around her knees. Maybe she should quit her job at Milo and Max and take up vampire hunting. She could wander the streets, luring fledglings to their death. One quick taste of her blood. One dead vampire.

"I could probably make a fortune," she muttered. On the other hand, maybe Andrei was right. Maybe becoming a vampire was the answer. She considered it a moment, then shuddered. No, there had to be a better solution. But what if there wasn't? Andrei said word that her blood was poison to fledglings would spread quickly through the vampire community, but the world was a big place. There was no way to contact every fledgling. And what about the vampires who weren't fledglings but not yet master vampires? Were they also hunting her?

She glanced at the doorway, wondering who Andrei was talking to, and how long he was going to keep her here. Not that she wanted to go back to her place. Her place! Bailey!

Tessa dug her cell phone out of her pocket, grateful her vampire-kidnapper hadn't thought to take it away from her.

"Bailey? It's Tessa. Are you all right?"

"I'm fine. Where are you?"

"I'm at Andrei's. I don't think you should stay at my place alone."

Bailey paused before saying, "I'm not. Tristan is here."

"Oh?"

"Do you have a problem with that?"

"I . . . I guess not. Keep in touch, okay?"

"Okay. I'm glad you're all right. Bye."

Tessa tapped her fingers on the phone, wondering just what was going on at her house. Bailey was young, impressionable, hormones raging. Tristan was a little older, handsome . . . and they had the house to themselves.

She looked up when Andrei stepped into the room. "Everything all right?"

"Yes. That was Luke. I asked him to look in on Bailey."

"I just talked to her. She said Tristan's there."

"Ah." There was a wealth of understanding in that simple exclamation.

"Yeah," Tessa muttered. "That's what I'm afraid of."

* * *

Bailey's heart skipped a beat when Tristan pulled her into his arms. "I'm crazy about you—you know that, don't you?"

"You're not just saying that to persuade me to be your life-mate, are you?"

"Of course not! Besides, I wouldn't take you for my mate if I didn't care for you. I mean, seriously, why would I want to spend the next hundred years or so mated to someone I couldn't stand the sight of?"

"A hundred years!" Bailey exclaimed.

"Yeah. Didn't you know? Were-creatures live a long time. I have an uncle who's almost a hundred and fifty. We don't age like normal people, either. Once you hit your twenties, the aging process slows way down."

"Wow, I didn't know that."

He nodded. "You'll be in your prime for a good long time."

She digested that a moment, thinking that being a were-panther was looking better all the time. "So, if I agree to be your mate, will we get married, like in a church? I've always wanted to wear a long white dress."

"That comes later. Being life-mated is kind of like being engaged. We'll stand in front of the pack and pledge ourselves to each other. We'll get married when you're eighteen."

Bailey pondered that a moment. It was just as well that they weren't getting married now because there was no way she could afford a wedding dress. Or a wedding. The Fischers certainly wouldn't pay for it, not that she would think of asking them! "I'd like Tessa and Andrei to be there."

"I don't know if that's permitted. I'll have to ask, since outsiders aren't usually welcome." His arms, corded with muscle, tightened around her. "I love you,

Bailey. I knew you were meant to be mine the first time I saw you. Say yes and I'll do everything in my power to protect you and make you happy."

She gazed into his eyes, eyes that burned with a soft golden glow. She basked in the warmth of that glow, filled with a sudden inner peace and the sure knowledge that she was, indeed, meant to be life-mated to Tristan.

His kiss, when it came, was slow and sweet. It made her heart pound and her toes curl inside her sneakers. The warmth that had suffused her only moments ago quickly became a raging fire and she clung to him, her hands restless as they delved under his shirt to caress his skin. Skin that was firm and smooth. The mere touch inflamed her senses, as did his kisses and the sweep of his tongue.

All sense of propriety was swept away in that kiss. He wanted her. She wanted him. If they were destined to be mated, why wait?

Bailey was ready to surrender to the desire thrumming through her when someone knocked at the door. As one, she and Tristan sniffed the air and said, "It's Luke."

Sitting up, she straightened her clothing. "How soon are we supposed to life-mate?" she asked, breathlessly.

"Whenever you're ready."

"I'm ready," she said, and went to open the door.

It was odd, being in Andrei's bed. In Andrei's lair. Tessa grinned faintly. The lair of the lion. The lair of the dragon.

The lair of the vampire.

"I've seen too many horror movies," she muttered.

"Did you say something?" he asked, coming to sit on the edge of the mattress.

"No."

"The lair of the vampire?" he said, arching one brow in wry amusement.

She shook her head. "I've got to work on keeping those walls up."

"I'll take you home if you'll be more comfortable there."

"I like it here. It feels, I don't know. Kind of dangerous."

"You have no idea."

"I'm glad you've never brought anyone else here," she said, though, of course, she meant other women. "Will you marry me when my parents get home?"

"Is this a trick question?"

"Will you?"

"Any day you like, my sweet. Why the sudden rush?"

She punched him on the arm. "Why do you think?"

"Getting tired of saying no, are you?"

She nodded. "You have no idea."

"You think not?" Moving so that his back was against the headboard, he drew her into his arms.

"Why do you think my blood kills fledglings but not you?"

He blew out an exasperated sigh. "I don't know. It's a mystery to me, too. All I can think is that it's because I'm long past the fledgling stage."

"Why do you think Katerina wants me?"

"Her bite should have destroyed me. It didn't. I'm sure she wants to taste you, to see if your blood will increase her powers, or perhaps make her invulnerable to another master vampire's bite. Her sire's, perhaps."

"He's still alive?"

"As far as I know."

Tessa found it hard to imagine anyone living longer than Katerina and Andrei. Some people lived to be a hundred, perhaps even a few years more. But Andrei had lived in medieval times. It was mind-boggling, the things he must have seen in his long life, the changes in the world, in people, and technology. He had seen things and places that no longer existed.

Andrei drew her closer, his lips moving in her hair as he whispered, "Can we talk about something else now?"

"What did you have in mind?"

His gaze moved over her, hotter than any flame, as his hands caressed her. "What do you think?"

"You don't play fair!" she squeaked as his tongue burned a path along the side of her neck. She felt the touch of his fangs, knew he was waiting for her to say yes or no.

But refusing never crossed her mind. She was determined to wait until they were married before surrendering her virtue, that was true, but the sensual thrill of his bite and the exquisite pleasure that followed was not to be missed.

Tessa was still thinking about the uniqueness of her blood when she woke the following morning. Andrei rested beside her. He lay on his back, one arm across his waist, the other at his side.

Sliding out of bed, she tiptoed out of his lair and up the stairs to the living room.

Settling on the sofa, she called work and told Mr. Ambrose she didn't feel well and needed the day off.

Her next call was to her mother. "Mom? Hi. What? No, I'm fine . . ." She frowned as static came over the line, and then the sound of music. "I guess I caught you at a bad time."

"Not at all," her mom said. "I was going to call you tomorrow. We met the Harringtons in Sydney. They're on their way to New Zealand and your father and I decided to extend our vacation another few days and go with them. I mean, who knows when we'll be in this part of the world again? What was it you wanted, Tess?"

"I was wondering . . . I mean . . . do we have any psychics or mystics or anything like that in our family background?"

"Is that why you called?" her mother asked incredulously.

"It's important, Mom."

"Why the sudden interest in your ancestry now? I tried to get you to help me with our genealogy a few years ago with no success."

"I'll explain it all to you later, I promise," Tessa said, and hoped it was a promise she would be able to keep.

"Well, your paternal great-grandfather was a Cherokee medicine man rumored to possess mystical powers of some kind, but that's all I know. I tried to find out more about him once, but there was no one left to ask. His wife and children all passed away before he did."

"Mystical powers," Tessa murmured.

"What's that, dear?"

"Nothing. Do you happen to know his name?"

There was silence on the line. Tessa could almost see her mother's face scrunched up as she searched her memory. "It was Chea Sequah, I think. Yes, that was it." Her mother spelled it out. There was more static on the wire. ". . . means Red Bird."

"Thanks, Mom. When are you coming home?"

"We'll be back on the twenty-third, just in time for Christmas. You're coming home, aren't you?"

"Of course." Tessa worried her lower lip, debating whether to tell her mother about Andrei. In the end, she decided that the news that she was marrying a vampire should probably be conveyed face-to-face. She was about to say good-bye when static crackled over the line and the phone went dead.

Sitting at Andrei's computer, she logged on to Google, the researcher's best friend. "Chea Sequah," she muttered, typing the name in the search bar.

And there it was. Chea Sequah. As her mother had said, he had been a powerful medicine man. Those who knew him believed he could change shape and travel through time. There were rumors that he had dwelt in darkness and that his blood had magical powers. When freely given, his blood possessed the power to heal; when consumed by his enemies or taken by force, it had been fatal. . . .

Feeling cold all over, Tessa sat back in her chair. It was a story too fantastic to be true. And yet, her blood—freely given—had healed a bite that should have been deadly.

Maybe it wasn't Andrei who was destined to bring her death and life, but the blood of an old Cherokee medicine man that ran in her veins.

Andrei listened carefully as Tessa related her conversation with her mother. Some might dismiss what her mother had said about the Cherokee medicine man as so much nonsense, but not Andrei. He had spent time with some of the Plains tribes, seen things he could not explain, heard things that sounded impossible until he viewed them for himself.

He had seen a Lakota shaman who could shape-shift.

He had talked to a Cheyenne medicine man who claimed to be able to walk between worlds.

And he had seen a Comanche warrior who was also a vampire, and another who was feared because it was believed he was a witch. One and all, they had possessed mystical powers that could not be explained logically. Why not a Cherokee medicine man whose blood could heal or destroy?

"So," he said when she had finished. "Chea Sequah's blood killed his enemies or those who took it by force, but healed those he favored. Much like yours."

Tessa nodded. She hadn't really expected him to believe her and yet, why wouldn't he? If anyone knew there were things beyond mortal ken, it would be Andrei.

"So, what do we do now?" she asked.

"I'm not exactly sure how best to put this knowledge to use," he replied, choosing his words carefully. "Katerina knows your blood has had some effect on me. I don't know if she's figured out exactly what it is. Hell, I'm not sure, either. There's no telling if she wants to kill you or drink from you."

"Or both," Tessa said, grimacing.

Andrei nodded. "Probably." Katerina might be an ancient vampire, but she was also a jealous, vindictive female. He had no doubt that, given the chance, she would kill Tessa. He was reasonably certain that turning Tessa would protect her from most vampires. But nothing he could think of would protect the woman he loved from Katerina's wrath.

Except Katerina's destruction.

Chapter Thirty-Four

Tessa decided to spend the rest of the day at Andrei's. After assuring him that she would be fine while he took his rest, she found a piece of paper and a pen and wrote out her Christmas list. With all that had been happening, she hadn't given the holiday much thought, but it was fast approaching. She needed gifts for her parents, Jilly and Luke, Bailey, Mr. Ambrose, and Andrei, of course. She spent a few minutes admiring her engagement ring. What did one buy a vampire for Christmas, anyway?

But she had a bigger problem. And that was going to visit her folks over the holiday. Andrei had eaten prime rib at Thanksgiving. Since then, he had eaten a few other things, but never a complete meal. If they were only visiting for a day, it might not draw any attention, but three days? Of course, there was always a chance that Andrei wouldn't want to go with her. But, sooner or later, he would have to meet her parents.

Jilly called at noon to see why she hadn't come to work.

"I just decided to take the day off," Tessa explained.

"I hate to admit it, but I'm still a little shaken up by what happened. I keep thinking, what if Andrei hadn't come to my rescue? What if the vampire who took me had given me to Katerina?" She shuddered, just thinking about it.

"I don't even want to think about that. If it's any consolation, Luke assures me there aren't any other vampires in town."

"Well, that's good news. But there's always tomorrow. And the day after that."

Jilly sighed. "Are you coming to work tomorrow?"

"I'm not sure. I'll let you know."

"All right. Talk to you later. Stay safe."

Tessa spent the rest of the afternoon shopping online. Around two o'clock, she ordered a pepperoni pizza and a salad from the local pizza place. While eating, she decided if she was going to stay here from time to time, she should stock the cupboards with some canned goods—soup and tuna—stuff like that. Maybe some frozen lasagna and veggies.

When Andrei woke, she would ask him how he felt about buying a few appliances for his kitchen, like a stove and a toaster oven, and maybe a microwave. And some dishes. And silverware. And a toothbrush.

"Sure," he said. "Whatever you want. We can go tonight if you like."

"We can go another time. I need to go home tonight," Tessa said. "I want to take a shower and wash my hair and get ready for work tomorrow." She smacked her forehead with her hand. "And get in touch with Bailey. How could I have forgotten to call? I haven't heard from her. Have you?"

"No."

Suddenly worried, Tessa grabbed her phone and punched in the girl's cell number.

Bailey answered on the third ring. "Hey, Tessa."

She blew out a sigh of relief. "How are you?"

"I'm fine. I'm with Tristan and the pack. I've been meaning to call you, but . . . Where are you?"

"I'm still at Andrei's."

"Oh, well, tell him hi for me. Guess what? We're getting married, me and Tristan!"

"Married!" Tessa exclaimed.

"Well, not really married, at least not right now. We're being life-mated."

"I don't care what you call it. You just met. And you're only sixteen . . ."

"I know. But in the pack, you're considered an adult at my age. And I'll be seventeen in a few months."

Knowing he could hear the conversation, Tessa stared at Andrei, one brow arched.

He shrugged. "I think it has to be her decision."

"Will you be home tonight?" Tessa asked.

"Yes. I'll see you then."

"All right. Bye." Tessa shook her head as she tossed the phone aside "Life-mated at sixteen. It just doesn't seem right."

"Different strokes for different folks," Andrei said, grinning. "Are you ready to go?"

Andrei waited in the living room while Tessa showered. He glanced around, thinking how much his life had changed since they'd met. And how drastically he had changed hers.

And then there was Bailey. Had it been fate that had brought the girl into their lives?

Yes, his life had taken an interesting turn. In addition to a woman he loved and a teenage were-panther, he now had a hunter for a friend. He had sensed a change in Luke over the last few days. He was more sure of himself, more confident in his abilities, than he had been just weeks ago.

They were all changing, he mused. Growing closer together, stronger. It was odd to have friends after spending so much of his life alone, to feel at ease around Jilly and Luke and Bailey. To feel he could count on them if need be.

Katerina had also changed. Where he had grown stronger, she seemed to have lost not only some of her power, but her smug self-assurance as well.

He shook off his thoughts as Tessa entered the room. As always, she had a smile for him.

Her love seemed to flow across the room, its warmth enveloping him, filling the dark empty corners of his soul.

She frowned at him. "What?"

"I was just thinking how beautiful you are, and how much I love you."

She smiled at him, her eyes sparkling as she went into his arms. "Are you as happy as I am?"

"More so, I'm sure."

"Impossible."

"No man has ever loved a woman as I love you." His knuckles caressed her cheek. "Or waited as long to find happiness."

"Andrei, what a sweet thing to say."

"It's true." Lowering his head, he brushed his lips across hers. "How soon can I make you mine?"

She gazed up at him, her heart skipping a beat at the thought of giving herself to him. "My parents will be back on the twenty-third. They want me to come home for Christmas. Do you want to come with me?"

"Did you think I'd let you go alone while Katerina is still a threat?"

"Well, I thought I should ask. Anyway, we can discuss a date for the wedding while we're there. I was thinking sometime in January."

He blew out a sigh.

"Too soon?"

"Not soon enough," he growled.

Tessa bit down on her lower lip. She didn't want to wait that long, either. "What if we just get married at City Hall? My parents will be upset, but I'm sure they'll understand, since that's what they did."

His arms tightened around her. "Tomorrow?" he asked.

"That's a little *too* soon," she said, giggling softly. "How about Friday? That'll give me a couple of days to find a dress and give us the weekend for a honeymoon."

"Friday," he agreed.

She wrapped her arms around his neck as he claimed her lips with his in a kiss that inflamed her senses and seared her very soul. And made her wonder if she really wanted to wait until Friday.

Jilly was all agog the next day when Tessa told her the news. "Friday!" she exclaimed. "As in day after tomorrow? Isn't that kind of sudden? And what about your mom and dad . . . ?"

"I'm tired of waiting. As for my parents, they'll understand."

"Maybe. But, don't you want a church wedding with all the trimmings?"

"I used to, but it just seems too complicated, you know what I mean? And I can't help thinking what would happen if some fledgling vampire crashed the ceremony. Or if Katerina showed up and slaughtered everyone."

"That seems pretty far-fetched," Jilly said. "I mean, no one's seen her recently. Maybe she went back to whatever hole she crawled out of."

"Maybe, but it could happen, and that scares me. Better if it's just the five of us. Well, six, I guess, if Tristan comes with Bailey."

"We're invited then?"

"Of course."

"All right!" Jilly glanced at her watch, then jumped to her feet. "I've gotta get back to work. I'm late! Just let us know the time," she called over her shoulder, "and we'll be there."

Tessa was surprised to find Bailey waiting for her when she got home that night. She glanced around, expecting to see Tristan, since the two of them were practically inseparable these days.

Bailey smiled tentatively. "Hi."

"Hi. How are you? I haven't seen much of you lately."

"I know. I've been with Tristan. I have so much to learn about pack rules and etiquette. Sometimes I don't think I'll ever remember it all."

Tessa sat on the sofa and kicked off her heels, then stretched her legs out in front of her.

After a moment, Bailey dropped down beside her. "Where's Andrei?"

Tessa smiled. "He'll be here later. We're getting married on Friday." She had already arranged to take the day off and the following week as well. She had taken a lot of time off lately and although Mr. Ambrose hadn't said it in so many words, she had the distinct feeling that the next time she asked for time off, she'd be getting it. Permanently.

"Really? That's great. Funny, all of us getting married so close together," she said. "First Jilly and Luke and now you." She stared down at her hands, a smile playing over her lips.

"Something you want to tell me?" Tessa asked.

"Remember I told you that me and Tristan were going to be life-mated?"

"Yes, although I'm really not sure what that means."

"It's sort of like an engagement since I'm underage. We'll get married when I'm eighteen."

Tessa had a sudden image of the two of them in panther form, howling and mating under a full moon. She quickly shook the image away. "Are you sure that's what you want? I mean, aren't you awfully young to make a decision like this?"

Bailey shrugged. "According to Tristan, we were meant to be together. It's a were-thing—they just know when they've met the right person."

"Do you feel that it's right? In here?" Tessa asked, pressing her hand over Bailey's heart.

Bailey nodded. "When we're together . . . I don't know how to explain it, but it's like it's meant to be. You'll come, won't you? Andrei, too? Tristan's parents said it would be all right."

"Of course. And we'd love to have you there with us on Friday. Where will the two of you live?"

"With Tristan's parents, at least until we're married."

"I'll miss you."

"I'll miss you, too. You've been so good to me."

Tessa put her arm around Bailey's shoulders. "You'll always be welcome in my home, whether it's here or somewhere else."

"Thank you," Bailey murmured, sniffing back tears. "You saved my life, you know."

"And you saved Andrei's," Tessa said, smiling. "So I guess we're even."

Chapter Thirty-Five

He was getting married. The thought burned through Katerina's mind like acid. How dare he marry another when he was *her* husband!

Andrei had blocked her for days, but now that Tessa had returned home, it no longer mattered. She knew where to find him.

She had followed him for the last few days, careful to shield her presence, her thoughts. He could keep her out of his lair. Tessa's threshold might protect her home, but neither walls nor a threshold could prevent Katerina from listening to their phone calls and conversations. She had had opportunities to kill the woman, but she was waiting for the perfect moment. And now it had arrived. All the players together in one place at the same time.

She threw back her head and laughed, filled with the sheer delight of what was to come.

He was getting married Friday afternoon. At four.

Or so he thought.

Chapter Thirty-Six

After work on Thursday, Tessa and Jilly went shopping for Tessa's wedding dress. Andrei tagged along. He had spent the day in Tessa's office, invisible much of the time. She was sure he had been bored to death, but she had appreciated his presence more than she could say. He was an exceptional man, she thought. Not many would be willing to play bodyguard all day and then sit in a bridal shop while their future bride tried on wedding gowns.

"Pick out something sexy," he said, settling into a high-back chair covered in a pink-and-white stripe. He looked as out of place as a riverboat gambler at a prayer meeting.

"I'll do my best," Tessa said as she followed the saleslady into the dressing room.

"I'm Diane," the woman said. "Who's the bride?"

"That would be me," Tessa said. "This is my friend Jileen, and I'm Tessa."

"Pleased to meet you both. What are we looking for today?"

"Something pretty but not too fancy," Tessa said.

"Something sexy," Jilly reminded her with a leer.

"I'm sure we can find something suitable," Diane assured them. "Were you looking for floor-length?"

Tessa shook her head. "No."

"Jileen, why don't you wait here while Tessa undresses," the consultant suggested, indicating a padded chair outside the dressing room. "I'll be back with several selections in a moment."

Tessa stood in front of the mirror in the dressing room, staring at her reflection. The gown, of white silk and lace, was exquisite, simple yet elegant. The matching hat had a small silk flower on one side and a short veil.

"I look like a bride," she murmured.

"Hey, girl," Jilly called. "What are you doing in there? Do you need help?"

"No. Come in." She twirled around when Jilly stepped into the room. "What do you think?"

"I love it!"

"Me too. Do you think Andrei will like it?"

"Oh, yeah. The groom asked for something sexy, remember?" Jilly said, waggling her eyebrows. "And that one says sexy with a capital S."

"So, when do I get to see the dress?" Andrei asked. They had dropped Jilly off at her place on their way home. Bailey had left a note saying she was with Tristan, but would be home later. Now, they were sitting on the sofa in front of the fire, sharing a glass of wine.

"Not until tomorrow. Don't you know it's bad luck for the groom to see the bride's dress before the wedding?"

"All right, Cinderella. Just don't change your mind when the clock strikes twelve."

"Why would I do that?"

"Maybe you'll come to your senses before it's too late," he muttered.

"Andrei, what a thing to say!"

Setting the glass on the coffee table, he drew her into his arms. "I guess I still can't believe you're mine."

"Well, I am, so get used to it." She smiled up at him. "You haven't kissed me in the last ten minutes. Don't you think it's time?"

He laughed softly as he cupped her face in his hands. "I will kiss you as often as you like."

"After tomorrow we won't have to stop at kisses." She closed her eyes as his lips met hers. Excitement burned through her at the thought of being his wife, of being his in every way.

Chapter Thirty-Seven

Katerina rose early Friday morning. Most vampires preferred the night, but she enjoyed watching the sun rise. It gave her a sense of power, of superiority, knowing she could greet the dawn when most others of her kind could not.

She prowled through the hotel suite, admiring the lavish furnishings. It was the best suite the hotel had to offer. Later, she would order room service. She hoped they would send the handsome young man who had served her the day before. She hadn't eaten the breakfast she had ordered; instead, she had satisfied her hunger with a few sips of the waiter's blood, then wiped the memory from his mind.

She showered in the luxurious bathroom, remembering, as she did so, the crude accommodations of the past, when hot running water and flush toilets would have seemed like miracles. These times were so much better.

Once she had destroyed Andrei and disposed of his whore, she would take Noah and leave the country. Perhaps she would take him to Rome, or maybe Paris. The world was a vast place. For a vampire, it was like a giant smorgasbord. When she grew weary of dining on one nationality, she simply moved on.

Returning to the bedroom, she sat on the edge of the bed. Head tilted to one side, she regarded her fledgling. He lay still as death, eyes closed, face pale, not breathing. In a few hours, he would take his first breath as a vampire. See the world through vampire eyes. Know the insatiable thirst of a newborn, the thrill of the hunt, the sweetness of his first kill.

Tonight, she would begin his education. She would teach him—in ways both painful and unforgettable— who was the fledgling and who was the master.

Tomorrow night, she would show him how much fun it was to search for prey, let him discover for himself how prolonging his victim's fear made the blood so much the sweeter.

But first she had a wedding to attend.

She would wear red, she thought, a smile twitching her lips.

It wouldn't show the blood.

Chapter Thirty-Eight

Tessa woke smiling. Today was her wedding day. In a few hours, she would be married to the most wonderful man in the world. "Mrs. Andrei Dinescu," she murmured, and burst into a fit of giggles.

Too excited to stay in bed, she went into the kitchen and put the coffee on. Waiting for it to heat, she fired up her iPad and read the news. For once, there were no stories of bodies drained of blood. The word vampire wasn't splashed across the headlines.

"You're up early," Bailey remarked, shuffling into the kitchen.

"And you came in very late last night," Tessa replied.

"I know. We were at Tristan's house. His mother took me shopping for a dress to wear for the life-mating ceremony."

"That was really nice of her."

Bailey nodded. "They treat me like I'm already one of the family. Tristan says it's because they know our mating was meant to be. I don't know how that works, but he said his father can sense that I was born to be his son's mate. Isn't that weird?"

"Well, maybe a little," Tessa said. "But in a good way."

"His family is really nice."

"And they're all shifters?"

Bailey nodded.

"I bought you a dress to wear today," Tessa said. "I hope you don't mind, but you've been gone so much lately and there was no time to take you with me." She made a vague gesture with her hand. "I think you'll like it."

"You didn't have to do that. I could have just worn the one I wore to Jilly's wedding."

"No way. New wedding. New dress. It's hanging on the door in my bedroom if you want to try it on while I fix breakfast."

"Thank you!" Eyes alight, Bailey gave Tessa a hug and hurried out of the room.

"I want to see it on you!" Tessa called after her, then forgot all about Bailey and breakfast when her phone rang. "Andrei!"

"Good morning, bride."

"Good morning, groom."

"How did you sleep?"

"Not very well, I'm afraid. I was too excited. You?"

"I slept like the dead," he replied dryly.

"I don't think that's very funny."

He laughed softly. "I dreamed of you." His voice, low and intimate, caressed her. "I dreamed of us."

His words sent a rush of heat spiraling through her, reminding her of the sensual images that had surfaced in her own dreams. Had he put them in her mind?

"Tonight will be better than any dream," he promised.

And she had her answer. "How do you do that?" she asked. "How can you influence my dreams?"

"I'm a vampire," he reminded her, a hint of laughter in his voice. "You'll be surprised at what I can do."

"Really? More surprising than learning vampires are

real and that there are shape-shifters and werewolves and all manner of supernatural creatures lurking in the shadows?"

"I was thinking of things of a more intimate nature. Vampire males aren't like other men, you know. We never tire, and we are very inventive in the bedroom."

His words sent a thrill down her spine, and then she went suddenly still, remembering that she had never asked Andrei if vampires made love the way humans did.

Ask him now.

The words whispered through the back of her mind, but she couldn't bring herself to say them aloud. Of course, it wasn't necessary. He always knew what she was thinking. And his amused laughter proved it.

Walls, she thought, feeling herself blush. *You have to remember to build those darn walls!*

"Put your fears to rest, *dragostea mea.* I am as other men in all the ways that count."

She didn't know what to say, only knew she was glad he couldn't see her burning cheeks through the phone.

They were to meet at four o'clock at City Hall. Andrei had suggested a daytime ceremony. Tessa hadn't needed to ask why. Fledglings turned to dust in the sunlight. As for Katerina . . . Hopefully, she had left town. If not, well, there was nothing to be done about her. She was like an earthquake. You couldn't predict it, never knew when it was coming, but when it did, it left chaos and destruction in its wake.

Tessa felt a surge of motherly love when she saw Bailey. The girl looked lovely in an ice-green tea-length dress and white heels. She wore her hair pulled back and tied with a matching ribbon. It was hard to believe that a black panther lurked under that innocent exterior.

Tessa wore a coat over her dress and carried a small overnight bag. She and Andrei were spending the night in a hotel in the next town; Bailey was going to stay with Tristan and his family.

At ten minutes to four, Luke and Jilly came to pick them up.

"This is it," Jilly said as Tessa slid into the backseat. "No second thoughts?"

Tessa shook her head. "Not one. It just feels right."

"Well, let's get this show on the road," Luke said, taking the suitcase from her hand. "The groom awaits."

Tessa's eyes widened in surprise when she stepped into the room where she was to be married. Ordinarily it was rather plain. White walls. A black-and-white tile floor. A table. Today, there were flowers everywhere. They lined the walls, adorned the table and the window ledge. A dark blue runner led from the door to the table where Andrei stood, waiting for her.

He came forward when he saw her, his hands taking hers as he kissed her cheek.

"What's wrong?" she asked.

"I was afraid you wouldn't come," he admitted.

"Silly." She squeezed his hands. "Thank you for the flowers. They're lovely."

A side door opened and the justice of the peace stepped into the room. "Shall we begin?"

Andrei and Tessa took their places in front of the magistrate. Jilly stood beside Tessa, Luke beside Andrei. Bailey and Tristan stood to one side, holding hands.

"We are gathered here today to join Andrei Dinescu

and Tessa Blackburn in the bonds of holy matrimony. Marriage is an honorable estate, not to be entered into lightly. If there is anyone, here present, who objects to this union, let him speak now, or forever hold his peace."

"I object!"

Tessa didn't have to turn around to know Katerina stood in the doorway. Andrei's hand tightened on hers. Other than that, he didn't move.

"On what grounds do you base your objection?" the magistrate asked.

"On the grounds that he already has a wife, and that she stands here before you."

The justice of the peace looked at Andrei. "Is this true? Is this woman your wife?"

Andrei took a deep breath, his mind racing. If he refuted her, there was no telling what she might do. He heard Tristan shift from one foot to the other, heard a low growl rumble in Bailey's throat. *Do nothing*, he warned her.

"Mr. Dinescu?"

"Yes," he said. "She is my wife."

"Then there will be no marriage today," the magistrate declared.

Andrei nodded, his hand clenching around Tessa's. He wanted nothing more than to confront Katerina, to rip her heart from her chest, but she would not die easily. And there was no telling what mayhem she might cause before he destroyed her, if, indeed, he could.

He turned, very slowly, to face her.

Katerina glared at him, her eyes glittering, her expression one of smug satisfaction. And then, in a lightning-fast move, she was across the room.

Certain the vampire was coming for her, Tessa

stumbled backward, let out a horrified cry as Katerina's claws tore into the magistrate's chest and ripped out his still-beating heart, then threw it across the room. Drops of blood sprayed through the air like crimson rain, staining her dress, splashing across her cheek.

"He will never be yours!" Katerina screamed before vanishing from their sight. The echo of her maniacal laughter trailed behind her like smoke from a funeral pyre.

Jilly buried her face in Luke's shoulder.

"Dammit!" Luke exclaimed, staring at the body. "How are we going to talk our way out of this?"

"We aren't," Andrei said curtly. Concentrating, he gathered his power, wrapped it around each one of them, and transported them all to his house on the hill.

As soon as they reached Andrei's place, Tessa ran into the bathroom to wash the blood from her face. With hands that shook, she peeled off her dress and tossed it into the bathtub. She never wanted to see it again, wondered if she would ever forget the awful sight of the magistrate's face as Katerina brutally ripped the man's beating heart from his chest.

"Tessa?"

"I can't do this anymore," she said dully. "Enough is enough. Why did she kill that poor man? Why not me? He was no threat to her."

"Tess." He closed the door, then stood there, regarding her face in the mirror. She was pale, eyes red, shoulders slumped.

She shook her head. "I don't want to be the cause of anyone else's death. I'm tired of feeling helpless. Tired of always looking over my shoulder, always being afraid.

I want you to turn me." She took a deep breath. "Now. Tonight."

"Tessa." Andrei stared at her, unable to believe what he was hearing.

"It's what you wanted, isn't it? Now it's what I want, too."

"Maybe you should think it over for a day or two," he suggested.

Tessa shook her head. "I've made up my mind. Don't try to talk me out of it."

"I just want you to be sure." He wanted to go to her, to take her in his arms and assure her everything would be all right. But something told him it would be a waste of time. She had, indeed, made up her mind. He only hoped she wouldn't hate him when it was done. "I don't want you to have any regrets."

"I don't know what else to do. Katerina's never going to give up. She killed a complete stranger today. The next time it might be Jilly. Or my parents." Her tormented gaze met his in the mirror. "I want her dead, Andrei. That's the only way this will ever be over."

He nodded. Hadn't he had the very same thought not long ago?

Closing the distance between them, he took her in his arms. "Between us, we'll settle this once and for all."

Luke, Jileen, Bailey, and Tristan were huddled together in front of the fireplace when Andrei entered the room.

"Where's Tessa?" Bailey asked anxiously. "Is she all right?"

"She's made a decision," he said quietly. "It wasn't easy."

Jilly's eyes widened. And then she shook her head. "No. She didn't! Tell me she didn't?"

"Not yet," Andrei said. "She's waiting for me down-stairs." He had taken her to his lair before returning to the living room.

"I want to see her," Jilly said. "Maybe I can . . ."

"You can't talk her out of it. She's made up her mind. You're all welcome to stay the night here. It's the one place I know you'll be safe."

"Was this really her idea?" Jilly asked.

Andrei nodded. "I suggested she wait and think it over for a day or two, but she's determined."

"Have you ever done this before?" Luke asked.

"No."

"What if you make a mistake?" Jilly exclaimed. "She could die! Luke, stop him!"

Luke put his arm around Jileen. "I don't like this any better than you do, honey. But it's her decision."

Jilly glared at Andrei, then buried her face in her husband's shoulder, her body shaking from the force of her sobs.

Bailey sank down on the sofa, hands clasped in her lap. "As I understand it, you're going to drink Tessa's blood, right? And then she'll drink from you?"

"That's how it's done."

"Aren't you taking a terrible risk?" Luke asked. "Her blood destroys fledglings. I know you've tasted her before with no ill effects, but how do you know that taking it all won't destroy you?"

"I don't."

"So it's dangerous for both of you," Luke said. "And if her blood destroys you . . . what then? There won't be anyone to bring her across."

"If her blood proves fatal, it will destroy me before her life is at risk."

"Are you certain of that?" Jilly asked. "We're talking about Tessa's life."

"If I wasn't, I wouldn't attempt it." His gaze swept over them. "The house is warded. No one can enter. If you decide to leave, I would advise you to all stick together."

"Safety in numbers and all that," Luke muttered.

Andrei nodded curtly. "I'll let you know when it's done."

Chapter Thirty-Nine

Tessa paced the floor of Andrei's lair. She tried to relax, to convince herself she was safe, but to no avail. She couldn't forget the horror of what Katerina had done. Couldn't forget how scared she herself had been, how helpless she had felt. She never wanted to feel that way again.

Leaving town wouldn't solve anything. Either Katerina or other vampires would search her out wherever she went.

Andrei had been right. Becoming a vampire was the only answer. It was the only way to gain the strength to protect herself. And if her blood changed after merging with his, so much the better. She didn't want to spend the rest of her life being afraid, or depending on Andrei to protect her. And she didn't want her blood to be responsible for killing anyone else.

As for Katerina . . . Tessa sighed. If Andrei couldn't destroy her, what hope did she—as a mere mortal—have?

Tessa sank down on the edge of the bed. She would be helpless during the day, she thought. But once she was turned, she would stay here, with Andrei, in his lair.

She would be safe here in the daylight hours. And Andrei had promised that together, they could destroy Katerina.

She jumped when he suddenly appeared in the room.

"Sorry," he said. "I didn't mean to startle you."

Nodding, she wrapped her arms around her waist. Tension hummed through her, making her tremble from head to foot.

"Tess?"

"Just do it."

"You're still sure?"

"Yes."

He sat on the bed beside her, his arm slipping around her waist, drawing her close. "Do you trust me?"

"Y . . . yes."

"Just relax. Clear your mind of your fears. Don't think about what's to come." He stroked her back lightly, up and down. Up and down. "There's nothing to be afraid of."

She wanted to say she wasn't afraid, but the words wouldn't come.

"Relax. I'm just going to hold you, kiss you."

His gaze captured hers as he lowered his head.

Tessa's eyelids fluttered down when he kissed her, ever so gently at first, as if he was afraid she might break. His tongue swept over her lower lip, dipping inside to tease and tempt her until she forgot everything else. There was nothing to be afraid of when she was in his arms. Nothing at all.

Still holding her close, he spoke to her mind, telling her that he loved her, would always love her, promising that all would be well.

She offered no resistance when he lowered her onto the bed, then stretched out beside her. His tongue stroked the soft skin beneath her ear so that, when his bite came, there was no pain, only indescribable pleasure.

Andrei drank slowly, his senses turned inward, but he detected no ill effects from taking her blood, only an increase of strength and power.

Her heartbeat slowed. Her body grew limp in his arms. The color drained from her cheeks.

He knew instinctively when he had taken enough. Sitting up, he bit into his left wrist.

"Drink, love," he whispered as his blood dripped onto her lips. "Drink and be mine forever."

He held his breath as a few crimson drops slid into her mouth, blinked back tears of relief when she swallowed, then grasped his arm and pulled it closer.

With a sense of wonder, he watched his blood transform her, felt his preternatural power flow into her, reviving her.

Withdrawing his arm, he sealed the wound with a stroke of his tongue. Rising, he drew the covers over her, then leaned down to brush a kiss across her brow.

"Rest now," he murmured. "You will have new worlds to conquer when you wake tomorrow night."

Remembering that he had promised to let Luke and the others know when it was done, Andrei returned to the living room. He found Jileen and Luke on the sofa, staring into the fireplace. Bailey reclined on the love seat, her eyes closed, though she was still awake.

They all looked up when he entered the room, their faces betraying a range of emotion—fear and dread from Jilly, curiosity from Luke, an expression of acceptance from Bailey. He touched her mind with his and realized she already knew what had happened and that Tessa was all right.

"How is she?" Jileen asked anxiously. "Is she . . . ?"

"She's resting. Everyone's fine."

"Fine! How can it be fine? You turned my best friend into a blood-sucking vampire!"

"There are worse things," Andrei replied.

Jilly uttered a very unladylike snort.

"I'll bring her to you when she wakes tomorrow night so you can see for yourself. Until then, I bid you good evening."

Smiling inwardly, he decided to give them a little display of vampire magic. Dissolving into mist, he vanished from their sight.

Jilly's gasp of surprise was reward enough.

Chapter Forty

She woke to darkness, but it was a darkness unlike any she had ever experienced. There was no light in the room, yet she saw everything clearly, each object crisply defined. She had fallen asleep in her clothes. They were familiar yet different. She felt each individual thread against her skin. A glance at the ceiling revealed every tiny fault, every tiny crack.

An ant crawled across the ceiling. Incredibly, she could hear its movement as it made its way toward the corner.

She licked her lips, suddenly overcome with a ravenous thirst. Never before had she felt such thirst, or such pain. Something was wrong. Throwing back the covers, she moved toward the door. Andrei. She needed him.

She was reaching for the latch when the door opened and he stood in the opening. Silhouetted in the light from behind him, he looked tall and dark and dangerous.

When he opened his arms, she went into them gladly. He was here. There was nothing to be afraid of.

His hand stroked her hair. "How do you feel?"

"I don't know. I've never felt this way before. What's wrong with me? I'm so thirsty!"

"Nothing's wrong."

She looked up at him and it was like seeing him for the first time. He looked the same and yet different. It was as if she had been looking at him through a veil before and it had suddenly dropped away, revealing the true beauty of the man.

She was trying to comprehend the change when she became aware of a sound she had never heard before— a slow, steady beat that sang in her ears like music.

A heartbeat. The knowledge came to her, along with the realization that it wasn't a single heartbeat, but four. It spiked her thirst, made her whole body ache with need.

She licked her lips, let out a startled cry when her fangs ran out.

Fangs!

"Tessa, it's all right." His arms tightened around her as he sensed the panic sweeping through her. "There's nothing to be afraid of. What you're feeling is natural."

She stared up at him in silent horror as the memory of the night before flashed through her mind. The images were hazy, dull, but she clearly remembered demanding that Andrei turn her into a vampire.

She didn't have to ask if it was true.

The answer was there, in his eyes.

"I'm so thirsty."

"I know, love. You can drink from me, if you like, or I can take you hunting."

Hunting. She waited for a sense of revulsion to overtake her, to feel nausea churning in her gut, to be horrified by the mere thought of feeding on a fellow creature. Instead, the idea was oddly compelling.

But she was thirsty now.

And he was here.

She ran her fingertips along the side of his neck. She could feel the blood flowing there, smell the crimson tide just beneath the skin.

Driven by a force too strong to resist, she went up on her tiptoes, pulled his head down, and took her first bite into a new life.

Andrei closed his eyes as Tessa's fangs pierced his skin. Since he'd been turned, no vampire had ever fed on him. The feeling was orgasmic.

He had been able to read her mind before; she had been able to hear his thoughts. Now it was as if their hearts and minds and bodies were one. He knew her deepest thoughts, felt what she felt as she drank from him—surprise, satisfaction, a growing hunger for human blood.

When she'd had enough to ease her thirst, he pulled away. "Not too much, love."

She licked her lips.

"Tessa?"

"Don't let me kill anyone."

"I won't."

Wrapping her arms around her middle, she rocked back and forth. "I'm still hungry."

"I know. That's why we're going hunting. It's nothing to worry about. It will come naturally. And I'll be there to make sure you don't take too much."

Walking down the streets of the neighboring town, Tessa felt as if she had been reborn, which, she supposed, she had. Sights and sounds and smells assailed her from all sides. Her new vampire senses were amazing.

Her vision allowed her to see things mortals never saw. Her hearing, sense of smell and touch, were equally amazing. And always, like a song that played over and over in her head, the alluring symphony of beating of hearts.

She glanced at Andrei. How did he stand it without going insane, this constant barrage of sensory perceptions?

"With practice, you'll learn to tune it out," he said.

A short time later, Andrei found a young couple leaving a restaurant. Taking Tessa by the hand, he followed them to their car.

Tessa watched as he approached the couple. He mesmerized them both with a look.

She watched as he took the woman in his arms, ran his tongue along the side of her neck, then buried his fangs in her throat. When he finished, he licked the twin wounds in her neck.

"Your turn," he said.

"I don't know . . ."

"Put aside your human preconceptions," he said. "Listen to the beat of his heart. Let his blood call to you. Follow your vampire instincts."

"How will I know when to stop?"

"You'll know. And I'll be here," he said, smiling. "Just in case."

Listen to the beat of his heart. Let his blood call to you.

Tentatively, she pulled the man closer, felt her fangs run out as the scent of his blood enticed her, a river of rich red nectar flowing just beneath his skin. Almost before she realized what she was doing, she ran her tongue along the side of his neck. He tasted of salt and fear. It sparked her hunger and then she was biting him, drinking from him. His blood was not as thick or rich or satisfying as Andrei's had been, but it eased her thirst in a way his had not.

She knew without knowing how when she had taken enough.

She sealed the tiny wounds, licked the blood from her lips.

Why had she feared this?

She smiled at Andrei.

And he smiled back, his expression smug with satisfaction. "Didn't I say you might like it?"

Jilly sat on the sofa in Andrei's living room, nervously chewing on her thumbnail. "Where do you suppose they are?"

Luke glanced at Bailey, one brow raised, and Bailey nodded. It was obvious, at least to the two of them, that Andrei had taken Tessa hunting.

Sighing, Bailey closed her eyes. Tristan had gone to tell the pack what was happening and to make final arrangements for tomorrow night when they would be life-mated. She had only a vague idea of what was to take place. Had no idea if Tessa would be in any condition to attend. What was it like, to be a new vampire? Was Tessa filled with uncontrollable bloodlust? Bailey had only had dealings with two vampires—Andrei and Katerina, and they were as different as night and day.

All things considered, Bailey decided she'd rather be a were-panther.

Rising, Jilly paced to the window and stared out into the darkness. "Luke, go find them."

"I'm sure they're fine. She's with Andrei. He won't let anything happen to her."

Jilly whirled around to face him. "What if she's turned

into a monster? What if that's why they've been gone so long? What if something went wrong and he had to . . . to . . ."

Taking Jilly in his arms, Luke said, "Honey, calm down. Andrei would have let us know if there was anything wrong. I know this is hard for you, but try not to worry."

"She's my best friend!" Jilly exclaimed, her voice rising. "How can I not worry?"

Urging Jilly to sit down again, Luke went into the kitchen. He returned moments later with a glass of wine. "Here, drink this. It'll help you relax."

"I'm sorry. I know I'm overreacting, but I just can't help it." She sipped the wine. "What if we can't be friends anymore?"

"Tessa's fine," Bailey said.

"How do you know?"

Bailey shrugged. "I just do. I can sense it through Andrei. They're on their way home."

Jilly's eyes widened.

And then she drained her glass.

Andrei slid his arm around Tessa's shoulders. "Are you ready to go home?"

"Yes."

"No regrets?"

She shook her head. "No. I think, deep down, I always knew this was inevitable." And then she frowned. "I don't feel like a monster."

"You're not a monster. You're a beautiful woman."

"Who just happens to have a craving for blood. Will I be dead all day?" Funny, she hadn't worried about that when she considered everything she'd be giving up. But it was too late now.

"I wouldn't call it dead, exactly, but you'll probably have to rest when the sun's up, at least for a while. But don't worry, love, I'll be there beside you."

"When *do* you rest?" she asked. "You're usually with me during the day, and most of the night, too."

"I catch a nap when I can. I don't need to rest as often as I once did. Or feed as often," he remarked, his expression thoughtful. "And I've been eating normal food. I think it's all because of your blood."

"So I've made you more human?"

"In a way." He grunted softly. "But you've also made me stronger. Come on, let's head back. This might be a good time for you to practice willing yourself from one place to another."

"Seriously? How do I do that?"

"Gather your power around you, then think about where you want to . . ." He laughed as she vanished from his sight. "Be."

Following their blood bond, he found her waiting for him outside his house.

"That was kinda scary and fun at the same time," she said, eyes sparkling.

"What are you doing out here?"

"All of a sudden I feel a little nervous about being around Jilly and Luke." She could hear the two of them whispering, wondering if she would be a "civilized" vampire, like Andrei, or like one of those out-of-control fledglings who attacked without provocation or remorse. She might have been offended, angry, even, if she hadn't wondered the same thing herself.

"Not Bailey?" he asked.

"No. She's sort of like one of us. But Luke's a hunter. And Jilly . . . she's my best friend. What if I want to drink her blood?"

"I think you're worrying for nothing, but there's just one way to find out." And so saying, he took her hand in his and opened the front door.

The conversation in the living room came to an abrupt stop when Tessa and Andrei entered the room.

Luke looked wary.

Jilly worried.

Bailey merely curious.

"I'm still me," Tessa said. "I promise not to eat you."

Luke snorted. "I don't mean any disrespect, Tess, but you're a vampire now. In my experience, fledglings are highly unpredictable."

"Luke!" Jilly admonished.

"It's true!" Luke exclaimed. "And if the time comes when it's your life or hers, you'd better know which side I'm on."

"I think we all knew that," Andrei said dryly. "But I can assure you that Tessa's no threat to any of you."

"Yeah? How can you be so sure? You might have had hundreds of years to learn to control your powers and your appetite, but she hasn't."

"She carries the blood of a master vampire and that makes all the difference. She's stronger and more powerful than ordinary fledglings. She won't be plagued with an insatiable thirst or an overwhelming desire to kill."

Luke nodded, but he still looked doubtful.

There was a moment of tense silence in the room. It was Bailey who broke it. Getting off the sofa, she embraced Tessa. "You're still coming to the life-mating ceremony tomorrow night, aren't you?"

"Of course," Tessa said, smiling. "I wouldn't miss it."

Chapter Forty-One

Katerina lifted her head, the man in her grasp forgotten.

"What is it?" Noah, who'd been feeding beside her, looked around, searching for some sign of danger.

"He's turned her!" She cast the half-dead man aside like so much garbage. "He's made her one of us!"

"Who?"

"Andrei, you fool! He's brought that woman across, made her one of us."

"I don't understand."

"I wanted her blood. I needed to find out what powers it possessed. Andrei should have died from my bite. Instead, he recovered and grew stronger."

"You were his sire," Noah said, brow furrowing. "But your bite would have destroyed him?"

"Yes," she snapped.

He took a step away from her. And then another. "So, now that she's a vampire . . . ?"

"Her blood is now his and his is now hers."

"So, whatever healed him doesn't exist any longer?"

"No." She clenched her hands, her fury growing with every passing moment. Tessa's blood had increased

Andrei's paranormal powers, made him strong enough to survive her bite.

She fixed her gaze on Noah. Andrei might be beyond her grasp, but here was the perfect target for her fury.

Seeing the rage in her eyes, he took an instinctive step away from her.

It was the last thing he ever did.

Chapter Forty-Two

Bailey went home with Tristan late Saturday night, saying there were a few last-minute things they needed to do for the life-mating ceremony tomorrow.

Jilly and Luke had left earlier, with Jilly pleading a headache.

Alone at last, Tessa thought, snuggling on the sofa with Andrei. He had turned off all the lights. The soft glow from the fire in the hearth cast dancing shadows on the walls.

"It's nice," she murmured, "just the two of us together."

Andrei nodded.

"Do you think Jilly will ever feel comfortable around me again?"

"In time."

Staring at the flames, she said, "I don't know what I'm going to do about Christmas. I always go home."

"We'll figure something out."

Tessa sighed. "I was looking forward to seeing my folks. And eating my mom's pumpkin pie." She glanced up at Andrei, bit down on her lower lip when she saw his face. His eyes were dark with guilt, his jaw clenched.

"I don't have any regrets," she said quickly. "Honest! I love the new bond between us. I know now there was really no other way for us to truly be together. It's just . . ."

"You don't have to explain," he said. "I've been where you are."

"We haven't talked about our future," Tessa said tentatively. "Maybe you don't feel the same way about me anymore."

"You're worried about that *now*? Seriously? I love you, Tess. Nothing will ever change that." Cupping her face in his hands, he kissed her.

There was something different about his kisses. It took her a moment to realize that, in the past, he had always been careful not to hold her too tightly for fear of hurting her. His kisses were deeper now, more intense. She was surprised to realize he had also kept her from reading his more intimate thoughts.

Lost in his kisses, basking in his caress, she surrendered to the magic that was Andrei. Somehow, she found herself lying on the rug in front of the hearth, wrapped in his arms, their bodies pressed intimately together, so close she couldn't tell where she ended and he began.

His hands were cool against her heated flesh. For the first time, she let herself caress him in places she had not dared touch before. He groaned softly, a wordless plea she could no longer resist.

Tessa ran her hands up and down Andrei's back. She loved the feel of his skin beneath her palms. Because of the bond between them, she knew what he was feeling, thinking, knew he was keeping a tight rein on his own desires, determined to let her go as far as she wished. Her vampire senses heightened the intensity of every need, every desire, overpowering every other emotion she had ever known.

She wanted him, wanted him desperately. Always before, she had been able to draw the line before things went too far, wanting to take Jilly's advice and wait until her wedding night. But tonight there was no turning back.

She was lost, drowning in a world of sensual desire that would not be denied. Their clothing disappeared as if by magic and for the first time, she knew what it was like to feel the wonder of bare male skin against her own. It was a feeling beyond description, like silk brushing silk. All her inhibitions fell away under the touch of his hands. She couldn't stop looking at him, touching him. He was beautiful, his shoulders broad, his chest solid, his arms and legs firm and well muscled. He was, she thought in a rare moment of lucidity, a study in sheer masculine perfection.

She writhed beneath him, her hands restless as they skated up and down his back.

He whispered to her in a language she didn't understand, but it didn't matter. His husky tone, the fire blazing in his dark eyes, told her everything she needed to know.

His mind brushed hers, a question looking for an answer, and she raised her hips in silent invitation.

There was no pain as his body melded with hers, only indescribable pleasure as he moved deep within her. She cried his name, desperately yearning for something that hovered just out of reach, then exploded within her, leaving her breathless and feeling oh so complete.

* * *

Andrei rose on one elbow, his hand brushing a wisp of sweat-dampened hair from her cheek. "No regrets, *dragostea mea?*"

His tone was light, but Tessa saw the worry in his eyes, the fear that now, no longer caught up in the heat of the moment, she would wish they had waited. "How could I be sorry when you're such an incredible lover?" she asked, trying, and failing, to stifle a grin.

"You ain't seen nothing yet," he said, flashing a wicked grin of his own. "I took it easy on you because this was your first time."

"Oh, my!" she exclaimed, widening her eyes in mock horror. "I am *so* afraid. Maybe you should do it again and get it over with."

"As always," he said, his eyes growing hot as his body covered hers, "your wish is my command."

Tessa sighed as Andrei washed her back. It was a night of firsts, she thought, because she had never showered with a man before. The feel of his soapy hands aroused her in new and exciting ways. Apparently, it was having the same effect on him, she mused, catching sight of their reflection in the glass.

Having made love twice, she wondered if there was something wrong with her, that she wanted him again so quickly. Would he think her a wanton if . . .

The thought had no sooner crossed her mind than he was carrying her back into the bedroom, sitting on the bed, pulling her down on top of him.

So many ways to make love, she thought. How glad she was that she had waited for Andrei to teach her.

Later, locked in his arms, his breath cool against her cheek, she grew increasingly aware of time passing. In a few hours, the sun would rise and she would . . . what? Lose consciousness? Fall asleep? Andrei had never told her what it was like to succumb to the darkness.

"Andrei?"

"Yes, love?"

"What will happen to me when the sun comes up? Is it like falling asleep?" she asked hopefully.

"Not exactly." It had been terrifying for him, the first time. The sudden lethargy, the sense of falling into nothingness. There were no dreams, no sense of time passing, no sense of anything until the sun went down and he awoke abruptly.

"Tell me."

"I won't lie to you. It was scary the first time. One minute you're awake and the next you're waking up with no memory of what happened in between. It doesn't hurt. There are no dreams, good or bad . . ." He paused. That was no longer true for him. Since tasting Tessa's blood, his existence had changed. He dreamed while at rest. He was able to partake of mortal food from time to time.

Seeing the pensive expression on his face, she asked, "What aren't you telling me?"

"Maybe it will be different for you."

"Why?"

"Your blood is different from most mortals. Or it was. I'm not sure if that's true now that you're no longer human. But I've had dreams, something I hadn't experienced for more than seven hundred years until I tasted your blood."

"You'll stay with me, won't you?"

"The whole time, if you want me to."

"At least the first time." She worried her lower lip. "You're sure I'll wake up again?"

Andrei laughed softly as he gathered her into his arms. "I'm sure, love."

He lay beside her, her head pillowed on his shoulder, as the sun came up and she slipped into the sleep inherent to their kind. She had always been lovely, but now, her beauty subtly enhanced by the Dark Gift, she was truly the most beautiful creature he had ever seen.

Even though he could be active during the day, it was natural for him to take his rest when the sun was up. Holding Tessa close, he let himself slip into the familiar darkness.

Yawning, Tessa rubbed the sleep from her eyes and sat up. There was no clock in the lair to tell her the time, no windows through which to judge the hour, yet she knew it was midafternoon. And that she should be trapped in the dark sleep.

Why wasn't she?

She glanced at Andrei, lying beside her. And smiled. She loved him, she thought, her fingertips tracing his lower lip. Loved him with every fiber of her being.

"As I love you." Capturing her hand, he kissed her palm, then drew her down beside him. "I had a feeling the dark sleep wouldn't be able to hold you."

"Did you?"

He grunted softly. "Your blood has enhanced my powers, as mine have enhanced yours. We are both the stronger for it."

She smiled, vastly relieved that she wouldn't have to be unconscious during the daylight hours.

"You won't be able to go sunbathing, or stay out in

the hot sun for long periods of time," he warned, "and you may have to wear dark glasses for a while."

"I don't care!" She kissed him soundly. "I was dreading having to sleep all day and now I don't have to!"

Andrei rose over her. "As long as you're awake . . ." he said, flashing a wicked grin.

"What did you have in mind? As if I didn't know."

He kissed her cheek, then nipped her earlobe. "Any objections?"

She started to say no, then stared up at him. "Wait! You're not going to bite me, are you?"

"I thought I might, why?"

"Why? Because I'll die from the bite of my sire, that's why!"

Andrei threw back his head and laughed. "Is that what you think? That I waited all this time just to turn you on Friday and do away with you two days later?" Lowering his head, he kissed her. "There are bites," he said, lightly raking his fangs along the side of her neck, "and then there are bites."

"If I taste you now, will it be as amazing as it was before you turned me?"

"Better, my love. From now on, everything only gets better."

Chapter Forty-Three

Sitting cross-legged on the bed, Bailey glanced at the time on her cell phone. It was almost three o'clock. In little more than two hours, she would be life-mated to Tristan.

The enormity of what she was about to do hit her for the first time. She was only sixteen. She had never dated anyone except Tristan and after tonight, she would never have that option again. Once they were mated, the bond between them could not be broken.

What if she was making a terrible mistake? Did she want to spend the rest of her life here, with Tristan's pack? She used to feel all grown up, but now, faced with the reality—the finality—of mating with Tristan, she was beset by doubts.

Maybe Tessa was right. Maybe she was too young to make such a decision.

She stared at the dress hanging on the door of the bedroom she used when she stayed with Tristan's family. It was long and white, not really a wedding dress, although it looked like one. Tristan's mother had bought it for her. She had waved Bailey's protests aside. *"I want to do this for you,"* Mrs. Kavanagh had said. *"You're going to be my daughter now."*

"Bailey?"

She glanced over her shoulder to see Tristan standing in the doorway.

"Can I come in?"

"Of course. It's your house."

Stepping into the room, he said, "In a couple of hours, it will be yours, too."

She nodded, somewhat reluctantly.

"What is it?" he asked, eyes narrowing. "What's wrong?"

She shook her head vigorously. "Nothing."

"Bailey, you can't lie to me. Don't you know that?" He closed the short distance between them and drew her gently into his arms. "Tell me what's bothering you."

She looked up into his eyes, beautiful green eyes filled with love and concern.

"Will you kiss me?"

"Anytime you want me to." He cupped her face between his hands, a faint smile curving his lips before he covered her mouth with his.

Bailey went up on her tiptoes, her arms sliding around his neck. How could she have ever doubted that being with Tristan was the right thing to do? He was the other half of her heart, the missing part of her soul. Only with him did she feel whole, complete.

Lifting his head, he gazed into her eyes. "Do you want to tell me what's going on now?"

"Nothing," she said, smiling. "Nothing at all. Just some last-minute jitters, I guess."

"I love you," he whispered. "All the years I followed you, I loved you. When I was old enough to know what old man Fischer was doing to you, I wanted to kill him but my father forbade it, saying it would bring trouble down on the pack. If you hadn't run away when you did," he said, his expression fierce, "I would have killed him, the safety of the pack be damned. You're mine now," he whispered fervently. "And no one will ever hurt you again."

With a sigh, Bailey rested her cheek against his chest, home at last.

Tessa stood beside Andrei, curious as to what being life-mated actually entailed. Earlier, they had spent a few minutes with Bailey, who had thanked them for coming, then introduced them to Tristan's family.

Tessa glanced at the faces of the other guests. There were perhaps twenty people of various ages gathered in a loose circle at the top of a flat ridge a few miles out of town. She wondered if they were all were-panthers.

A large black bowl sat on a square stone table in the center of the ring.

Tessa bit down on her lower lip. The soft rhythmic sound of so many beating hearts called to her, making it difficult to relax.

Andrei squeezed her hand. "Slow, deep breaths," he whispered. "Don't think about anything but Bailey. You'll be fine."

Tessa nodded, hoping he was right. Her enhanced vampire perceptions heightened every sense, both internal and external.

As the sun set in a glorious blaze of crimson and ocher, a tall woman in a long, gray robe strode into the center of the circle. Three young girls clad in white gowns followed her. One carried a torch, the other two carried crystal goblets filled with a clear golden liquid.

From somewhere beyond the circle, a drum beat slowly, softly.

When it fell silent, Tristan entered the circle. He wore black pants and a white shirt open at the throat.

The drum beat again and when it stilled, Bailey took her place beside him.

Wearing a long, white gown, with several flowers braided into her long, brown hair, she looked radiant. And happier than Tess had ever seen her.

The woman in gray took the torch from the first girl and touched it to the bowl in the center of the table, and a tiny flame flickered to life.

"We are gathered here this blessed night to unite Tristan Kavanagh and Bailey Fairchild. To be life-mated is a promise for their future, and for the future of the Kavanagh pack." Her gaze touched that of the young couple, and then she pulled a small knife from inside her robe.

Taking first Tristan's hand and then Bailey's, she made a shallow cut in each of their palms, then pressed their hands together.

She motioned the two girls to come forward. Lifting Tristan's hand, she held it over one of the goblets, letting a single drop of blood drip into the liquid. She held Bailey's hand over the second one.

"Drink now."

Gazing into each other's eyes, Tristan and Bailey drained the glasses.

"Blood to blood," the woman intoned. "Life to life. From this night forward and for all the days and nights to come."

She bowed her head a moment, and it was as if the whole earth held its breath until she lifted it again. "It is done."

As soon as the words were spoken, the circle closed in around Bailey and Tristan.

Power drifted on the breeze, sang through the night. There was a rustle of clothing and when the crowd parted, Tessa saw that Bailey and Tristan had shifted into their were-panther forms.

"Go now," the woman said, "rejoice in the bond made between you this night."

Throwing back his head, Tristan howled before darting toward the trees. With an answering cry, Bailey ran after him.

Tessa glanced at Andrei as they pulled onto the road that led back to town. "Well, that was different. Kind of beautiful, in its own way. I hope they'll be happy together."

"I think they have a good chance."

Tessa sighed. "I had a text from my parents earlier. They'll be home tomorrow afternoon and I'm still not sure what we should do."

"You should go home and see them," Andrei said.

Tessa nodded. He was right. If she decided not to tell them about becoming a vampire, the time would come when she wouldn't be able to see them at all because there would be no way to explain why she wasn't aging. "You're going with me, right?"

"If you wish."

"I'm not going without you." She stared out the window. If she told her parents, would they understand? Would they be able to accept a daughter who was a vampire? Would they still love her? Or would they be so horrified, so repulsed at the mere idea, that they'd never want to have anything to do with her again?

"You're their daughter," Andrei said. "Their only child. They love you. That won't change. They might be shocked when you tell them, but they'll get over it."

"Are you sure about that?"

He flashed her a crooked grin. "About ninety-nine percent."

Tessa looked out the window again. It would make things a lot easier if they knew. She wouldn't have to explain why she couldn't eat Christmas dinner with them. . . . "Do you think I can eat mortal food?"

"I don't know, why?"

"Well, since I can be awake during the day, if I can eat a little at breakfast and dinner . . . maybe they won't have to know."

"It's your call, love."

"Can we stop at the store before we go home?"

"Sure."

Turning down Main Street, he pulled up in front of the market. "What are you in the mood for?" he asked, amusement evident in his voice as he followed her inside.

"I'm not really in the mood for anything," she retorted. "But I need to see if I can keep anything down."

Andrei trailed behind her as she pushed her cart down the aisles, pausing to select a small, precooked chicken, cans of sweet potatoes, corn, and cranberry sauce, a package of buttermilk rolls. At the last minute, she added a pumpkin pie and whipped cream.

At the register, he paid the bill. Smiling faintly, he followed her back out to the car.

"What are you grinning at?" Tessa asked as they pulled away from the curb.

"Just curious to see what happens. I mean, it took me over seven hundred years to be able to consume mortal food and you've been a vampire, what? Forty-eight hours, give or take a few minutes."

"You said we strengthen each other," she reminded him. "If I can be awake during the day, maybe I can eat, too."

"And if you can't?"

"I guess I'll cross that bridge when I come to it." She shrugged. "If it seems like the right thing to do, if there's no way around it when we get there, then I'll tell them. This is all so new to me, I'm just feeling my way."

Andrei reached over to squeeze her hand. "I know, love. And you're handling it a lot better than I ever did."

Twenty minutes later, Tessa sat at her kitchen table. They had come to her house to prepare the meal, since there were still no appliances at Andrei's to cook or store the groceries, and no dishes or silverware, and not likely to be any in the near future, if ever.

She frowned at the food before her. She really wasn't hungry for anything she had bought, but she figured if she could keep down a bit of chicken, sweet potatoes, rolls, and pumpkin pie, she would be able to eat at least a little of her mother's Christmas dinner.

Andrei sat across from her, looking bemused by her hesitation. "I'm sure your mother would have told you to eat it while it's hot."

Tessa huffed a sigh as she picked up a roll and cut it in half. And took a bite. "It has no taste!" She tasted a forkful of potatoes, a spoonful of corn. And shook her head. "Does food taste good when you eat it?"

"It has flavor. I'm not sure I would call it good. If you

don't want to dine at your mother's, I can exert a little vampire magic to make them believe we're eating."

"Well, it's good to know I've got an option." Pushing away from the table, she caught his hand and tugged him to his feet. "I really am hungry, though, so what do you say we go out and find something more suitable to quench my thirst?" Going up on tiptoe, she kissed him, then nipped his lower lip. "Then we can come back here and have dessert." She blew out a long, slow sigh. "And then I'll pack."

Katerina prowled the edge of the grounds that surrounded Andrei's lair.

He took his rest here. With the woman.

Hands clenched, she stared at the house. Even knowing that she couldn't cross the threshold, she had tried, on several previous occasions, to get past his wards, but to no avail.

She had endeavored to steal her way into Andrei's mind. And failed.

She had sought to invade the woman's mind. And failed.

What had changed? It had to be the woman's blood. Somehow, her blood had made Andrei's powers stronger. She snarled softly. If Andrei wouldn't share the woman, there was only one thing to do. Destroy her. But how? Nothing she had tried so far had worked.

Feeling her outrage growing, she picked up a large rock and hurled it at the house with all her might. It broke one of the front windows with a satisfying crack.

Ha! She might not be able to get inside, but . . . she smacked her forehead with her hand. Of course! Why hadn't she thought of it before? He had warded his lair

against intruders but not against nonhuman invaders.
Like rocks. And flames . . .

She paused a moment. It was a beautiful old house.
She almost felt a twinge of guilt at the idea of destroying it.

Almost.

All she needed was a bottle, a rag, a little gasoline.
And a match.

Chapter Forty-Four

Andrei paused as he parked the car in the driveway.

"What is it?" Tessa asked. They had gone hunting earlier and, after making mad, passionate love in her bedroom, she had packed her suitcase.

He jerked his chin toward his lair. "Someone broke a window." He rolled down the car window and inhaled sharply. "Katerina."

"She was here?" Tessa glanced around. Darn! She thought they'd seen the last of that witch.

Andrei switched off the engine. "Come on," he said, grabbing her suitcase from the backseat. "I'll throw a few things in a bag and we'll be on our way to see your parents."

A thought transported them inside the house. It took him only moments to pack.

"How are we going to get there?" Tessa asked. Until now, she hadn't given it any thought.

"Vampire Airways." He tucked her suitcase under his arm, picked up his bag, then wrapped his free arm around her waist. "Hang on tight."

He had transported the two of them before, but never so far. All the other times, the trip had been over before she had time to really experience what was happening. But this time . . . it was, she thought, the strangest feeling she'd ever had. It felt a little like hurtling down a long pitch-black corridor, yet there was no real sense of moving through time or space, just a faint hum in her ears and a queasiness in the pit of her stomach.

When the world righted itself, they were in front of a brightly lit hotel.

Tessa blinked up at Andrei. "Wow."

"It's a little late to be calling on your folks," he said. "I thought we'd spend the night here." He frowned at her. "Are you all right?"

"I feel a little dizzy."

He nodded. "Once you've transported a few times, it won't bother you anymore."

"Next time we're taking a trip, remind me not to have dinner first."

He laughed softly. "I promise."

"What if they don't have a room?"

He looked at her, one brow arched. "Seriously?"

"Sorry for doubting you," Tessa muttered as she followed him into the lobby.

Five minutes later, she stood in the middle of a luxury suite while Andrei tipped the bellboy, who gushed his thanks as he backed out the door.

"How much did you give him?" she asked.

"Fifty bucks."

"Fifty dollars!"

Andrei shrugged. "He needs the money. He supports his invalid mother and younger sister."

"Oh." Tessa shook her head. She loved Andrei, but there were times, like this, when she realized she really knew very little about him. Who would have thought that a seven-hundred-year-old vampire would feel compassion for a mortal he didn't even know? He really was a wonderful guy, she thought.

"You just finding that out?" he asked, drawing her into his arms.

"I always knew you were wonderful," she said. "But you still manage to surprise me."

"Really?" He smiled down at her. "There's a big, oval bed in the other room," he said. "If you're game, I have a few other surprises I can show you."

"Will I like them?"

He dropped butterfly kisses on the tip of her nose, her lips, the curve of her throat. "I can guarantee it."

Wrapping her arm around his neck, she murmured, "Then I'm definitely game."

In the blink of an eye, she was lying on her back on the big round bed. Her clothes—and his—had magically disappeared and she was wrapped in his arms.

"You are still going to make an honest woman of me, aren't you?" she asked, and then, as his hands caressed her and his mouth covered hers, she forgot the question, forgot she needed an answer, forgot everything but the fire that swept through her as his kisses worked their sweet magic, carrying her away to a place where there was no need for words or promises, only the joining of his body with hers, her heart with his.

"I'm so nervous!" Tessa stood in front of the hotel closet, frowning. "Should I wear this? Or this? Or . . ."

Andrei shook his head. "Tessa, they're your parents. They don't care what you wear. Just pick something. If you can't relax, they'll know something's wrong without your saying a word."

She whirled around, a blue dress in one hand, a lavender print in another. "Relax!" she exclaimed. "Relax!

How can I? This isn't like bringing home a prom date. I'm a vampire. You're a vampire!"

"It's not like a scarlet letter," he said, his voice laced with patience and amusement. "It doesn't show."

"Oh! How can you make jokes?"

Taking the dresses from her hands, he tossed them on the bed and drew her into his arms. "Tessa, it'll be fine. Forget that you're a vampire. You're just a young woman going home for Christmas. We'll visit for a while and see how it goes. If you can't handle it, I'll know, and I'll make some excuse for why we have to leave. All right?"

She took a deep breath. He was right. She looked pretty much the same as always. There was no way her parents would jump to the conclusion that she was a vampire.

Murmuring "Thank you," she picked up the blue dress.

Thirty minutes later, Andrei knocked on her parents' front door.

It opened almost immediately. "Tessa!" Beaming, her mother threw her arms around her. "Come in, you two. Did you have a nice flight?" Alice Blackburn asked, ushering them into the living room.

"Tess." Smiling, her father wrapped her in a bear hug. "Welcome home, sweetie."

She hugged him back, trying not to notice the beating of his heart, the scent of his blood. This was her father, not prey.

"Mom, Dad, this is Andrei. Andrei, my parents, Alice and Henry."

Andrei shook her father's hand. "Pleased to meet you, sir."

Henry nodded. "I've heard a lot about you."

"All good, I hope." Andrei bowed over her mother's hand. "Mrs. Blackburn."

"Let's sit down, shall we?" Alice suggested. "Have you had lunch?"

Andrei glanced at Tessa, then said, "We ate on the plane."

Alice nodded. "Well, I hope you saved room for dinner. I made Tessa's favorite homemade lasagna and garlic bread."

"Thanks, Mom." She sat on the love seat and Andrei sat beside her, while her parents sat on the sofa. "The house looks good, Mom. I like the new carpet and drapes."

Alice smiled. "We redid the upstairs, too. Except for your room, of course. I didn't want to do anything without asking you first."

"Mom, it's your house."

"But it's your room. I want you to know you always have a place here."

"So, Dinescu, tell us about yourself," Henry said. "Tessa mentioned you're in the antiques business."

"Yes, sir. I'm doing pretty well."

"You should see his house," Tessa said. "He has some beautiful pieces. And the house itself is amazing."

Her father nodded.

"Are you planning a long engagement?" her mother asked.

Tessa glanced at Andrei. "We haven't decided."

"I suppose you'll want to get married in Cutter's Corner."

"I don't know, Mom. We've only been engaged a short time."

"You girls can talk about all that wedding stuff later,"

Mr. Blackburn said. "Right now, I'll bet Andrei would like a piece of that apple pie you've got in the kitchen."

"Of course," Alice said. "Would you like coffee with that, Mr. Dinescu?"

"Andrei, please. And coffee would be fine. Black, no sugar."

Tessa fell back on her bed, arms outstretched.

Andrei sat on the edge of the mattress, his fingers threading through her hair. "I think it went well," he said. "Don't you?"

"I guess so. I don't think they suspected anything. Do you?"

"Not a thing. I almost forgot you were a vampire."

Lifting her head, she stuck her tongue out at him. "Tomorrow's Christmas! I've got to go shopping! I don't have a single present for my folks. Or for you . . ."

Stretching out beside her, he drew her into his embrace. "I don't need anything, *dragostea mea*," he said, kissing her lightly. "I've already got everything I want."

Tessa's parents were very understanding when she said she and Andrei needed to go Christmas shopping. Before she left, she took her dad aside to ask if he knew of anything her mother wanted, then took her mother aside to ask about her dad.

Her father generously offered to lend them the car.

"So, did you get any ideas?" Andrei asked as they pulled out of the driveway and headed for Omaha, because Tessa said there were a lot more places to shop there than in Ashland.

"Not really. Parents are so hard to buy for. I mean, by the time their kids are old enough to actually buy them nice gifts, they already have everything they want or need."

Andrei laughed. "Yeah, I guess that's true."

Tessa glanced out the window. Ashland was a small town with a rural charm she had loved while growing up. It had been fun, knowing almost everyone in town, feeling safe and secure. When she graduated college, she headed for the Big Apple, thinking she'd had enough of being a small-town girl. To her chagrin, she didn't like living in a big city. Not wanting to go back home, she had settled in Cutter's Corner.

She slid a glance at Andrei. Had she stayed in New York, or gone back home, she never would have met him.

"Pretty country out here," Andrei remarked.

"Yes." She turned on the radio and lowered the volume.

"Have your parents always lived in Nebraska?"

"Yes, and their parents, too." She glanced at a road sign, announcing Omaha just ahead. "Did you know that the TV dinner was invented by a man from Omaha?" she asked, then laughed. "I don't suppose you've ever eaten one."

"You'd suppose right. But I've seen them on the tube."

"Cake mix was invented there too. And the ski lift."

They reached Omaha some thirty minutes later. The weather was gray and cold. Although vampires didn't feel the cold, Tessa had worn boots and a heavy jacket because her parents expected it, and insisted Andrei do the same.

Andrei had never been much for shopping but he loved Tessa, so he let her drag him from store to store while she tried to decide what to buy her parents.

She finally settled on a chess set for her father and a nightgown and matching robe for her mother.

While waiting for the clerk to wrap her mother's gift, Andrei leaned over to whisper, "Now can we go somewhere and make love?"

Christmas morning dawned clear and bright and cold. Since there weren't any kids in the house, no one was in a hurry to get up, for which Tessa was grateful, since no one would think it strange if she slept late.

She missed resting with Andrei but, because she knew her parents wouldn't approve, she had spent the night in her old room. Andrei slept in the guest room down the hall.

Turning onto her side, she listened to the sounds emanating from downstairs—the drip of the coffeemaker, the quiet hum of her parents' conversation, the steady beat of their hearts . . .

It bothered her that the scent of their blood called to her. They were her parents, for goodness' sake! She shouldn't want to bite them, but the urge to drink from them was strong. Why? Because they were family? She would have to ask Andrei when she saw him.

Andrei.

Yes, love?

I miss you.

Come and get me.

A thought took her to his side. Being a vampire definitely had its perks, she thought, as he wrapped her in his arms, then slid his hand under her gown to stroke her thigh.

"Did you come for a quickie?" he asked, eyes twinkling with mischief.

"I wish."

"I can be very quiet," he said. "I don't know about you."

She made a face at him, thinking she had never

been happier in her whole life. The things she had given up paled in comparison to the joy she felt in his arms, the love she read in his eyes.

"I smell breakfast," he said. "No doubt your mother will be coming to wake you up . . . Yep, I hear her footsteps on the stairs. Better scoot back to your own room if you don't want to shock her."

Stealing a quick kiss, Tessa willed herself back to her room. The sooner they went back home, the better!

Her mother served Belgian waffles, bacon, and eggs for breakfast. It had once been Tessa's favorite breakfast, but looking at it now, she knew there was no way she could eat it. She sent a helpless glance at Andrei, who nodded almost imperceptibly. *Just follow my lead.*

He helped himself to a waffle and a generous serving of bacon and eggs, complimenting her mother's culinary skills all the while.

Following his lead, Tessa filled her plate.

Her father said grace and her parents ate as if nothing unusual was happening, even though Andrei and Tessa never touched a bite.

When the meal was over, Tessa insisted on clearing the table, unable to believe that Andrei's mind tricks had somehow fooled her mom and dad.

With the dishes done, they gathered in the living room to open their presents.

Her father was pleased with the chess set; her mother said the robe and nightgown were exactly what she needed. Tessa's gifts from her parents were a Coach handbag, a pair of boots, and a bottle of her favorite perfume. They had even bought presents for Andrei—a box of monogrammed handkerchiefs and a black leather wallet.

The rest of the day passed in lazy fashion. They watched *The Greatest Story Ever Told* on TV; later, they played cards. Still later, her mother brought out the family album.

Tessa groaned as her mother proudly showed Andrei photos of Tessa growing up—from plump, rosy-cheeked baby to gangly teenager and all the embarrassing years in between.

"She's always been a lovely girl," her mother said, putting the album aside. "Never gave us a moment's trouble."

Andrei nodded.

"There's something about her now," her mother remarked, studying Tessa's face. "I can't quite put my finger on it, but she's radiant in a way I've never seen her."

Tessa sent a worried look at Andrei. *They know!*

He shook his head, the movement almost imperceptible. *No way.*

"It must be love," Henry said, grinning.

"Of course." Alice beamed at Andrei. "That must be it!"

"I do wish the two of you could stay longer," Alice said, squeezing Tessa's hand as they walked out to the porch.

"I know, Mom, me too. But I have to go back to work on Monday."

Alice sighed. "It was wonderful to meet you, Andrei. Take good care of my little girl."

"You can count on it," Andrei said. He stood back as Tessa's parents hugged her, obviously reluctant to see their only child leaving home yet again.

Tears sparkled in Alice's eyes as she hugged Tessa

one last time. "Have a safe trip. Call us when you get home."

"I will, Mom. Thanks for everything."

Andrei noticed tears shining in Tessa's eyes as well, as they climbed into the cab that was, as far as her parents knew, taking them to the airport. In reality, it was only taking them a few blocks away.

"I'm glad you talked me into coming," she said, sniffling.

He nodded. "You're lucky to have parents who love you."

"Didn't yours love you?"

"I suppose they did, in their way. But my father was more concerned with running the estate. My mother spent her days looking after castle affairs and keeping my father happy. My brothers and I were raised by nursemaids and tutors."

"Andrei, why was I so tempted to drink from my parents? The urge was so strong, stronger than anything I've felt with anyone else. Is that normal?"

"I don't know. My parents were dead by the time Katerina turned me. But if I had to make a guess, I'd say it's because their blood is still a part of you."

Tessa considered that while Andrei told the cabbie to pull over. After gathering their suitcases and handing Tessa their gifts, he tipped the driver and when the cab was out of sight, he put his arm around Tessa and willed the two of them back to his lair.

Only it wasn't there.

Chapter Forty-Five

Andrei dropped their suitcases on the ground. "What the hell!"

Tessa stared at the burned-out wreckage of what had been Andrei's home. The front door hung askew, wisps of smoke curled through the broken windows, the luxurious velvet drapes were little more than blackened cloth.

She shook her head. His beautiful house, all those wonderful antiques, gone. "How could this have happened?"

He swore a vile oath. "Katerina happened. Damn her black soul to hell!"

"She did this? How can you be so sure?"

"Even the acrid smell of the fire can't cover her foul stench."

Frowning, Tessa opened her vampire senses. And then she smelled it too. The unmistakable scent that was Katerina. "But, why would she do this?"

"Because she's an evil, vindictive, selfish . . ." Clenching his fists, Andrei took a deep breath and let it out in a long, slow sigh. "It doesn't matter why," he said flatly.

"It's done." He glanced at the sky. It would be dark soon. Picking up their luggage, he clasped Tessa's hand. "Looks like we'll be spending the night at your place."

Her condo seemed empty without Bailey there, waiting to welcome them home. Putting their Christmas gifts on the coffee table, Tessa walked through the house, turning on the lamps. She could see perfectly fine in the dark, but it just seemed more like home with the lights on.

Someone—Bailey, she guessed—had cleaned out the refrigerator and the cupboards, disposing of all the perishable food items. The bed in Bailey's room was neatly made, the drawers empty of the clothing Tessa had bought her.

With a sigh, Tessa sat on the edge of the bed. How quickly her life had changed.

"You okay, love?"

She looked up to see Andrei standing in the doorway, arms crossed, his shoulder resting against the jamb.

"I'm fine."

"You look like you're about to cry."

"Maybe I am. I guess it just hit me. Bailey's gone. Jilly's married. I'm a vampire. My life will never be the same again."

A muscle twitched in his jaw. "Regrets?"

"What? Oh, no. It's just that it all happened so fast. I guess I need to call Mr. Ambrose and let him know I won't be coming back to work."

"Is that what you want?"

"I don't know. I love my job, but . . . it just doesn't fit anymore."

"Well, I know how to fill your days and nights."

Moving to the bed, he sat down beside her. "We need to find a place to live. So, do you want to stay in Cutter's Corner?"

"If we can. Jilly's here."

He nodded. "Then the next question is, shall we rebuild or buy something new?"

"I don't know. What do you want to do?"

"Rebuild. It's hard to find a new home with a big basement and we need a secure place for a lair. Something defensible," he said. "And fireproof."

Smiling, Tessa rested her head against his shoulder. "I love you."

"I love you, too. There's just one more thing we need to decide."

"What's that?"

"When we're getting married."

She looked up at him, eyes wide. "Seriously?"

"Damn straight. We're through living in sin, woman. It's time to make it legal."

"The question now is where?" She grimaced, remembering what had happened to the justice of the peace.

"Here," Andrei said. "In the living room. That way we don't have to worry about any unwelcome visitors."

"Then I guess the next question is when?"

"I'll leave that up to you. Just make it as quick as you can."

Tessa nodded. "I'd like to invite my parents, but they'd expect us to get married in a church, and probably the one they attend in Ashland."

"Whatever you decide is fine with me."

"I'm not willing to take the risk of having it in a public place. I originally planned to say we eloped and I think I'll just stick with that and tell them that we'll come visit them again in the spring."

* * *

Sunday afternoon, Tessa called Jilly to let her know they were back in town and staying at her place.

"She burned down his house!" Jilly exclaimed. "Well, I'm not surprised. It sounds just like something that evil woman would do."

"I know, but still . . . anyway, we're going to rebuild. But that's not why I called. We're going to try getting married again, only this time at my place. I'm not sure when. I need to find another dress because I sure can't wear the other one."

"Do you want me to come along?"

Tessa paused. Was it her imagination, or did she hear a hint of reluctance in Jilly's voice? Was her friend afraid to be alone with her? "Sure, if you want. I'd love a second opinion."

"All right. Just tell me when. Are you coming to work Monday?"

"No. I've decided to quit my job."

"It won't be the same without you."

"I'm going to miss it, but . . . I just don't think I can handle it right now." It had been difficult being around her parents, listening to the sound of their hearts, smelling their blood. How much worse would it be in a crowded office building, surrounded by coworkers and people she didn't know? What if she couldn't control the urge to feed? What if Katerina came looking for her?

"I understand, I guess. Listen, I need to go make Luke's lunch . . . anyway, I'm free any night you want to go dress shopping."

"Okay, talk to you soon. Tell Luke hi for me."

Tessa's next call was to Bailey, but she didn't answer the phone, so Tessa left a message, then went into the bathroom to fill the tub, thinking a nice hot bubble bath was just what she needed.

She was relaxing in the tub, eyes closed, up to her chin in lavender-scented bubbles, when Andrei slipped into the tub behind her. She sighed as his arms slid around her to make a slow exploration of her body from her hips to her shoulders, lingering at the inter-esting hills and valleys in between.

There was magic in his touch and she moaned with pleasure as his hands drifted over her skin.

He nipped at her ear, then nuzzled her neck. And all the while his hands moved over her, arousing her. When she thought she might burst with wanting him, he rose in a single fluid motion with her in his arms and carried her to bed.

At any other time, she might have worried about dripping soapy water on the mattress, but not now, when she was on fire for him.

He fell back on the mattress with her straddling his hips and it was her turn to tease and touch and taste until, with a wordless growl, he rolled over, carrying her with him. His eyes burned with heat as his body melded with hers, the fire between them so intense she was surprised the sheets didn't go up in flames.

And then there was only wave upon wave of sensual pleasure beyond words or description, and Andrei's voice, whispering that he loved her, would always love her.

Later, after Tessa had fallen asleep, Andrei returned to the ruin that was his former lair. He picked his way through the debris, quietly cursing Katerina. He'd had a fortune in antique furniture and paintings, pieces he had collected in the last seven hundred years.

His insurance would cover the cost of rebuilding the house, but the paintings by some of the Old Masters—Botticelli, da Vinci, Raphael, Tintoretto—could never be replaced.

The stairs leading down to his lair were gone but it was an easy jump for a vampire. He brushed aside the wreckage of his bed, revealing a floor safe. It opened with a creak of protest. He withdrew several small velvet bags, a metal box, and an ornate sheath that held a silver-bladed knife. The weapon had been doused in holy water and blessed by an Italian bishop over five hundred years ago. The hilt was encrusted with rubies that glittered like drops of fresh blood in the pale shaft of moonlight that penetrated the gloom in his lair.

It was an antique more valuable than anything else he had ever owned—an ancient, deadly weapon crafted solely to destroy master vampires.

He felt the power of the blade hum in his hands as he turned it over. He had acquired it a century ago, solely for the purpose of destroying his sire.

Chapter Forty-Six

Tessa called her boss first thing Monday morning to tell him that, due to a sudden illness, she was quitting her job. She apologized for the short notice. Mr. Ambrose was both annoyed and sympathetic, and assured her that he would make certain she received whatever funds were owed her. To her surprise, he told her there would be a place for her should she ever wish to return.

After disconnecting the call, she returned to bed. Though she could be awake during the day, she sometimes found it difficult to stay awake when the sun was up.

"It's more normal for you to rest during the day," Andrei had told her on more than one occasion. "That will change as you get older."

"But you prefer being awake during the day," she'd said. "And I want to be with you."

"Not so, my love. I only kept those hours to be with you."

She smiled as she slid into bed beside him. He had been unusually quiet and withdrawn since returning home. She knew he was upset over what Katerina had done, but then, who could blame him?

Resting her head on his shoulder, she breathed in his scent. Soon, they would be married. What would their lives be like? A thought could take them wherever they wanted to go—across the street or across the world. They had no jobs to tie them down, no responsibilities. No children . . . Did Andrei ever wonder what it would have been like to have children? Did he ever think about it? Was it something he missed? Would she regret not having a family in years to come?

Blinking back tears, she closed her eyes and let the darkness steal her away.

Tessa met Jilly at the bridal shop on Tuesday evening. As he had before, Andrei tagged along. His presence reminded her that Katerina was still out there somewhere, still a threat.

Sitting in the dressing room with Jilly, waiting for the consultant to bring some dresses in, Tessa blew out a sigh. "Seems like we just did this, doesn't it?"

Jilly nodded.

"Is something wrong? You've been awfully quiet."

"No," Jilly said quickly. Too quickly.

"Is it me? Do I make you uncomfortable now?"

"No, silly. It's just that . . . well, I have news but I'm not sure you want to hear it."

"What kind of news?"

"Here we are," the consultant said, sweeping into the room with several dresses draped over her arm. "If none of these work," she said, hanging them up, "just give a holler."

"Thank you."

"I don't know how you'll ever decide," Jilly said. "These are even more beautiful that the last ones we looked at."

"They are, aren't they? But I want something completely different from the last one."

"Maybe a mermaid gown?" Jilly suggested. "Or a princess style?"

Tessa looked them over, then picked one with a sweetheart neckline and a full skirt adorned with brilliants.

"Oh, I like that one!" Jilly said. "You look like Cinderella."

Tessa smiled at her reflection in the mirror. "I love it."

She tried on several others, but always came back to the first one. When the consultant brought her a long veil to try on, she was sold.

"I'll just go ring this up for you while you change," the consultant said.

Tessa waited for the clerk to leave, then said, "Okay, Jilly, what's your news?"

"I'm . . . that is . . . we're pregnant."

"That's wonderful! I'm so happy for you. Why didn't you want to tell me?"

"Well, I just wasn't sure how you'd feel, because . . . you know."

"Oh, right." Vampires couldn't reproduce. "But I'm still happy for you and Luke."

"He's decided to give up vampire hunting. Says it's too risky a job for a married man with a baby on the way."

"He's right. You tell him I said so." She stepped into her boots and opened the dressing room door. "I'll call you when we decide on a date. It'll probably be in a day or two, now that I have a dress."

"All right. Just let me know."

Tessa hugged her. "I really am happy for you."

* * *

It was true, Tessa thought as she hung her dress in the closet at home. She *was* happy for Jileen and Luke. They were very much in love. They deserved to have a family and live happily ever after.

She stared at her wedding gown. It was beautiful. She felt like a fairy-tale princess in it. And she had her very own Prince Charming.

So why did she suddenly feel like crying?

She quickly shut the closet door when she sensed Andrei's presence. "Hey, you can't see the dress until the wedding," she said, forcing a note of cheerfulness into her voice.

"Right. I forgot." He leaned his shoulder against the doorjamb. "Everything okay?"

She nodded. "Why wouldn't it be?"

Stepping into the room, he closed the distance between them, his gaze searching hers. "You wouldn't lie to your future husband, would you?"

"Everything's fine."

"Uh-huh. What's wrong?"

"Nothing." She sank down on the edge of the bed, hands clasped in her lap.

Andrei blew out a sigh, wishing he had never taught her how to block her thoughts because the wall she had built in her mind was ten feet high and rock solid. "Are we still getting married?"

"Of course. Anytime you want."

He nodded. "How about Friday?"

"No!" She shuddered, remembering all too clearly what had happened at the last ceremony. "Fridays are bad luck for us."

"Right. How about tomorrow?"

"Can we find someone to marry us so soon?"

"Leave that to me."

"All right. Oh! Tomorrow's New Year's Eve."

"And I can't think of a better way to start the new year. You call Jilly and Bailey. I'll bring the priest." With a last, speculative glance, he left the room.

When she was certain he had left the condo, Tessa collapsed on the bed and let her tears flow.

Andrei stood on the landing, hands fisted over the railing as he tried to figure out what was bothering his bride-to-be. Women were complicated creatures. In spite of centuries of experience with females—human and vampire alike—he didn't think he would ever understand them.

It troubled him that Tessa wouldn't confide in him. Was it something major worrying her, or just a case of pre-wedding jitters? His biggest fear was that she was suddenly regretting her decision to become . . .

Vampire!

Andrei swore as the wind shifted and a familiar scent stung his nostrils. Katerina! Damn the woman. What was she doing lurking around here? Did the vindictive witch intend to burn down the condo, too? Not that he'd put it past her.

Hands curled into fists, he opened his preternatural senses, but it was too late. She was already gone. Nevertheless, her scent lingered in the air, an odious reminder of unfinished business that would mean the end of one of them.

Or perhaps both.

Chapter Forty-Seven

Tessa stared at her reflection in the mirror. It was her wedding day. Again. Hopefully, this one would end better than the last. Andrei had assured her last night that there was no way Katerina could cause trouble this time. She couldn't enter Tessa's house, couldn't mess with Tessa's mind as long as she kept her walls up.

Praying Andrei was right, she lifted a hand to her veil. It was as light and airy as finely spun sugar.

She heard the doorbell, the sound of voices as Jilly and Luke came in, followed by Bailey and Tristan.

Jilly was starting to look pregnant.

Tessa sighed. Why was she letting her friend's good news upset her so? Given a choice, she would rather have Andrei than a dozen babies fathered by another man.

There was a knock on her bedroom door. "Tess?"

"Come in, Jilly. You too, Bailey."

Faces wreathed in smiles, they stepped into the room.

"Oh, Tessa," Bailey murmured, "you look just like Cinderella going to the ball."

"Told you so," Jilly said. "Seriously, girlfriend, you look beautiful."

"Is Andrei back yet?" Tessa asked.

"No."

"Maybe he couldn't find a priest willing to marry us on New Year's Eve."

"I'm pretty sure Andrei can persuade just about anyone to do just about anything," Jileen said dryly.

"I'm sure you're right," Bailey remarked, grinning.

"We brought a wedding cake," Jilly said. "Even if you don't eat it, I thought you should have one. I hope you don't mind."

"Jilly, that's so sweet! Of course I don't mind. Thank you." Tessa glanced toward the living room, her heart suddenly beating faster. The way it did whenever Andrei was near. "The groom's arrived. And he's not alone."

Jilly nudged Bailey. "Time to take your place out front."

Bailey winked at Tessa, then left the room. She and Tristan were going to be their witnesses.

"Are you ready, Tess?" Jilly asked.

She nodded. This was it. Finally.

Moments later, Luke poked his head into her room. "Ready?"

"Yes." More than ready, she thought, as a million butterflies of excitement took wing in the pit of her belly.

Jilly took her place and Luke and Tessa fell in behind her. Tessa placed her hand on Luke's arm, took a deep breath, and then they followed Jilly down the narrow hallway into the living room.

Andrei and the priest stood in front of the fireplace. Tristan and Bailey stood to one side, his arm around her waist.

Tessa's heart skipped a beat when she met Andrei's gaze. He was all man, she thought, admiring the width of his shoulders, the inky blackness of his hair, the heat in his eyes. All man. And all hers.

She and Luke stopped in front of the priest. Luke stepped back and Andrei took his place at her side. He smiled as he took her hand in his. *Hello, beautiful.*

She squeezed his hand.

The priest cleared his throat. "We are gathered here today to join Andrei Dinescu and Tessa Blackburn in the bonds of holy matrimony. Marriage is an honorable estate, not to be entered into lightly. Andrei, do you take Tessa to be your lawfully wedded wife, to love her and cherish her as long as you both shall live?"

"I do."

"Tessa, do you take Andrei to be your lawfully wedded husband, to love and to cherish as long as you both shall live?"

"I do."

"Then, by the power vested in me by Holy Mother Church, I now pronounce you husband and wife. Andrei, you may kiss the bride."

"In a moment." Andrei reached into his pocket and withdrew a wedding band studded with diamonds—the mate to her engagement ring. Slipping it on her finger, he drew her into his arms. "I will love you and no other as long as I live," he murmured, and kissed her.

It was, Tessa thought as his mouth closed over hers, the sweetest, most gentle sign of love and affection she had ever received.

"All right," Luke muttered as Andrei deepened the kiss, "break it up, you two."

Tessa laughed softly as Andrei growled low in his throat, kissed her again, then let her go.

Bailey and Jilly stepped forward to hug her while Luke and Tristan congratulated Andrei.

"Time to cut the cake," Jilly said.

"And drink a toast to the bride and groom," Luke added.

"Cake first," Jilly insisted. She had not only brought a small wedding cake, complete with a little bride and groom on top, but paper plates, and a knife tied with a white bow as well.

"Ladies first." Taking the knife from Jileen, Tessa cut a thin slice of cake. She hesitated a moment. Many brides and grooms smeared the dessert over their partner's face, but she didn't want to make light of the occasion. She fed it to Andrei, then handed him the knife. His gaze met hers as he cut a small piece and offered it to her. She ate it quickly, then licked her lips. Even though she couldn't taste it, she still remembered the taste of cake and buttercream.

Luke filled seven glasses with champagne and Bailey and Tristan passed them out.

Smiling benignly, the priest joined in the toast.

"Time for a wedding photo," Jilly said, digging her phone out of her handbag. "This is a day we want to remember."

Feeling as though she had swallowed a piece of the sun, Tessa stood beside Andrei. Her husband. She glanced at her wedding ring. In all the fuss and excitement, she'd forgotten to buy him one. Something she intended to remedy at the soonest possible moment. He was a married man now, and she wanted everyone to know it.

The party broke up a short time later amid lots of winks and smirks. Jilly and Luke offered to drive the priest home so that the newlyweds could "start their honeymoon right away."

"Happy New Year," Jilly said, giving Tessa a hug. "Let's hope the new year is Katerina-free."

"I'll drink to that," Tessa said, laughing.

"Luke and I are going out dancing at the Stardust later. If you and Andrei get bored before midnight, come find us."

Tessa glanced over to where Andrei and the others were standing by the door, chatting with the priest. She could hardly wait until they were alone. She grew warm all over just thinking about being in Andrei's arms, running her hands over his hard body, testing the strength of his arms, hearing his whiskey-rough voice murmuring love words in her ear.

"Tessa?"

"What? Oh, thanks, but I don't think that's going to happen."

"No, I guess not," Jilly said, following Tessa's gaze. "Happy New Year."

Andrei closed the door. "I thought they'd never leave."

Tessa nodded, surprised to feel suddenly shy now that they were alone.

"We did it," he said, slipping his arms around her waist.

"So we did."

He gazed down at her, his brows drawn together. "You okay?"

She stared up at him, felt her cheek grow hot under his probing gaze. "I should cover that cake and put it away."

"Now?" He nuzzled her neck. "I had something else in mind."

"Did you?"

"Can't you guess?"

Her gaze slid downward to the obvious evidence of his desire. "No guessing required," she muttered, then burst out laughing.

"I hope you're not expressing an opinion of my masculinity," he said dryly.

With a shake of her head, Tessa took him by the hand and led him to the bedroom. "Have no fear. I know just how to ease your problem."

Andrei's grin stretched ear to ear. "I know you do, love. I'm counting on it."

In the bedroom, he drew her into his arms, then turned her around so he could unfasten her gown. He whistled softly when she stepped out of it, revealing a lacy white bra and matching bikini panties.

He groaned softly. "I'm not sure you're solving my problem."

"In time," she promised as she removed his coat and tie.

He obligingly toed off his boots and peeled off his socks.

He sucked in a breath as she unbuckled his belt, unzipped his fly. He kicked his trousers aside, then scooped her into his arms and carried her to bed.

"I love you, wife," he murmured.

"Love you more."

"Impossible." His hands played over her body, lingering in those places he knew aroused her most, carrying her to the peak, then backing off until she thought she might go mad with wanting him.

She clutched his shoulders as, with a lustful growl, he thrust into her, carrying her over the edge of desperate need into ecstasy and beyond.

* * *

Tessa was drifting off to sleep when her cell phone rang. She sat up, instantly alert. People never called with good news at three a.m.

"Who is it?" Andrei asked as she reached for her phone.

"Jilly." She mouthed the word before answering. "Jilly, what's wrong?"

"I'm afraid Jilly can't come to the phone right now."

"Katerina!"

"Sorry I missed the sham of a wedding. Do tell *my* husband hello for me."

"What do you want? Where's Jilly?"

"Oh, she's right here. The hunter, too. And the priest who dared to marry you."

Tessa stared at Andrei. With his preternatural hearing, he could listen to both sides of the conversation.

He took the phone from her hand, his expression grim, his eyes as hard as flint. "What do you want, Katerina?"

"I want what's mine. But since you don't want me, I don't want you to have anyone else. So, tell your whore that if she ever wants to see her friend and the hunter again, to come and meet me."

"That's not going to happen."

"Then put her on the phone so she can tell her friend good-bye."

Tessa snatched the phone from Andrei's hand. "What do you want?"

"I've decided to fight for what is mine. If I win, I get Andrei. If you win, you get your friends back. I'm afraid it's too late for the priest."

"You killed him?"

"I never could control my temper."

"Just tell me where you are."

"We're in the high school gym. Be here in ten minutes, or she's dead. Oh, and come alone. I'll know if you don't."

There was a loud click as Katerina ended the call.

"Are you crazy?" Andrei exclaimed. "You can't fight her."

"Well, I can't let her kill Jilly and Luke." She jumped out of bed and went to her closet.

"I'm not letting you go alone."

"She'll know if you're there."

"I don't give a damn," he said, following her across the room.

Tessa pulled on a pair of jeans and a sweater, tugged on a pair of fur-lined boots.

"Dammit, Tess, she doesn't play fair. For all you know, Jilly's dead already."

"Katerina loses her leverage if she kills her. Because I'll know if Jilly and Luke are alive as soon as I get there."

Andrei bit out a curse.

Tessa put her arms around him. "You know I have to go, don't you?"

"Yes, dammit, I know. I've been expecting her to pull a stunt like this. Stay strong, love. I won't be far behind."

As soon as she left the house, Tessa's courage deserted her. Katerina was ancient. She was a fledgling. But she had Andrei's blood in her veins. And by extension, Katerina's, too. Hopefully, that would make all the difference.

When she arrived at the school, all the windows were dark. After vaulting over the fence, she made her way to the gymnasium. One of the doors stood open. It was pitch-black inside. Pausing, she opened her senses. Katerina was inside. So was Jileen. She could smell her friend's fear. And Luke's. And overall, the smell of blood and death.

Taking a deep breath, she entered the gym's yawning maw.

"So, he let you come alone."

In the darkness, Katerina's voice seemed to be disembodied.

Tessa's gaze swept the room. Jilly and Luke were bound to metal chairs. The priest lay dead in the far corner, his blood congealing.

There was no sign of Katerina. But she was there.

Tessa moved to the center of the floor, her hand reaching into her back pocket for the weapon Andrei had thrust into her hand as she left the house. "Let's get this over with. I'm on my honeymoon, you know. Andrei's in bed, waiting for me."

With a growl, Katerina materialized and launched herself at Tessa. Hands like claws, teeth bared in a feral snarl, she grabbed Tessa's arm and hurled her across the room.

Tessa bounced off the wall and scrambled to her feet. Whirling around, she deflected the blow she saw coming. Katerina fought like a wildcat, her nails scoring Tessa's arms and cheeks while she hurled insults.

The smell of fresh blood filled the air.

Tessa fought back as best she could, amazed by her own strength. She had never been in a physical fight in her whole life. And never a fight to the death. She thought of Jilly and Luke. If she died, they would die. She thought of Andrei, of how much he loved her. How much she loved him. If she lost, she would never see him again.

It was that thought that spurred her on.

At Katerina's next charge, Tessa feinted left, then lowered her guard. And waited.

With a cry of impending victory, Katerina sprang at Tessa. Tessa fell heavily and Katerina landed on her chest, eyes glowing red.

"All too easy," Katerina crowed as she pinned Tessa's shoulders to the floor. She leaned down, intending to sink her fangs into Tessa's throat.

"You think so?" Tessa retorted, and plunged the dagger Andrei had given her into Katerina's back.

Katerina let out a shriek of pained surprise as the silver-bladed dagger penetrated her heart. She stared at Tessa in shock for stretched seconds before she toppled sideways.

Tessa scrambled to her feet, eyes growing wide as the vampire disintegrated into a pile of dust and ashes.

Swallowing the bile that burned the back of her throat, Tessa crossed the floor to turn on the lights before hurrying toward Jilly and Luke. She quickly untied them.

"Are you two all right?"

"We are now!"

Luke glanced around. "Where'd she go?"

Tessa gestured to the pile of ashes in the center of the floor. A silver-bladed dagger winked in the light. "That's her."

"You destroyed her?" Jilly asked. "All by yourself?"

"I had a little help from an ancient weapon," Tessa said, retrieving the knife.

"Where the hell's Andrei?" Luke asked.

"Right here," he said, materializing in the doorway. "You didn't think I'd let Tessa confront Katerina alone, did you?"

Luke shrugged, his expression sheepish.

"It's over, isn't it?" Jilly asked, her voice touched with awe. "Really over?"

Tessa nodded. "Come on, we'll take you home."

"I destroyed her," Tessa said, crawling into bed beside Andrei. "I can't believe it."

"I can." He smiled at her. "In fact, I think you were the only one who could."

"I couldn't have done it without your dagger."

Andrei grunted softly. "I'm not sure about that. I think your blood would have been just as deadly."

"Really? Even now, when I'm a vampire, too?"

"I don't think becoming a vampire would have altered the curse. I think anyone who takes your blood by force will pay the ultimate price."

"Well, that's something you'll never have to worry about," she said, snuggling into his arms. "Because I'm giving you permission to taste me as often as you like, as long as I can taste you, in return."

"Good to know, Mrs. Dinescu." Stretching out on the bed, he drew her down beside him.

"Mrs. Dinescu," she repeated. "I love the sound of that."

"You're gonna love this, too," he growled as he rose over her.

They had made love before, but it was different now, she thought, more meaningful, more intimate.

Later, wrapped in the warmth of her husband's embrace, she smiled, thinking Jilly had been right. It *was* better when you were married.

Epilogue

Tessa stood beside Andrei, staring in wonder at their new home. He had found the original plans to the house Katerina had burned down and had it rebuilt, with a few improvements, and a lair that was impenetrable and looked like a bedchamber fit for a king. The final touches had been completed only yesterday. Tessa hadn't been surprised when Andrei erased all memory of their hidden lair from the minds of the builders.

The last two years had seen many changes in their lives. Their friendship with Luke, Jilly, Bailey, and Tristan had grown deeper, stronger.

Luke had joined the Cutter's Corner Police Department. Jilly had quit her job. She was pregnant again, this time with twin boys, to Luke's delight.

Bailey and Tristan were married now, and expecting a child of their own.

Tessa still hadn't found the courage to tell her parents that their daughter and son-in-law were both vampires. She told herself she was waiting for just the right moment but so far, she hadn't found it. Andrei said waiting wouldn't make it any easier, but she just couldn't find the words.

Andrei gestured at the house. "So, what do you think?" he asked, giving her hand a squeeze. "Is it everything you hoped it would be?"

"It's exquisite."

"All those empty rooms," he remarked, seemingly apropos of nothing.

Tessa looked at him askance.

"I was thinking we could fill them up with children."

"It's a wonderful idea, but not likely, unless you plan to kidnap them."

"I was thinking of adoption."

Tessa shook her head. "No adoption agency in the world is going to give two vampires a baby."

"I don't see any need to mention that, do you?"

"Do you mean it?"

"I always wanted a houseful of children. I'm sure we can afford a dozen or so."

"Oh, Andrei, you really do mean it, don't you?"

When he nodded, she threw her arms around his neck. "I love you!"

"And I you. Always and forever."

He kissed the tip of her nose, then swung her into his arms. "We have a new house," he said, carrying her up the porch stairs. "And a brand-new king-size bed that's calling my name."

"Just *your* name?" she teased with a grin.

"I'm sure it'll be fine if I bring a friend." He carried her across the threshold and, minutes later, into their own paradise.

Read on for an excerpt from Amanda Ashley's

TWILIGHT DREAMS,

available now in paperback or online!

"A tender paranormal romance exploring love and
family ties . . . tinged with intrigue and vengeance . . .
This portrait of new love is sweet and endearing."
—*Publishers Weekly*

"Author Ashley is no stranger to paranormal
romance . . . Intriguing."—*Kirkus Reviews*

Holly Parrish has never met anyone like Micah
Ravenwood: his dark eyes, his movie-star smile, the
indefinable way he looks at her. Even when she
thought he was no more than another client for her
investment firm, her lust overpowered her logic.
But she never expected this attraction to whisk her
from her busy Southern California life
to a silent and eerie ghost town in Wyoming.
Only vampires call the deserted place home—and
one of them is Micah. He says he's brought her to
Morgan Creek for her safety, that vicious creatures
are hunting her. But how can Holly trust him?
One look and she can see the need barely restrained
behind Micah's polite words. The heat of his kiss,
the pleasure of his touch—none of it can tell her
whether he wants her as his lover—or his prey. . . .

Micah sat at the long ebony bar inside The Lair. He had been coming here long enough to recognize most of the patrons—women looking for a one-night stand, men looking for a woman—any woman—to ease their loneliness for a night or two. He had been in Southern California less than two weeks and had already reached the conclusion that coming to the City of Angels had been a mistake. He had been wandering from one goth hangout to another in hopes of finding a lady vampire, someone to take his mind off his loss, his loneliness, but if there were any vampires here, he hadn't been able to find them. The state seemed to be filled with nothing but movie stars, wannabe movie stars, surfers, and beach bunnies.

He was about to leave the club when he saw her—a young woman who stood an inch or two over five feet. Long, blond hair fell in soft waves over her shoulders. Even in the dim light, he noticed her eyes. They were an unusual shade of blue, almost turquoise. Contact lenses, perhaps? A gray sweater and a pair of blue jeans caressed a petite but perfect figure. He guessed her to be in her mid twenties.

She glanced around the bar, obviously looking for someone. To Micah's surprise, she lifted a hand in greeting when she saw him at the bar and hurried toward him.

"Joseph Burke?" she said, smiling. "Sorry I'm late. I'm Holly Parrish."

"Pleased to meet you, Miss Parrish. Can I buy you a drink?"

"A vodka martini, please," she said, taking the stool beside his.

Micah relayed her order and asked for another glass of wine for himself. "Holly," he murmured. "I'm guessing you were a Christmas baby."

"Good guess." She smiled that enchanting smile again. "Mr. Gladstone is very anxious to have you on our team, Mr. Burke. He's prepared to pay you twice what Lindor-Beakman is offering, along with the usual perks, of course—a company car, a three-week vacation, and the best health insurance on the market."

Micah sipped his wine. "I must admit, it sounds like a very generous offer."

She nodded. "You won't find a better one." Lifting her glass, she took a swallow.

His gaze moved to her throat, his nostrils filling with the warm, rich scent of her blood, the flowery fragrance that clung to her hair and skin, her perfume. The faint, musky scent of woman. She might be short and petite, he mused, but she was all female.

Setting her glass aside, she licked her lips. "So, if you're willing to accept Mr. Gladstone's offer, we can close the deal right now. I have the necessary papers in my bag."

"I'd be more than happy to accept, Miss Parrish, if I was Joseph Burke."

She blinked at him. "Excuse me?"

"I'm not Joseph Burke. My name is Micah Raven-wood."

Books by Bestselling Author
Fern Michaels

___The Jury	0-8217-7878-1	$6.99US/$9.99CAN
___Sweet Revenge	0-8217-7879-X	$6.99US/$9.99CAN
___Lethal Justice	0-8217-7880-3	$6.99US/$9.99CAN
___Free Fall	0-8217-7881-1	$6.99US/$9.99CAN
___Fool Me Once	0-8217-8071-9	$7.99US/$10.99CAN
___Vegas Rich	0-8217-8112-X	$7.99US/$10.99CAN
___Hide and Seek	1-4201-0184-6	$6.99US/$9.99CAN
___Hokus Pokus	1-4201-0185-4	$6.99US/$9.99CAN
___Fast Track	1-4201-0186-2	$6.99US/$9.99CAN
___Collateral Damage	1-4201-0187-0	$6.99US/$9.99CAN
___Final Justice	1-4201-0188-9	$6.99US/$9.99CAN
___Up Close and Personal	0-8217-7956-7	$7.99US/$9.99CAN
___Under the Radar	1-4201-0683-X	$6.99US/$9.99CAN
___Razor Sharp	1-4201-0684-8	$7.99US/$10.99CAN
___Yesterday	1-4201-1494-8	$5.99US/$6.99CAN
___Vanishing Act	1-4201-0685-6	$7.99US/$10.99CAN
___Sara's Song	1-4201-1493-X	$5.99US/$6.99CAN
___Deadly Deals	1-4201-0686-4	$7.99US/$10.99CAN
___Game Over	1-4201-0687-2	$7.99US/$10.99CAN
___Sins of Omission	1-4201-1153-1	$7.99US/$10.99CAN
___Sins of the Flesh	1-4201-1154-X	$7.99US/$10.99CAN
___Cross Roads	1-4201-1192-2	$7.99US/$10.99CAN

Available Wherever Books Are Sold!
Check out our website at **www.kensingtonbooks.com**